S0-FEP-102

HURON PUBLIC LIBRARY
333 WILLIAMS STREET
HURON, OHIO 44839
www.huronlibrary.org

Also by the author:

Story collection:

A History of Things Lost and Broken
Catholic Boys

Plays:

"The World of Flesh and Blood," (one act)
"Little Houses of the Dead,"
"Gun Hill Road,"
"Everglades City,"
Love in the Age of Dion
"Love in the Age of Dion," (one-act version)

THE BRONX KILL

Philip Cioffari

Livingston Press

The University of West Alabama

Copyright © 2017 Philip Cioffari
All rights reserved, including electronic text

ISBN 13: 978-1-60489-186-7, hardcover
ISBN 13: 978-1-60489-187-4, trade paper
ISBN: 1-60489-186-6 hardcover
ISBN: 1-60489-187-4 trade paper
Library of Congress Control Number 2016958353
Printed on acid-free paper
by Publishers Graphics
Printed in the United States of America

Hardcover binding by: Heckman Bindery
Typesetting and page layout: Amanda Nolin, Joe Taylor, Teresa Boykin,
and Sarah Coffey
Proofreading: Joe Taylor, Ciara Denson, Hannah Evans,
Jessica Gonzalez, Jessie Hagler, Patricia Taylor
Cover design: Amanda Nolin

Cover photo: Philip Cioffari

The author wishes to thank Joe Taylor and the staff at Livingston Press, as well as Jaden Terrell, Lisa Rast and Raymond Mosser, for their help in preparing this manuscript for publication.

This is a work of fiction:
any resemblance
to persons living or dead is coincidental.

Livingston Press is part of The University of West Alabama,
and thereby has non-profit status.
Donations are tax-deductible:
brothers and sisters, we need 'em.

first edition
6 5 4 3 3 2 1

THE BRONX KILL

PROLOGUE

August, 1998

Four of them, stripped to their shorts, stood on the riverbank, eyes fixed across Hell Gate at the lights of Queens.

This had been Charlie's idea. *Let's swim it.*

No one protested. Not Johnny or Danny. Not even Mooney, the weakest swimmer among them. No one dared.

No sweat, Charlie said. *Can't be more than half a mile. Can't be.*

Across the river the lights flared, spur-like, diffused, beyond the roiling currents.

Tonight it's ours. They had tried before and failed. But that didn't matter. Not this night. Not for this, what Charlie called the grandest challenge of their youth, the ultimate test of their manhood. *Let's do it*, he said.

They'd been drinking and their bodies leaned tentatively toward the water. Uncertain. Unsteady. Charlie with the broadest shoulders, the biggest build, the others thin pale shadows of him.

Above them the rush of cars on the bridge lifted into the night like a primal chant.

Come on.

Come on.

Come on.

Charlie stumbled forward, he was no pansy, feet slipping on wet rocks, arms swinging in broken circles, propeller-like, powering him into the waist-deep water at the river's edge.

Johnny followed quickly, then Danny, mud sucking at their feet. Only Mooney hesitated, watching from the shoreline.

Come on, Charlie shouted. *Prove you got some balls. Prove it.*

Mooney shook like he was cold. Thin flat chest, flat belly, thin arms and legs—bird-like, delicate—his face tinged with a blush of shame but his body white as bone.

Come on! Charlie said again, this time Johnny and Danny joining in. Three voices shouting: *come on, come on, come on.*

Charlie came out of the water, talking under his breath to Mooney, jabbing at his face, his chest, his arms. Softly at first, almost playful. Then harder, *harder*. Grabbing him and lifting him, turning sharply as though he might fling him into the water.

Mooney slipped free. He hung back on the bank, shoulders hunched in apology. Then the girl appeared. Out of nowhere, it seemed. Stepping from the shadow of the bridge. Sun-bleached hair blown back in the breeze, her smile an arc of whiteness in her deeply tanned face. She had a slow, easy way of walking, an offhand way of saying, *I'm coming, too*. No chance they wouldn't go now. No chance any of them would chicken out. They watched her—Mooney less intently than the others: he'd seen her naked before—as she lifted her halter top, unzipped her shorts. In her bra and panties, she stood on the bank, unflinching under their scrutiny, before entering the water, striking out for the far shore.

Charlie leading the way, the three of them surrounded Mooney then, shouting *Timmy Timmy Timmy*, pulling at his thin arms, dragging him into the water.

Nobody swam in this river. Too dirty. Too dangerous. Too rife with chemicals, disease. Too subject to strong and unpredictable currents. As rough at times as Hell Gate to the south. At night the ship traffic couldn't see you. You were flotsam, debris tossing in the waves.

But Charlie plunged ahead, swimming hard to overtake the girl, Johnny following close behind, then Danny, and Mooney dead last.

The water's black grip felt colder than Danny, the youngest of them, expected this time of year; slick and oily, it yanked him downward. When he fought his way to the surface, coughing, spitting through gritted teeth, he turned to be sure Mooney was following—and he was, arms flailing, feet kicking hard, an awkward but determined pantomime of a swimmer. The others, ahead of Danny, were already nothing more than dark blurs on the water, marked now and again, brief silver flashes.

Danny got his bearings then and swam harder, gaining on the others because he knew without thinking it this test of their manhood involved not only making it to the other side but making it there *first*. It was as much now about *her* as it was about proving himself to the guys.

Fifty feet from shore the current began to strengthen. He

stopped to rest, treading water, gulping mouthfuls of air, watching the pinpoint of a ship's light gliding by on the river, watching the shoreline glide by too as he drifted southward. Then he was swimming hard again, fighting the current, trying to make up lost ground.

What happened next happened without warning. A wave from the passing ship swamped him. When he re-surfaced, spitting the sour-tasting water, eyes tearing, thinking *we're all going to die out here*, he saw Charlie swimming back toward him, heading for shore.

Too rough, Charlie shouted. *We can't make it.*

Then Charlie was past him, head down, doing the flawless overhand stroke he'd won medals for. Johnny was close behind, swimming in his wake, face tight with strain as he too headed back.

I can make it, Danny thought. *We're almost a third of the way and I can make it. I can. I can.* No longer could he see any trace of the girl, Julianne—he was in pursuit of the *idea* of her, his fantasy of her—so he began swimming again, riding the ship's waves which were less severe now, small rounded hills of water breaking over him.

In a matter of moments, though, he saw Charlie was right. The current swiped him from all sides, held him captive, dragged him southward toward the bridge. It took all his effort to break free, to spring from its grip, to point himself toward shore where they'd left their clothes.

That was when he saw Mooney coming toward him, arms flailing, feet sending back fantails of spray as he labored into the current.

You won't make it, Danny shouted.

Mooney kept swimming his awkward, blundering stroke. Danny stopped him, grabbing at his shoulders, his neck, the water rising in furious waves around them, everything—Mooney's slick skin, Danny's clawing hands, the stinging burn in his eyes, his throat—all of it inseparable from the river's raging assault; and then Danny stopped reaching for him, slowly backing away from him as the dark water swirled between them.

Treading water, his heart pounding so hard he gasped for breath, Danny watched him struggle to stay above water. He kept his head turned toward Danny. He seemed to be waiting for something. The look in his eyes said that.

Before he began swimming again, Mooney's face lifted above the river. He was grinning, or so it appeared, his mouth twisted in an odd, unexplainable way as he leaned back into the current.

PART ONE

CHAPTER 1

June, 2003

Mooney's ghost, it seemed, had come back with a vengeance.

For five years it had been a frequent visitor to his dreams, a stalker at the edge of his consciousness. Sometimes, in those dreams, it was Moon himself making an appearance, recognizable and distinct. Blond hair, thin almost girlish face with its perfectly formed features, wide smile that won you to his side the instant you met him. Other times, the nightmare version, he came in many guises: a shapeless mass sinking beneath the waves; a lost soul wandering without purpose or direction through empty streets; a bodiless cry for help that Danny would follow through darkened hallways and alleys, never reaching the source. Often it was unclear whether the cries for help came from Mooney or himself.

On certain days, certain weeks, the boy was beside him constantly like a living being. Then he would disappear for a while, or seem to. But when the letter came in early June, on a bright-hot Florida afternoon, Mooney's ghost in all its forms gathered full force.

There was no way he could turn it away.

No way he could not go home.

Charlie's letter had been brief: *Johnny leaving seminary, marrying Lorraine. Engagement party, Saturday the 12th. Wedding date TBA. Looking forward to a Renegades' reunion.*

On the cab ride from the airport, Danny Baker re-played the last sentence of it in his mind: *Looking forward to a Renegades' reunion.* What they had called themselves: the Renegades. Outlaws, outcasts, rebels. Though what they were rebelling against—other than themselves—he couldn't say now.

From the Tri-Borough Bridge Manhattan's timeless grey slate of pointed and flat-roofed towers dominated the skyline; but when the cab came off the bridge they were in the southern tip of the Bronx where the buildings were far less impressive: a haphazard collection of squat factories and warehouses, many of them abandoned, cordoned off from one another by chain-link fence and barbed wire.

He asked the driver to stop alongside a long-neglected wasteland overgrown with grass and weeds.

This had been their hangout. Vacant lots, abandoned rail yards, three square miles of mostly flat land pockmarked with occasional clumps of trees. Running through it was a channel of murky, sluggish water that connected the Harlem and East Rivers.

The *Kill*.

What the early Dutch settlers had called that strip of water, pure and fast-flowing then, clear and clean.

Now the Kill's water was dark and sluggish, channeling through the most desolate of surroundings. Urban blight at its finest: what had been their teenage Garden of Eden.

Where it all began the day Julianne walked into their lives.

Coming down here like it was nothing, he'd thought then, crossing the train tracks with a slow thoughtful walk, dreamy rather than sassy, her mind not on the walking but on something else, her sandals scraping the hard soil of the Kill's bank.

She didn't hesitate approaching them, saying she'd seen them down here before, though none of them could remember seeing her.

She'd just moved into the project, didn't know anyone yet. Could she hang with them?

Girls don't come down here, Charlie told her, they're too scared.

She didn't care, she said, she wasn't like other girls. Besides, she'd rather hang out with guys any day. She stood with her shoulders high and jaunty. A dare in them, like the way she walked, the way her eyes looked when she smiled.

The kind of look that could bring a man down hard.

"Somethin' you're lookin' for?" the cabbie was asking. His face in the rear view said his patience had run out.

Danny stared out the window at the wall of weeds and grass.

Pictures, not words, came to him: the flash of Mooney's arms as he battled the current, his cryptic grin as he swam away. His pale, shriveled flesh the next day when the police fished him from the river at Hell Gate, a mile south of where Danny had last seen him.

Julianne's body, though, had never been found. What he saw when he thought of her, in dreams or in waking, was the heaving muscle of the river, empty and dark and endless.

"Terrible, this place," the cabbie grumbled. "Asshole of the earth. Why you wanna look at this?"

Danny settled back into the seat. From here the Kill and the riverbank that had been their jumping off point weren't visible, only the acres of weeds and marsh leading there, and the bridge ramp arcing skyward toward Queens.

"Visiting a grave," he said.

CHAPTER 2

His father came to the door quickly, spry as ever. Without hesitation he reached for his son's bag.

"I got it, I got it," Danny said, holding the door with his foot, but his father insisted, taking the leather overnight bag and setting it down in the narrow foyer.

"Been waiting for you all morning. Took the day off so I'd be here."

"I told you what time I'd be in."

"Yeah, yeah, but that was an hour and a half ago."

"I made a stop."

His father grunted, a vague acceptance of the fact that things rarely turned out as you expected. He was the same height as his son, six feet, maybe a shade over. His face had maintained its ruddy glow, a result of all the walking he did on his daily rounds. That had kept him trim and lean, as well.

"You're looking good," his father was saying, sizing him up. "Real good."

"It's my clean living."

His father looked at him sharply. "Making fun of your old man?"

"Couldn't be any cleaner if I was a monk. I swear." He had to laugh at how true that was. Other than for work or school or for a movie, he didn't get out a hell of a lot, which was just the opposite of his life before he moved south.

The worst of it was he'd stopped writing. The book he was working on, liked to *think* he was working on, had stalled out. It existed now mostly in his mind, a far off corner of his mind at that, a place he rarely visited these days. For Danny, that was more serious than it might first appear, because simply living his life had never been enough for him. Writing it down mattered as much, if not more. On the page he could say things he couldn't say in real life.

As for what others thought of him, they saw what his father saw: a decent-looking guy with a tan. It looked as if all was right in his world, and he was content letting them think that.

"I never liked change," his father said before Danny could say the apartment felt as familiar as it always had: the framed paintings of Tuscany villas and vineyards; the foyer smell of musty, plaster walls still embedded with odors of his mother's cooking—basil, garlic, olive oil; the notebook at one end of the dining room table where his father kept his accounts.

"Why we standing here all cramped up?" He ushered Danny into the living room with its sixth-floor view of the playground across the street and, beyond the remaining buildings of the Chester Hill housing project, a partial glimpse of the Kill.

"Okay to sit, you know." His father indicated the arm chair by the window.

Danny stood by the chair but didn't sit, distracted by activity on the street. In the playground shirtless teenage boys in over-sized pants were embroiled in a heated game of basketball. Sweat glistened on dark skin.

"First thing you did when you could walk was climb onto that chair. You always had to know what was going on outside."

"Still do." He laughed at himself. "Makes it a little bit easier to bear what's going on inside."

"What's that supposed to mean?"

"I'd rather deal with other folks' problems than my own."

His father shook his head in disappointment. "Ever since that damn accident—"

Danny knew the rest by heart. How many times had he been lectured? You can't let one event define your life. The world's too big a place for that—his father's argument went on and on.

"Let me get you some coffee," his father was saying as he shuffled toward the kitchen. "I been keeping it warm."

Danny lingered by the window. On the basketball court bodies ran, turning fast, arms raised beneath the net. A fight broke out. Two guys at first, their teams gathering around them in a tight circle, before it turned into a free-for-all: a melee of shouts and swinging arms and clenched fists that widened in ripples across the court. "Fight outside," he called toward the kitchen.

"There's always a fight outside," his father said back. "I don't even bother calling the cops anymore."

Danny watched the fighting stop as quickly as it had begun. The game resumed: the ceaseless ebb and flow across the court,

The Bronx Kill 17

passions re-focused.

With the apartment's silence eating at him, he wandered down the short hall past his parents' bedroom to the room he'd lived in for nineteen years. It was, as he knew it would be, as he left it: ordinary but adequate with its single bed, its blond walnut dresser and matching desk. Two shelves above the desk held books and the few trophies he'd earned. But it was the framed photo on the dresser that held his attention. The four Renegades at the beach. July 4th, 1996. Charlie Romano, Johnny Whalen, Tim Mooney and himself. In their bathing suits. Arms around each other. Mooney's smile the biggest and brightest.

The room's unaltered state, he decided, was more disturbing than it was a comfort.

In the kitchen he watched his father pour the coffee, hand steady, controlling the flow of dark liquid.

He handed his son a steaming mug.

In the cramped room, the air hung heavy and close. The wall clock above the fridge counted off the seconds as they stood leaning on opposite ends of the counter, between them the space of years and things unspoken.

His father's head was bowed and Danny could see how few the hairs were that still clung to his scalp. He remembered when he'd first discovered the small bare spot on his father's head, how it had become a joke between them, the ever-widening circle of baldness that Danny would trace with his fingers, pretending to measure it. They were close back then and he missed that closeness now.

He had blamed it on life, the inevitable distance that grows between a son and his old man; but if he were honest with himself he knew the cause was more particular than that, that it had begun the night of the "accident," with all the things he'd never been able to talk about: his secrets, his shame.

His father looked across the counter at him as if he knew what his son was thinking. And what he said next was said in apology, as if it proved his advice to forget about the accident, that it was a thing of the past, had been—if not dead wrong—at least premature. "Mooney's brother came by."

Danny didn't understand. "Tommy Mooney? Why?"
"Had some questions."
"About what?"
"The accident."

"Why? *When?*"

"Last week. Thursday maybe, or Friday. He's a detective now. NYPD. Said he wanted to talk to you."

Danny hadn't thought about Tommy Mooney in years. Back in the day the guy had only been a beat cop, finishing up his law degree nights at St. John's. Bottom line: he was a wise-ass with a fast mouth. At his brother's funeral, though, he hadn't said a word. He'd kept his head down and wouldn't look at anyone.

The wall clock ticked into the silence.

The phrase *he wanted to talk to you* had set Danny's nerves on edge. "What'd he want to know?"

"He didn't say."

CHAPTER 3

He had to talk to Charlie.

If anyone knew what was going down, he was the man.

The place he managed, the MoonGlow Bar and Grill on East 177th, was a throwback to the '50s—discolored dust-encrusted glass in the windows, ceiling pipes that knocked and hissed in a perpetual rant through the winters, old songs on the jukebox— a second home to the Italians, Irish and Germans who for one reason or another had hung on in the Bronx.

A *WELCOME HOME, JOHNNY* sign hung across the mirror behind the bar where Charlie stopped halfway through drawing a draft to come around to greet Danny.

A booming "hey, look who's here," a big hug—tight, brief—then they were patting each other on the back, exchanging how-the-hell-you-beens.

"Let me get you a beer," Charlie was saying and Danny sat beside three old-timers at the bar. They couldn't get over what a fine-looking man he'd turned into, how he'd filled out. Not the same scrawny kid they remembered. They were sure as hell glad he was back. Florida had the sunshine but the Bronx had the gusto. Nothing like it anywhere else. No way, no sir, no how.

Early though it was, they were calling it a night—so much for the gusto, Danny thought—but they were happy as hell, they said, to see he'd come back to the land of the living. They'd be sure to see him around.

In a matter of moments, it seemed, they were alone and Charlie sat across the bar from him in the evening quiet.

"Great to see you, man. Great to see you." Charlie beamed brightly, his ruggedly handsome face aglow in the bar light.

Danny tried to muster an equal amount of enthusiasm but his friendship with Charlie had always been a complicated one. For him at least, if not for Charlie. Competition was Charlie's game and there was never a time when he wasn't competing for something: a girl, a ball game, attention. Most irritating of all was that Charlie always won, whatever the prize.

"When Whales gets back," Charlie was saying now in the pink glow of the bar light, "it'll be good times again."

"When's he getting in?"

Charlie straightened up, looking annoyed. He was solidly built with broad shoulders, a squared face and wide forehead. In addition to being a swimmer, he'd played football for their high school team, all-city quarterback two years in a row, and he'd kept himself in shape. "Supposed to be back yesterday," he was saying. "Big crowd in here last night waiting for him. Never showed, though."

"What happened?"

"Who knows? I called the Sem. They said he'd already left. I checked with his mom. Lorraine, too. Nobody's heard from him."

"Maybe he's afraid to come back."

"Why in hell would he be afraid?"

"The investigation. Maybe he heard about it."

Charlie seemed taken aback. "Who told *you*?"

"My old man. Mooney's been to see him."

Charlie settled in again, arms on the bar, leaning forward. "He's been here, too. Nosing around."

"What's he want?"

"Didn't say. All he said was some new things had come to light, something unexpected—with regard to the *crime*."

"He called it a crime?"

"Yeah."

"He thinks we *killed* Moon?"

"I don't know. He didn't say that exactly. But he's calling it a crime, not an accident. So I figure, you know, that's what he means."

"Jesus!"

"Yeah, it sucks, right?"

The entire time he'd been in Florida, Charlie had been sending him letters—which was so uncharacteristic of a guy like Charlie—sometimes three or four pages in length written late at night from the bar when things were slow, keeping him up to date on neighborhood events.

"How come you didn't tell me?"

"I knew how intense you'd get over it. Besides, it just happened. I knew you'd be coming back for the wedding."

"Yeah, but still—"

It seemed to Danny that something had given way inside

The Bronx Kill 21

him, that whatever had been holding him together these past years had broken loose—*like the time he was drowning, that awful sensation of knowing he was up against something that would destroy him*—and knowing too that from this Charlie wouldn't be able to save him, that he needed to grab onto something quick. What he reached for was his beer and drank deeply.

"My source at the 4-3 says he's become a real badass," Charlie was saying.

"Yeah? *How* badass?"

"Like out of control badass. Planting evidence. Setting guys up. Whatever it takes, you know, to get a collar. Apparently he's been trying to build a case against us for a long time." He thought before adding. "What Mooney said to me was he's not happy with the way the cops handled the investigation back then. Too many unanswered questions."

"Like what?"

"Like I said, he didn't get into specifics. Which says to me, he's probably got nothing. Maybe he's tryin' to justify his promotion to Detective. Prove he's some kind of a hot shot. Who knows? Anyway, I told him go fuck himself. I never liked that guy. Even back when we were kids. And I'm sure as hell not going to let him spoil Johnny's wedding. That is, *if* St. John of the Cross ever shows up."

Danny tried to take comfort in Charlie's bravado but Timmy Moon was calling to him again, not with words but with his smile, slow and easy and cryptic, as he undressed on the riverbank, dropping his pants and shirt onto the muddy ground, turning to face them, the same smile Danny would see again out on the river when Moon swam past him, deeper into the current.

CHAPTER 4

By midnight, Danny couldn't take any more nostalgia: friends and acquaintances drifting in and out, timeless oldies on the jukebox, Charlie working the room, purveyor of drinks and jokes and all around good cheer.

It had been fun for a while. No sign of Johnny Whales, though. No one had heard from him yet.

There had been only one other sour note.

About half past nine two men from outside the neighborhood came in and sat at the bar. No problem until Charlie noticed one of them was packing. He took away their drinks, told them to get out. They refused—until Charlie took out his cell phone and called 9-1-1—then they left grudgingly, cursing Charlie first, calling him a motherfucking pansy. "You all motherfucking pansies," one of them shouted before the door slammed shut.

Charlie's face had flushed with anger. "I'm no racist," he told the room. "But I'll be damned if I'm going to tolerate firearms in here."

Other than his own, he meant. He'd shown it to Danny during a quiet moment when they were alone at the bar. A short-barreled .38 that fit the palm of his hand. He kept it under the bar, behind a roll of paper towels.

When Danny left the bar, he passed the playground where he'd worked after school. Swings, monkey bars, a dodge-ball pit, two side by side basketball courts in the center. He'd loved the job, his responsibility for boys in the 10—13 age group, and he remembered one of them in particular, a painfully shy boy named Rashad Taylor.

He wondered what had become of the kid.

Rashad never got into a game because he couldn't handle a basketball very well, so Danny had worked with him, hours at a time, teaching him lay-ups, jump shots, how to shoot from the foul line—until the kid was finally able to hold his own on the court. It was because of that job Danny decided he wanted to be a teacher when he finished college, and it was writing he wanted to teach since

The Bronx Kill 23

it was the one thing most important to him. That was still his dream, *if* he ever finished college, *if* he ever got back to the book that was waiting for him.

It was on the street beyond the playground that he realized he was being followed.

The slow purring of a car behind him.

A sudden, empty feeling in his gut.

When the car didn't pass him he turned around, saw it half a block behind, a black Mercury Marquis moving slowly, keeping pace with him.

Never run. Never show fear. You learned that as a kid in this neighborhood. Act cool. Dignity over panic, any day of the week.

So he simply quickened his pace, crossing the street, turning right at the corner.

The car accelerated behind him. He heard it hit the brakes at the STOP sign then come slowly past him. He thought it might be the two men from the bar but the windows were tinted too dark to see.

Several blocks ahead the car disappeared in traffic and he exhaled in relief. He crossed the street thinking he was safe now but when he reached the next corner the Merc sat double-parked alongside a truck that had concealed it from view.

He was about to cross the street and turn back when the car door opened and a familiar figure stepped out. Older now and heavier, the beginnings of a gut making itself manifest beneath his dark three-piece suit, premature grey in his thinning hair, Tom Mooney took a step toward him. "Got a minute?"

"What if I don't?"

"Come on, let me buy you a beer. Just wanna talk."

"Not really in the mood."

"Only be a minute. One beer. I promise."

"Promises, yeah."

Mooney came toward him, pointed to a bar farther up the street.

"You going to leave it like that?" Danny said, nodding at the Merc.

"They know my car here. No problem, man."

"Cops get all the breaks."

They crossed the street to a bar called Mexicali Rose. "Heard you got back," Mooney said.

"You hear fast."

"Not much I don't know about in the neighborhood."

"Why's that?"

"It's my baby. Got to keep it safe. Got to keep it orderly."

"Big job."

At the bar Mooney ordered two Coronas.

"I'll pay my own way," Danny said.

Mooney shrugged. "Suit yourself."

The place was garishly lit, out of season Christmas lights blinking from all sides of the room, loud Salsa music from the jukebox. The almost exclusively male crowd huddled around an old-fashioned jukebox in the room's center or sat at the long tables along the back wall. There'd been no Mexicans in the neighborhood when Danny left.

Mooney tipped his head back and drank straight from the bottle. When he set the bottle down he kept his hand on it, contemplating it with satisfaction. "You guys were my brother's heroes, you know. Back then."

"Oh?"

"He thought you were so cool, so . . . hip."

"We were ordinary guys. Nothing special."

"Yeah, but Timmy loved you guys. He would of done anything for you."

Danny stared into his beer. "He was a good kid."

"Too good to die so young."

Nobody knew that more than Danny. He stared at the detective, tried to find in his face the cocky guy he knew back then. There was arrogance in the tilt of his head, in the wide flat high forehead, the rigid jaw line beneath which jowls were beginning to stake a claim. But that arrogance was tempered now by something harder: a resoluteness that kept his eyes steady, unyielding. "Yeah. He was."

"So you can see why I'm interested in what happened that Friday five years ago."

"Because you made Detective."

Mooney grinned at the cynicism. He'd taken a blue poker chip from his pocket and was manipulating it from finger to finger, the way some people might play with their keys. "Because I have resources at my disposal I didn't have before."

"You *know* what happened. It's in the police report."

"That's just the point. It's *not* in the police report." Mooney smiled but his eyes remained hard. "Oh, there's a description of what happened that night. The facts. Some of them, at least. But there's more to the story. I've always felt there was more to the story."

"Like what?"

"Like what happened *before* you guys decide to do the marathon swim thing."

"We went to the beach first, then we went to a dance."

"Yeah, yeah. That's in the report. But I hear there was some kind of contest going on, some kind of competition."

"Who said that?"

Mooney drank from the bottle again, set it down carefully. "Let's just say I heard it, all right? There was some kind of contest involving my brother."

"I don't know what you're trying to prove, man, opening this up again."

"I'm not trying to prove anything. I'm tryin' to understand why my brother died that night." He was working the chip between his thumb and forefinger, rubbing it as if it was some kind of charm.

Danny felt the old anger rising in him again. He tried not to sound defensive but failed. "It was an accident. A lousy, rotten accident."

A burst of laughter broke from the men at the jukebox. Mooney glanced at them, annoyed at the distraction. He leaned closer to Danny, spoke low under the music, the heavy chatter of jumbled Spanish. "Tell me about this contest."

"It was a private thing. Over a girl. Between me and Charlie. Nothing to do with Timmy. Nothing to do with that night."

"Let me decide that."

"Is the case officially re-opened? That what you're telling me?"

"Right now I just have a few questions, that's all." He drank from his beer, offered a smile meant to be reassuring. "I hear there was some trouble at that dance you guys went to."

"Says who?"

"Told you. I hear things."

Danny straightened up at the bar. "I don't like the way this is going, man. Maybe I should have a lawyer here."

Mooney's eyes softened. "Take it easy. I just want to understand, that's all. This is off-the-record."

"Nothing's off the record."

"You watch too many cop shows."

"Maybe I just don't trust you."

A note of desperation crept into the detective's voice. "He was my brother. I've got a right to know."

"It was an accident, man. I told you." Danny slid the beer away and turned to leave.

"The truth," Mooney shouted after him, gripping the blue chip tight in his fist. "The truth's what I have a right to know." Under his breath, he added: "What I'm *gonna* know. You can bet your worthless ass on that."

CHAPTER 5

The truth, Danny thought as he walked away. What he had been trying to find these past five years.

A truth he could live with.

A truth that wouldn't kill him.

He knew this much at least: what happened that night, as Tom Mooney was suggesting, didn't begin with that night. Julianne had set things in motion long before, her simple presence among them a disruption, an *aggravation*. Everything, no matter how trivial, had become a contest designed to get her attention. Who could hit the baseball farther, who could dance better, who could swim stronger, faster.

Charlie vs. Danny.

Timmy Moon and Johnny watched from the sidelines.

The friction between them had smoldered like brush fire all summer long. The longing, too, inside him—until he had fallen hopelessly, irreversibly, in love with her.

The night before the drownings he took her on a date—their one and only.

He couldn't remember how the idea originated. Charlie's brain-child most likely: they would each take her out. Then she would have to choose which one of them would be her boyfriend. Why she went along with it, he realized afterward, was only to make Timmy jealous. It was Mooney she loved, all along.

He crossed the street but instead of entering the project with its narrow walkways, its brick canyons in which the night's stagnant air collected—he turned and walked south toward the Kill.

Where he had taken Julianne that night.

When he reached the marginal road where the cab had taken him earlier in the day, he stopped before the wall of tall grass that had grown wild above the rotting, disjointed sections of chain-link fence. Beyond it lay the overgrown fields and lowlands that surrounded the Kill where it emptied into the East River. Certainly not a romantic place. Certainly not.

And yet...

He shoved his hands in his pockets and hunched his shoulders, as he would have as a teenager, and walked along the fence. He couldn't yet bring himself to enter this violated land.

"Why'd you take me here?" She wanted to know as he led her along the water's edge. On one side of the promontory, across the water to the east, the houses of Queens were already in shadow. To the west, the sun's rim touched the buildings of Manhattan, the last golden light spinning toward them across the water. "I want to show you something."

"This?" She wore a jersey and shorts, her usual outfit, and she leaned close to nudge him playfully. "This pile of rocks?"

He shrugged. "I like it here, I guess. It's quiet."

She laughed at that. "Yeah, right."

He laughed, too. "If you don't count the barge horns, or the cars on the bridge. The quiet's not so much about sound as it's a mood thing."

He stopped himself. If he explained what he meant he'd sound even more foolish.

He took her hand and led her toward the wall of the bridge, and for a time he was aware of nothing but the soft, moist feel of her palm and the sound of her step behind him. Then they were in the bridge's underbelly, enclosed by massive cement buttresses that were graffiti-scarred and magnificent, rising to the roadway. It was darker here. Pigeons flapped in the high spaces. Traffic hummed in the stone.

In the shadows, the hulks of rotting cars sunk on their rims into the mud.

"So what is this?"

"Nothing, really."

"You wanted to show me nothing?" she chided.

She gave him a long look. In the dim light it was hard to read her face. But she smiled when she said, "You know, you're the strangest boy I've ever known."

She grew silent then. The tightness in her face made him think she'd fallen to some deep place where there was no room for him. "You mad at me?"

She seemed startled by the question. "Why would I be mad?"

"For not taking you on a normal date. Like Charlie did. To the movies and dinner at someplace fancy."

"That wouldn't suit you." The way she said it, so automatically and without any note of disapproval made him feel better about himself.

He led her farther back into the tunnel like passage beneath the bridge. It was barely light enough to see the objects he pointed out: a car chassis painted red, white and blue, with an American flag hanging from the spokes of each of its four rusted wheel-rims; a wreath made out of a circle of rocks painted red and gold; and a few yards beyond that, positioned in the center of one of the open arches of the bridge, a tree made out of driftwood with stars hanging from its branches.

They stood before the tree without speaking. In the failing light the tinfoil stars glittered with a light of their own.

"It just showed up here one day," he said.

"It's pretty. And weird."

"You mean it's pretty weird," he said and laughed.

Because the ground was damp he took off his shirt and spread it for her. He sat beside her, bare-chested and self-conscious. She was looking at him and smiling. He blushed.

"Showing off your muscles?"

He held his arms crossed to hide his chest. "I have to start working out. I'm too skinny."

"You're real hard on yourself, aren't you?"

"I guess."

"Me, too." She had turned inward again but she made an effort to smile.

"Everyone in my family is so damn hard. My father—" She stopped talking and bit her lip.

"What about him?"

"He's always had a temper, but it's worse now. His job contract's over. All he does is sit around the house and get angry. He threatens us all the time. Says he's going to put my mother in a home, take me back to Peekskill. His brother has a house there."

"Can he do that? To your mother, I mean."

She shrugged, said she didn't know. "She's never been well. I mean, she's okay for a while then she's not okay. There's a long history."

His stare was fixed on the water, on the passing light of a boat heading downriver. "What will you do there? In Peekskill?"

"Work, I guess. He doesn't have the money for me to go to college." She spoke without regret or bitterness, as if her future was something she had long since decided not to fight. "School was never really my thing, anyway."

"Can't you—?" He didn't finish. He had no solution to offer.

She put a hand on his shoulder and he looked out at the water again with the lights of Queens far off. "Muscle Man," she said and pinched his chest.

There was a smirk on her lips and he thought she must be thinking how skinny he looked hunched on the rock beside her, how useless he was in the face of her problems, but then he saw how her face had softened, her eyes shining with what he thought might be appreciation, though what about him that she was appreciating he couldn't say.

This was a time and place when he could tell her how he felt. Do it now, a voice inside him said, do it now. He leaned toward her and there was a moment that he might have kissed her but the moment passed and then she was smirking again, her head drawn back and he thought you can still tell her, you can tell her now, but that moment seemed to pass too and she turned to stare off at the water and at the long upward sweep of the bridge, and all of the things he felt for her he kept inside.

Julianne.

He shook his head to clear away her image, but she lingered in his thoughts, refusing to be pushed aside. Once they had walked under the EL, holding hands. The sun had been shining brightly, falling in thin slanted offerings through the tracks above. He could still remember the feel of her hand, the easy way it cupped itself into his.

He had reached the street's end and he turned away from the wall of tall grass and the cursed history that lay beyond it.

There would be no answers tonight.

Only memories.

Bearing pain, as always, without insight, without remediation.

Something caught his eye and when he turned, the street that had been deserted before, now had another visitor. A black Merc parked halfway down the block.

A coincidence, most likely.

He wanted to think so. After all, there had to be more than one black Merc with tinted windows in this city.

Yet there was something about the car that seemed uncomfortably personal. The angle maybe. The way it waited there, lurking, engine off. The way it seemed pointed in his direction, watching him.

CHAPTER 6

"I saw Timmy Moon tonight."

The words, coming through Danny's cell phone as he walked back from the Kill, stunned him. Briefly it took his mind off the Merc which hadn't yet made an appearance on the street behind him.

"I saw him, Danny. I swear." In the misty rain that had begun to fall, Johnny's voice sounded as skittish and fragile as the wisps of fog slithering up from the black surface of the street. "I swear I saw him. Couple of minutes ago. I swear. Right there on the street. Right there—"

"Slow down, man. Slow down—"

"It scared me, Danny. It scared the hell out of—"

"You saw somebody who *looked* like Timmy. Timmy's dead, remember? We saw him when they pulled him out of the river."

"I don't know, this guy was the spitting image, the spitting image. He couldn't have looked any more like Timmy if he was his twin brother, I swear to—"

"Calm down, Whales. Get a hold of yourself."

"Just standing there. On the street. Like he'd never died at all."

"Take a deep breath and settle down. It wasn't Timmy. You know that. Somebody maybe who looked like him, that's all. That's all it was."

"Sorry. I'm sorry. I'm real sorry but I can't help it." Johnny was crying then. Heavy sobs that he tried to choke back. "It scared me so much. It brought the whole thing back, you know, like it just happened, like it—"

"Where are you?"

A silence followed and it seemed Johnny wasn't going to tell him.

"Times Square."

"Times Square?" Danny couldn't make sense of it. "Why?"

"In a hotel."

"What the hell you doing there? You're supposed to be—"

"I don't know, I don't know." Johnny was crying again. A wheezing, high-pitched sound as if he couldn't catch his breath. "I'm all messed up. I'm—I'm—I don't know what I am."

"Stay there, all right? I'm coming down."

He'd been walking in the middle of the street. That was how he negotiated neighborhoods like this. Keeping himself away from the shadows, from doorways and alleys. Giving himself enough space so he could see what was coming at him, so he could break into a run to avoid it.

A light rain began to fall.

Before he reached the avenue where, at least, he had a *chance* of hailing a cab, he glanced behind him again.

The street was clear.

So maybe that hadn't been Tom Mooney's black Merc on the marginal road, after all.

It gave him comfort to think not.

He found Johnny in a fifth floor room on 45th Street, off Seventh Ave.

When Johnny opened the door, he stood there awkwardly, as if he wasn't quite sure what was expected of him. They shook hands, shared a tentative embrace which Johnny pulled back from quickly. His pale blue eyes, the thin slant of his face, his drawn-in shoulders all suggested apology. They'd had no contact beyond Christmas cards and an occasional phone conversation in the past five years. So maybe, Danny thought, that explained the contrite look. Or maybe it had to do with Danny seeing him like this: holed up in a crummy hotel, a poorly lit cage with its threadbare throw rugs and its smell of musty bed covers.

Vaguely was he aware of the sounds of life around them: a faucet turned on in the room above, a toilet being flushed. In other rooms, in distant hallways, voices murmured as if secrets were being kept. At the far end of the corridor the elevator door opened, a voice was raised in anger then quickly fell silent; and closer, across the hall, someone was crying: man or woman, he couldn't tell.

"How long you been here?"

Johnny shrugged. Another apology. He dug his hands into his pockets and stood by the only window. "All day."

"Doing what?"

"Mostly this." He nodded at the window. "Staring out at the street. That building over there. Deciding what I should do."

Through the rain-streaked glass, Danny could see the neon sign that blinked the word MASSAGE in endless repetition, its ghost light smearing a blue veil across the window glass; and below that, on the basement level, an amber sign advertised the services of a PSYCHIC ADVISOR.

"Body or spirit," Johnny said, "don't know which needs healing more."

"The neighborhood's been expecting you."

"I know. I know." Johnny's face flushed. One more reason to feel guilty. "I'm—I—I guess I'm too afraid."

"Of what?"

"Lorraine. Seeing her again."

"She loves you, man. She's been waiting for you."

"I know. I know." He sat on the bed, his shoulders hunched, eyes fixed on the floor. When he finally looked up, his eyes were wet. "What's wrong with me? Why am I here in this room, when I have a woman like her? I mean, she's been so faithful, so patient. All that time in the Sem, she wrote to me every week, twice a week. I mean those letters meant so much to me. I'd tuck them under my pillow and wait till lights out before I'd read them, so I could be alone with them in my bunk."

He grew silent, eyes fixed to the floor again, as if he might be contemplating how incomprehensible her devotion was, how unworthy it made him feel.

Danny leaned back against the door, tried to close his ears to the low, steady sobbing from across the hall.

"I try to imagine our life together," Johnny was saying. "What it would be like living with this woman who'll be a loving mother, a faithful wife, who's so giving, so understanding, so pretty. Most likely we'll live in a two-family house, if not on the same street as her parents then at least nearby. She'll continue working at the bank until our first child comes, then she'll become a stay-at-home mom. I'll take the subway to and from my job in the city—at a bank or an insurance company, mid-level management of some sort. Evenings I'll help feed the kids and put them to bed. Weekends will be for running errands, taking the kids to the playground, Sunday dinner with her parents.

"That's as much as I can imagine, as far into the future as

I can see. And sometimes it seems like enough, *more* than enough. Other times, though, it seems like a plan for someone else's life, not my own."

"You need time, that's all. To get used to things. To get used to being back."

Johnny looked at him hopefully. "You think so? You think that's all it is?"

"Sure. That's probably all it is."

"That fortune teller," Johnny said.

"What fortune teller?"

"The one across the street." He nodded toward the window. "I finally went over there. *Me*, a seminarian, an *ex*-seminarian, a student of the Holy Mysteries. I'm sure it was a sin. *I am the Lord thy God, thou shalt not have strange gods before me*—that sort of thing. Anyway, she knew about Lorraine. I didn't tell her anything but she knew. And you know what she said? She said, 'Sometimes love is the shadow of a shadow. It sings with many voices at the same time, like a Devil's Choir.'"

He looked at Danny closely. "What the hell does that mean? What do you think she meant by that?"

Danny shook his head. "I don't know. I'd have to think about it."

"It's deep, I know that. It's real deep."

The crying from across the hall seemed to have grown louder. Danny thought if he had to listen to it much longer in this dreary room, after the night he'd had plagued with memories and the knowledge that Tom Mooney was now on his tail, he'd break into tears himself. "Come on. Let's go home."

But Johnny didn't move from the bed. "First," he said, "I have to show you something. Where I saw Timmy Moon."

The rain had let up but the air was still wet. Traces of fog hung in the alleys, in the branches of the trees in playgrounds, as he followed Johnny through streets that ran west of Broadway.

With gentrification the area had lost much of its sordidness but still, tucked in among tenements and restaurants, he saw traces of what it had once been: an occasional gentleman's club with its velvet rope out front and dark-suited doormen passing judgment on those who entered; XXX video stores with blacked-out windows; a lingerie

The Bronx Kill   35

shop called Naughty Nighties.

Soon they were on Eighth Avenue, in the fifties, at a point where the crowds had begun to thin. A digital clock on the side of a building said: 2:48. Cabs hissed by looking for riders.

Johnny, hair wet and flat on his head, his still-damp shirt and pants pressed against his skin, stopped mid-block. "There." His hand shook as he pointed. "He was standing right there."

A grey mist lifted from the sidewalk, dulled the gaudy lights of an All-Male Triple X video store. A young man, resolute and alone and staring blank-faced into the street, stood in the shadows around the window's light.

"Where that guy's standing. Same posture. Same attitude. Same thing for sale."

"A trick of the eye," Danny said. "The rain, the shadows, that's all it was."

"Blonde hair just like Timmy's, combed to the side. Something soft and gentle in his face despite the hard look in his eyes. Like he'd been through hell but he hadn't lost *every*thing. Like he was still the Timmy Moon we loved. He stood there staring at me and I could see that he knew me, that he was trying to tell me something, that he wanted to give me a *message*."

Johnny's eyes had narrowed as if he was seeing the boy again, not in his mind but in the flesh, a mere sidewalk's width away. "I stopped dead in my tracks. My heart stopped beating, I swear."

Danny was reminded of another time, years before, that Johnny had used that phrase, *my heart stopped beating*. It was not long after Timmy had joined the Renegades—he'd come from Ohio, because there was some trouble "*back home*," to live with an aunt who didn't like him very much—and Johnny couldn't seem to take his eyes off him.

Once, late on a night they were drinking beers in the park, Danny caught Johnny in an unguarded moment staring at Timmy Moon in a way that could only be described as adoring, a stare that was both intimate and distanced at the same time. Johnny had turned then and saw Danny watching him. Later that night he confessed that sometimes he couldn't help himself, he was totally fascinated by the guy. "It freaks me out. It's like I'd look at him and my heart stopped beating," he said. Then, embarrassed or ashamed, he'd quickly asked, "You think there's something wrong with me? I mean, it's weird, right?"

"No big deal," Danny had said and let it go at that. They never discussed it again.

Now, on the sidewalk outside the All-Male video store, Danny stared at the teenage boy who watched him impassively from his post by the window, his face blurred in the mist which, like smoke from a hidden fire, continued to lift from the pavement. "A trick, Whales. What else could it have been?"

But even as he said that his heart thumped hard against the walls of his chest, as if he could see Timmy too, standing there forlorn but resolute, a figure wrenched from his dreams, a fallen angel promising in the wee small hours hope for the damned, as if he were neither a deception of the eye nor a figment of Johnny's overwrought imagination.

CHAPTER 7

It was Danny's idea not to say anything, until *after* the engagement party, about Tom Mooney re-opening the case.

"I'm with you a hundred percent on that," Charlie agreed. "The kid's got enough on his plate. Let's not spoil it for him. This is his time right now. No way that son-of-a-bitch is gonna ruin it. Not if I can help it."

It worried Danny, though. Since the detective had already visited each of *them*, it was only a matter of time before it would be Johnny's turn. He hoped it would be later rather than sooner. Judging by Johnny's stressed-out condition last night, the guy was spooked enough already.

He made his first appearance at the MoonGlow that night.

In the doorway he wore a sheepish grin, hands thrust into his pockets, his wisp of a body drifting in the draught, or so it seemed, not quite rooted to earth. He stood there, squinting into the room's murky light.

Time stopped.

Then he stepped forward into the blue shimmer of jukebox light and the neighborhood crowd gave him a standing ovation. He stood silhouetted against the doorway, hands still in his pockets, head bowed, thin frame listing sideways toward the wall's anonymous wood paneling. A helpless grin appeared and disappeared on his flushed face. If he could have turned around then, walked out and slipped unnoticed into the night, Danny felt sure he would have.

Charlie had come from behind the bar and ushered him to a stool. The regulars mobbed him. Whistling. Shouting. Pounding his back.

One of the guys said, "So, what, priests don't eat? Look how skinny this kid is. Get him a meatball parm before he fades outta sight."

Somebody else said, "Getting it regular again will put some color into those cheeks."

Across the room Tony Mancuso, the butcher, pumped

quarters into the jukebox and shouted above the din. "So, what was it like up there?"

All eyes on Johnny: waiting for him to sum up nearly five years in the seminary, thousands of hours of mystical solitude and debate between man and his God before both of them decided to call it quits. It had to be quite a story, Danny thought, but it looked as if they weren't going to hear it this night. Johnny stared into the polished wood of the bar, drew his breath in a momentous pause, then delivered his response straight-faced with no apparent irony. "Different."

"*Different*," Tony echoed. His laughter rolled in waves across the room. "Least they didn't take away the kid's sense of humor."

Sinatra began singing about high hopes, the bowling machine clunked into action, and one by one the regulars drifted away.

Charlie bought beers on the house. In addition to his joy at having Johnny back, he'd won the neighborhood pool as to *when* Johnny would arrive. 10:10 was his pick, and Johnny showed up at exactly 10:13. Winning at anything, even something as silly as this pool, Danny knew well, still meant a lot to Charlie, and the more witnesses to his victory the happier he was.

When the jukebox finally quit, a heavy silence hung in the room. The crowd had thinned. Only a few people lingered in the booths, leaving Danny and Johnny alone at the bar. Charlie was wiping down the wooden surface, but his mind wasn't on it. He'd been holding back his questions all night. You could see them stacking up behind his eyes. He stood in front of Johnny, the rag still balled in his fist. "So, when you gonna tell us what happened up there?"

"Nothing to tell really."

"You spend five years locked up studying to be a priest, then one day you up and walk away? *Some*thing must have happened."

Johnny kept his eyes lowered, fingering his beer glass. "I've had my doubts for a while."

"Yeah, yeah we know. You thought about quitting how many times? Three, four hundred? You kept postponing your ordination. You kept leaving. But you always went back."

"This time is different."

"Why?"

"It's not for me."

"Yeah, *so* ? The realization just popped into your head

The Bronx Kill 39

you're sittin' on the crapper one morning: it's not for me?"

Danny saw something shift, a nearly imperceptible movement in Johnny's eyes as he scrambled to explain himself.

"Grace," Johnny said.

"What about it?"

"I didn't feel it. Not once in all those years. I said to myself, how can I be a priest if I don't even know what grace feels like."

"Grace?" Charlie spread his arms to embrace what was before him. "This is grace. The three of us back together again. Here in the Glow."

"Yeah," Johnny said, struggling to match his enthusiasm.

Charlie scowled. "You don't sound happy."

"I'm a little nervous, that's all."

"Yeah? About what?"

Johnny shrugged. "Everything, I guess."

"Relax, man. Getting it regular again will take the edge off."

Johnny brushed his hair from his face, raised his glass and drained it. "That's one of the things I'm nervous about. We haven't done it yet."

"Not rushing things." Charlie bobbed his head knowingly. "Not my style but hey, you've got plenty of time."

"No. I mean we haven't done it yet."

Danny was surprised at that, but Charlie's jaw dropped in total incomprehension. "*Ever?*"

Johnny's lowered head, his silence, answered for him.

"You've been going out since Junior High."

"Yes."

"So what'd you do all that time?"

"Kissed and stuff."

Charlie wiped the rag across the bar again, contemplating something. "Kissed and stuff, huh?"

"Yes."

"Well, kiddo, it's never too late for love."

"But what if it is?" Johnny rocked forward on the stool. His eyes raked theirs for reassurance. "We've waited so long. All that anticipation. I mean, she's going to expect *a lot*."

Charlie leaned across the bar and clamped his arm around him. "And in true Renegade spirit, you're going to give it to her. Now that God's stepped aside."

"I hope so," Johnny murmured.

"Confidence, man. Confidence." With exaggerated swagger, Charlie hoisted his glass in the air. "Renegades forever."

Johnny, pale-faced, his shoulders drooped, raised his glass without conviction.

Danny followed suit, lifting his glass slowly in an effort to muster the old brotherhood spirit.

In that moment each of them, in his own way, was keenly aware of the ones who were missing.

CHAPTER 8

For two days Tom Mooney kept a low profile. No sign of the black Merc in the neighborhood, no sign of the man himself.

The afternoon of the engagement party Danny and a few regulars were at the MoonGlow, helping with the decorations, when Johnny stopped in.

Charlie had been rushing around, directing operations with the exactitude of a mother managing her unruly children. Watch out for the jukebox. Don't break that lamp. Careful with the bowling machine. He treated every object in the room with a tenderness and concern that belied his tough guy demeanor. He treated the place like he owned it which was, of course, precisely his dream. It was no secret he lived for the day Uncle Sal would sell it to him. But when Johnny came in, his face coloring at the rows of crepe paper wedding bells hanging from the ceiling, he stopped what he was doing and ushered the groom-to-be to a bar stool and poured him a beer.

"I'm here to help," Johnny said.

No way, Charlie declared. This was *his* party and his only responsibility was to sit there like a prince, drink free beers, and tell them how it felt losing his almost twenty-five year old cherry at long last.

Johnny's face flushed even deeper as he reached for his beer. With his fine reddish-blonde hair that fell across his forehead, and his small cherubic face, he still looked like the altar boy he once was.

"Geez, man," Charlie prodded, "you can tell *us*, your buddies. Gives new meaning to the words *Holy Communion*, right?"

"We haven't done it yet," Johnny said.

"You've been home almost three days."

"I know." Johnny seemed to shrink in his seat. "I haven't found the ideal time yet, I guess."

"It's always the ideal time for love. Right, Danny?"

On the step-ladder, Danny was hanging another bell from the ceiling. He was thinking of Julianne—*if it's with the right person*—but what he said was, "Yeah, always."

"See?" Charlie said. He turned back to Johnny. "Tonight. After the party. You couldn't ask for a better time than that, right?"

"Yeah, I guess."

Charlie bristled. He'd heard something he didn't like. Maybe it was Johnny's body language too, the way he slumped there without definition on the stool. "Come on, we're gonna get you into shape. Physical, mental, emotional. Starting now."

As he would have in the old days, he appointed himself quarterback and brought them out into the street alongside the bar. He tapped the football in his grip, twirled his arm to loosen up, sending Danny first then Johnny out for passes.

In a matter of minutes they were playing hard, sweating in the June air, each of them pumped with excitement, and Danny was thinking this was what, for better or worse, he'd left behind when he went to Florida: guys with a shared history, who knew the best and the worst about you, who most of the time knew what you were thinking even before you had time to say it.

He was running neck and neck with Johnny. Charlie uncorked a pass that sailed high above their heads, landing a good thirty feet beyond them. "Hustle," Charlie was yelling at them. "I want to see some hustle out there."

Johnny quit running and called for a time-out.

It was then Danny noticed the black Merc double-parked near the playground at the street's end. Charlie noticed it, too, at the same time. They exchanged glances and a moment's silence passed before Charlie straightened up and said, "Come on, what are we, pansies? Let's rock and roll."

He sent Johnny out for another long pass.

Danny glanced again in the direction of the playground. The Merc was gone. Just passing through.

Long enough to leave a message, though.

The seminary stint had left Johnny rusty: he'd forgotten how to negotiate the narrow street. You had to keep one eye on the ball and one eye on the cars parked on either side. Though Charlie threw perfect spirals, Johnny would bobble the ball, weaving as he fought for balance and for a grip on the pigskin.

"You got rocks, man, use 'em. Take control of the damn ball." Charlie let go a bullet that carried halfway down the block. Johnny veered into a yellow Toyota and went down hard but he managed to hold onto the ball and come up smiling, arms raised high.

"That's it! That's it! A Renegade may fall but he rises again," Charlie yelled. He stood in the middle of the street like he owned it. His thick black hair lifted in imposing waves from his forehead but his squared, normally solid-looking jaw line quivered and his eyes momentarily lost their aggression. He looked to each of them with gratitude.

Something lost had been returned to him.

CHAPTER 9

On his way to the party that night, dressed in a new suit for the occasion, Johnny had his turn for a Tom Mooney visit. The detective was parked under the EL, the elevated tracks casting long shadows on the street. When Johnny came around the corner, the big man stepped from the car and came toward him, flashing a wide grin. "Tommy Mooney. Remember me?" He held out his gold shield and Johnny stepped back as if he'd been struck.

"Sure, I remember you."

"Big night tonight."

"Kind of, yeah."

His bewildered expression made the detective smile. "Your friends didn't tell you, huh?"

"Tell me what?"

"That I'd been around."

"No. Why—?" Johnny stepped back, away from the detective's aggressive leer. With his back against the window of a live chicken market, he felt cornered and stared helplessly at the man before him.

"Unfinished business," Tom Mooney was saying.

"What do you mean?"

"I think you know what I mean."

Johnny's eyes darted wildly from the detective to the street. Life was going on as usual; no one paid them the least attention. In his mind, he saw the Moon's face as it had been showing itself in his dreams, as it had been reincarnated two nights ago in the boy outside the sex shop. He knew what the man was asking him.

"That night—"

"We told the police—"

"I know what you told. What I want to know is what you *didn't* tell."

Behind Johnny, muted by the glass, came the squabble of chickens. "You saying we lied?"

"Come on, Johnny boy. You know theology. You spent years studying it." There was a hard light behind the steel-blue of his eyes.

He's nothing like his brother, Johnny thought. Too cold, too hard, too judgmental. Nothing like Timmy. "I—I don't know what

The Bronx Kill

you're saying."

The detective kept his face thrust forward, inches from his. "Degrees of lies. That's what I'm sayin'. Lies of saying too much and lies of saying too little. I want to know what you guys left out."

"We told what happened."

"Not what I hear." Overhead the uptown local rumbled by, erasing the sound of the chickens. When the train passed, Tom Mooney said: "Someone's come forward. A witness."

Johnny's voice trembled. "No one was there. Only us."

"That's what we thought."

"Who?" Johnny blurted. "Who?"

"It don't take a genius to see you're hiding something." The detective kept Johnny pressed against the window. "I want to know what."

Johnny was sweating visibly now. He felt like a child again, when he was sick with fever. "*Who?*"

"Don't matter who. It's *what* that matters. One of you was fighting with my brother the night he drowned."

Johnny's lip quivered. His hands, splayed against the warm glass, could feel the movement of the chickens in their cages.

"I came to you because you're a decent guy, a *moral* guy. You were gonna become a priest, for god's sake. You wanna carry this around inside you like a disease the rest of your life?"

"I don't have anything to tell you."

The detective stepped back then, gave him breathing room. But the hard blue of his eyes still levied their judgment. "I'm tryin' to make it easy for you. You cooperate now, the easier it'll be for you later."

"It was an accident," Johnny said. His eyes held Mooney's, but tentatively.

"Have it your way. Rest assured, though, I'm not quitting on this till I have answers. Don't care how long it takes me. I'll haunt you guys till I die, if I have to." He turned toward his car.

"Who?" Johnny asked again. "Who came forward?"

"You'll know when the time's right."

The downtown express clattered above them. Johnny moved toward the car to hear what the man was saying. Tom Mooney opened the door and turned toward him. His words were lost in the rush of sound, but Johnny could read his lips.

Till I die.

CHAPTER 10

Johnny stood, bewildered still, hearing the squabble of chickens through the glass behind him as he watched Tom Mooney's car merge into the flow of traffic beneath the EL.

What had just happened?

A scene born of his worst fears: the devil, or his surrogate, come to claim him as one of the damned.

He stared at the steel span of the EL and the anonymous procession of cars beneath it. What he felt was *exposed*, conspicuous, as though Tom Mooney had turned the light on him in front of all those passing by: a specimen to be observed in microscopic detail: every facet of his life, every choice he'd ever made would now come under scrutiny.

The detective's car was lost to view, which gave him at least some temporary relief as he walked away from the EL, seeking refuge in the anonymity of the sidewalk crowd. Focus on the now, focus on the moment, he told himself. You'll get through this. *You will. You will.*

He was already late for picking up Lorraine so he quickened his step. But when he reached her block he stopped at the corner and glanced back as if he'd forgotten something.

He thought at first it was Tom Mooney's visit that had given him pause. But, if he was honest with himself, he knew it was more than that. It was his self-doubt and fear, the reasons why his first stop after his departure from the seminary had been a squalid Times Square hotel.

It was full dark now and he stood in a building's shadow, his hands fidgeting in his pockets. Her house was midway down the block, fourth in a row of identical brick two-family homes. Since his last visit from the Sem, she'd moved upstairs to the second-floor apartment. Her own place, kind of, if you didn't consider that her parents lived downstairs.

All he could see from here was that the downstairs was dark and a single light shone in one of the second floor windows.

He could picture her watching the street from that window,

The Bronx Kill 47

her face strained, anxious, wondering which direction he'd be coming from—the way she had watched for him when they were dating. If he had come upon her by surprise, before she had seen him, before she'd had time to preserve her cool and withdraw from the window, he would be overcome by sadness for her, her undisguised need—and for himself too, because whatever good things he felt for her, he believed he could never return her devotion in equal measure.

What would she think of him now? Stalling like this, hesitant to take the last few steps to meet her on the night of their engagement?

What had she thought of him a few nights before when he'd proposed to her? An awkward business, at best. It had been like meeting her for the first time.

For the longest time it seemed he'd done nothing, simply stood there in her living room helplessly watching her. Then he'd gotten down on his knee because he knew that was what was expected in these situations and he had begun by telling her that all the while he was in the seminary he recited a rosary for her every day. Which *had* to be the least romantic preface in the history of proposals. Had to be.

What an idiot he was!

And then he followed with a string of apologies.

First, for not writing enough.

Second, for all his doubt and confusion—his alternating bouts of hope and despair, his relentless back and forth over the years about whether or not he had a vocation.

Third, for giving her hope, time and again, for each "leave of absence" he took—then crushing that hope when he returned to the seminary with his tail between his legs.

And finally—for ever having let God come between them in the first place. Because he should have known that loving someone he could see and touch would be a hundred times more satisfying than loving someone he could only imagine, whose image kept changing day to day.

Then he raised his eyes, if only briefly, to take in the woman she'd become: her hair shorter and flipped to the side now over one eye, sexier than the long straight, parted-in-the-middle style of their school days. Her body had lost its baby fat, her face thinner too, less round than it once was but still with that same disarming smile that held nothing back, that promised him the world.

In that moment his all too familiar fear had seized him once again: that he could never live up to the fullness of her beauty. Despite that, he reached for her hand, kneeling now on both knees—the way he might have knelt before the cross of Christ in the seminary chapel—and overcome by a similar reverence and humility, asked her to marry him.

A few minutes later he was still on the corner, still fidgeting. Finally he forced himself to move down the street. She was not, as he'd expected, watching from the window. In fact, he saw no movement in any of the rooms.

He hesitated only a moment, then continued to the block's end where he phoned her from one of the last remaining outdoor booths in the neighborhood. He had not yet bought a cell phone.

She answered on the second ring, breathless from apprehension or anticipation, he couldn't tell which. He told her something had come up, he had a few things to do. He'd see her shortly at the Glow.

He didn't say he loved her.

I've been away too long, and now I'm afraid, he muttered to himself. And then he said it again, aloud this time, to the night around him: "I've been away too long, and now I'm afraid."

He hurried under the El until he reached the park, circling the playground twice—as if his fast-paced gait might tire him, exorcise the demons that were driving him—before he settled on the bench, *their* bench in the shadow of the Sugar Maple trees, where the Renegades would gather to begin their nights together.

But the bench held demons of its own.

Timmy Moon forced his way into his thoughts: sitting dreamy and reflective at the end of the bench, Julianne beside him, as always. Usually—as he appeared in the image that came to him then—Timmy would be leaning forward in a thinker's position, hand cupped to his jaw, elbow resting on his knee. Whatever was happening *on* the bench, there was something else going on inside Timmy.

Or so it seemed to Johnny. And he would sit sometimes on the grass at his feet, gazing up at him, and sometimes his gaze would include Julianne and he would have the strangest of thoughts: that they were his parents and he was their child and he loved them both equally. That thought, that concept bringing him an odd kind of contentment. If he would simply keep that in mind, he believed then, he would remain safe from harm. Now, though, the memory made him anxious, added to his distress.

In the seminary, whenever Timmy would force himself into his consciousness like this, usually in the sleepless hours of night, he would drive him away by reciting prayers: Our Father's, Hail Mary's, Glory Be's, the words tumbling over one another, hurried, frantic, becoming one prayer without beginning or end, until he would hear himself saying the words of contrition: *O my God, I am heartily sorry, O my God I am heartily sorry, O my God I am, I am* . . . He would repeat the words until he fell into a delirium, from which he would eventually arise, and the memory of Timmy—at least for a while—would be gone.

But there on the park bench, no prayers came to him. No words were available to mesmerize him into forgetting. So he forced himself from the bench and began walking in the same hurried way—beyond the playground, past trees, other benches, past the lamplights that fanned blue light across the walkway, past lawns and ball fields and more trees and more benches—walking with his head down, without direction.

CHAPTER 11

It was past ten and Johnny still hadn't arrived at the party. Lorraine had been there an hour already, anxiously watching the door each time it opened. She'd put up a courageous effort not to appear heart-broken, but her smiles were beginning to look forced and a distinct tinge of moisture rimmed her eyes.

True to form, as he had whenever she'd stop into the bar, Charlie kept a solicitous eye out for her. While Danny was on the phone calling all over to find their missing buddy, Charlie brought her whiskey sours and took turns dancing with her, regaling her with jokes, making excuses for Johnny's absence. "The man of God has descended to earth," he told her, "and hence is now susceptible to the human failing of tardiness or perhaps vanity, if our boy has a grand entrance in mind." In between quips, he'd tell her how pretty she looked.

For the occasion, she and her sister had chosen matching satiny dresses, Lorraine's white, her sister's red, which happened to be the exact colors of Rheingold beer cans. Soon after they arrived, to Lorraine's embarrassment, everyone had begun ordering cans of Rheingold and making a point of toasting her.

On the dance floor, Charlie continued to charm—broad smile, broad shoulders, light and graceful on his feet—as he swirled her around the cleared space by the jukebox, whispering in her ear, amusing and reassuring her. Behind the bar, though, he was all business: checking on the baked ziti turning to mush in the silver warming trays, pouring drinks for the near capacity crowd of seventy people, alternately keeping an eye on the door, and on Danny—for a sign that his phone inquiries had turned up something.

By ten-thirty, having consumed one too many whiskey sours, Lorraine appeared to be on the verge of a nervous breakdown. She stood alone in a corner of the room, her only company a drifting flock of heart-shaped balloons and a few wayward crepe-paper wedding bells that had fallen from the ceiling. She refused to dance, refused even to talk to her closest girlfriends. When Charlie tried to coax her back onto the dance floor, she burst out sobbing and locked herself in the ladies' room.

A few minutes later she emerged, teary-eyed but head held high. Surrounded by her sister and a bevy of commiserating allies, her face now bestowed with a long-suffering dignity, she moved through the crowd of family and friends toward the door.

It was at that moment Uncle Sal made his appearance.

In his custom-tailored white suit, he moved comfortably through the room, shaking hands, patting backs or pinching cheeks, bestowing an occasional bear-hug on the anointed. Despite his size—he was barely 5'9"—he had a commanding presence and though he was, in actuality, nobody's uncle, he was like a distant relative to everyone in the neighborhood. He'd lived in Larchmont for a good ten years already but he made the trip to the Bronx at least twice weekly to check on his properties, of which the Glow with its reputation for out-of-this-world meatball Parmesan sandwiches was the most profitable.

When he reached the bar, Charlie had a double amaretto awaiting him. A dark look had replaced the smile on Uncle Sal's face, made even more solemn by his thick eyebrows and black, full moustache. "The *fianzata*. She's in the street, in tears."

"A little problem," Charlie said. "We're working on it."

"What is it with that kid?" His look swung from Charlie to Danny. "He still got to act like he's sixteen?"

Danny said, "He needs time to adjust, that's all."

"I'll give the kid an adjustment." He shook his head in disgust. "He oughtta be ashamed of himself—a good woman like Lorraine." He took his drink and headed back to his office. "Lemme know when Friar Tuck arrives," he said over his shoulder. "I got a thing or two to say."

Charlie stood with both hands on the bar, watching him walk away. He chewed his lip like he was deciding something.

Danny said, "Maybe now's not the best time to talk to him."

"I'll give him a minute. He'll cool down."

"I don't know. Maybe you should wait."

"How long?" Charlie's strong, handsome face softened, his eyes traveling long-distance. "*How long?*" It wasn't an answer he sought but a release of frustration. "I've been waiting too long already," he said. "I'm so damn sick of—"

Someone yelled to him from the end of the bar and he went off to pour another beer.

Minutes later, on the way to the men's room, Danny saw Charlie farther down the hall, knocking on the half-open office door. He leaned in, using his most ingratiating voice. "I'd like to talk to you, Uncle Sal, if you've got a minute."

"So talk," Uncle Sal said.

When Danny came out of the john, the door was still half open. He could see Charlie's back, the humble curve of his shoulders as he stood before Uncle Sal's desk. Uncle Sal spotted him lurking in the hall and called out, "Yo, Danny, come in here."

Charlie, holding a notebook, turned to watch him enter, his face bright with expectation.

"Charlie here's got some big ideas, ain't that right, Charlie?"

"I just wanted to, you know—" he shifted uneasily in front of the desk—"if you've got a minute, I just wanted to go over some figures." He began flipping through the pages of the notebook until he found what he was searching for. "My plan, you know, you said when I was ready—" He lay the notebook flat on the desk but Uncle Sal ignored it.

"I think I'm ready now," Charlie was saying. "I mean, I've got it all worked out. The bank will give me a small loan. If you could just let me pay off the rest over time, I—"

"Whoa! Whoa!" Uncle Sal raised both hands as if pushing something away. "Let's not get ahead of ourselves here."

"I'm not, I'm not. I mean, I'm really ready for this. I can feel it—"

"You're forgetting something, aren't you?"

"What? What am I forgetting?"

"I said I'd turn the place over to you when *we both* think you're ready—"

"So what you're saying—"

Uncle Sal lit a cigar and leaned back in his chair. "What I'm saying is you don't have a pot to piss in. You spend your time and money chasing skirts. You still think you're some kind of God's gift to womankind. You still got this King Kong complex thing, like you want to beat up everyone who looks at you cross-eyed. You still got this grudge thing, this whatever it is, like the world owes you something." He blew a steady stream of smoke in their direction. "You're the same kid you were in high school. You all are."

The room was small and crowded and hot. Danny, not wanting to be there, was about to excuse himself but Uncle Sal fixed

The Bronx Kill 53

him with his glare. "Ain't that right, Dan-o?"

"That's all gonna change," Charlie was saying. *I'm* gonna change. Now that Johnny and Danny are back. We're gonna be strong together. I can run this place. I can make it happen—"

"It's already happening. The Glow's been turning a profit since it opened in 1959."

"I know, I know, it's doing great. But I've got ways to make it better. Bring in the young crowd, live music, a little re-decorating. I got plans—"

"Yeah, you got plans." Uncle Sal looked at Charlie without blinking. "You'd follow your dick over a cliff you thought there'd be something to stick it in."

"No, I—"

"And your buddies." He gave Danny a pitying look. "We see where Johnny's at. Mr. No-Show. And you, Danny, the *artiste*. The writer who don't write nothing. How long you been working on this book that never appears?"

"I'm taking notes."

"*Notes*." That gave Uncle Sal a laugh. "That'll put food on the table." He shifted his gaze to Charlie. "I was your age I already owned three businesses. And I did it on my own. Nobody gave me nothing."

Danny started backing his way to the door, but Charlie wouldn't let it go.

"Jeez, Uncle Sal, I worked my ass off for you, like how many years now. I thought—"

"I know you did, son." The sneer was gone, replaced by the solemn, thoughtful gaze of Uncle Sal's face at rest. "You're a damn good bartender. Don't let nobody tell you any different. You got a job here long as you want it. I promised your father I'd never let you go hungry, and I won't. But this other business, this taking over the place, forget about it. You got a long way to go before we can sit down and talk."

Charlie wouldn't look at Danny as they left the office. He went directly into the storeroom to collect himself and Danny followed him, coming up with no better words of consolation than, "He's in a bad mood tonight, that's all. Maybe his blonde bimbo girlfriend dumped him."

Charlie stood with his back to the wall, arms crossed, staring at the cases of beer stacked in neat rows, floor to ceiling. "All my life he's been telling me how much like a son I was to him. I showed him respect. I gave my life to this place. And this—this is what I get."

Danny could think of nothing more to ease Charlie's stress. He'd been having his own issues this night, missing Julianne, missing Timmy Moon too, wishing they could have been here.

In the silence that followed, Danny glanced out the window. "Look," he said.

Beyond the shadow of the EL, Johnny sat on the steps of St. Cecelia's Church, staring blankly like a man whose future had suddenly quit on him.

CHAPTER 12

From the sanctuary door Danny saw Johnny in the church's dim nave: first row, right side, kneeling with his back straight, eyes raised to the altar. He looked, at least, more focused than on the church steps.

Danny slipped into the pew beside him, kneeling, eyes straight ahead on the altar, as if he was praying. Since the accident, he'd lost his belief in prayer but he still had feeling for the *atmosphere* of a church. This was the silence of eternity: heavy shadows, fluttering candles, the arms of saints lifted in rigid supplication, frozen for all time.

Beside him, Johnny blessed himself, settled back on the seat and stared ahead at the row of saints flanking the altar. "Why didn't you tell me about Tom Mooney?"

Danny took a deep breath. In his friend's eyes there was accusation and hurt. "We thought you had enough on your mind right now."

"He scared the hell out of me. Jumping out of a car like that. Cornering me. On the way to the party."

"The bastard. I was hoping—"

"Hoping what?"

"We didn't want you to worry."

He shook his head in disapproval. "You should have told me."

"We would have. Soon."

"What are we going to do?"

"I don't know. Nothing, I guess."

Johnny looked horrified. "We've got to do *some*thing."

"Like what?"

"I don't know. *Some*thing."

"It's Mooney's move. We've got to wait and see."

The silence rose up between them again. Johnny had turned back to face the altar, looking to the crucifix for answers.

Charlie waited on the steps of the church. "The Prodigal

Son," he said, smirking, when Johnny came out.

"Mooney paid him a visit tonight," Danny explained.

"Oh, yeah?" He tried to make it sound matter-of-fact.

As they walked toward the Glow, Johnny said: "It's been hard enough, my coming back. Now this."

"Nothing that can't be fixed," Charlie assured him.

But Johnny seemed unconvinced. He wouldn't meet their eyes. Several steps behind them, he walked with his head turned to the side as if the small park, the playground, the stanchions of the EL might offer him more comfort.

Finally he said, "So when were you going to tell me?"

Charlie pretended he didn't understand. "Tell you what?"

"About Tom Mooney. Asking questions."

"Oh that," Charlie said dismissively. "It's all bullshit. Nothing to get your panties in a wad."

"He's got a witness."

"He said that?"

"He says we'll find out *who* when the time's right." Johnny's voice shook, the way it did when his nerves took over. "What do you think he means by that?"

Charlie stopped at the corner, grabbed Johnny by the shoulders to steady him. "Cool down, dude. Don't get so hysterical."

"I'm not hysterical."

"You *look* it."

"I'm not."

"Yeah, dude, you are. He look hysterical to you, Danny?"

Johnny said, "How long's he been—*investigating*?"

"I don't know. Few weeks maybe. He came to me beginning of the month. He ran into Danny couple of nights ago. It's all bullshit."

Johnny looked doubtful. "How you know that?"

"It's a cop game. They bluff you into thinking they've got some inside info. They figure that'll make you spill the beans."

"He said he's got someone."

Charlie stopped again, glared at Johnny. "Who, Whales, who? Unless the Moon or Julianne came back from the dead, who's he got?"

"I don't know." Johnny looked genuinely perplexed. "But I've been having these dreams."

"What kind of dreams?"

The Bronx Kill   57

"About Timmy."

"What about him?"

The pact was not only to not *speak* about that night, but not even to *think* about it. Danny had broken that second part more times than he could ever count. He'd broken it a dozen times already that night. Now it was Johnny's turn, breaking both parts of the pact with reckless disregard.

"In the latest ones, since I've been back," Johnny was saying, "he's walking through the neighborhood like nothing's happened, or he comes dripping out of the river. In his underwear like that night. But the thing is he's smiling. In every dream he's smiling. He's coming right towards me and smiling."

"Better to shut the hell up about it," Charlie said.

But Johnny couldn't help himself. "I've had dreams about him for years, off and on. But since I decided to leave the Sem and marry Lorraine, I have them all the time. Every night, almost."

"We're gonna start thinking you got a thing for the guy, you don't shut the hell up about him."

Johnny blushed but covered it quickly. "But what do you think it means? It's got to mean something, doesn't it? Why would he be smiling?"

CHAPTER 13

At the bar only a few die-hards from the party remained. With his jacket off and his tie loosened, Johnny sat on a stool, nursing a beer. He looked so morose Charlie finally relented. "Listen, Whales, if it'll make you feel any better I've got a friend at the 43rd. I'm gonna call him now. If Mooney's got some secret witness, he'll know about it. If he *doesn't* know, he'll find out."

He went into the office to make the call and came back a few minutes later. "My man's on it," he reported. "He's gonna check around."

In the men's room a few minutes later, Danny and Charlie side by side in front of the two ancient enamel urinals, Danny said, "This guy at the 43rd, I know him?"

"Better we don't use names. Let's just say he's been drinking gratis here for years. He owes me." He glanced at Danny's brooding face. "*What?* Don't tell me Mooney's got you spooked, too?"

"I don't trust him, that's all."

"Hey, it's bad enough I got Nervous Nelly out there. Don't you go south on me, too."

"I'm fine," Danny said. "I'm fine."

"Good. Because we've got to get our boy up to speed tonight." Charlie turned back to face the urinal and sighed in relief.

The walk-in urinals, the regulars called them, because they were so over-sized. Originally they might have been white or cream but over the years they had darkened to the color of coffee stains. Whatever it was—their size or age or inescapable man smell or the enamel solid as an altar—the place had become a shrine to masculine secrets, a place of revelation.

In the time it took to relieve yourself, wash and dry your hands, guys were known to pour their hearts out in synopsis form, especially in times of distress. Charlie was no exception. He rattled on about how he could never figure why Johnny wanted to be a priest in the first place, what with a girl like Lorraine in the picture. She wasn't the best-looking girl in the neighborhood, he said, nor even the best-built. But she had the sweetest disposition, a smile that got his heart pumping.

The Bronx Kill

"I prefer blondes and redheads," he said, "as you well know. I like 'em big-chested and glamorous, but Lorraine, Lorraine—" He didn't finish the thought. "You know, she'd stop in the bar sometimes, usually after a date with some guy who asked her out. She'd tell me about him, you know like she was confessing something, apologizing, and I'd always find something negative to say about the guy, 'cause in my heart I wanted her to save herself for Johnny. But I felt guilty about that, like maybe I wasn't doing the right thing. Now that our boy's back, though, I'm glad I did it. I think it was the right thing to do."

He zipped his fly and looked over at Danny. "So, what do you think?"

"About Johnny?"

"Yeah."

"He's overwhelmed."

"So what do you think? We should get Lorraine over here, get them to talk."

"I don't think we should force the issue. Not right now."

"What should we do?"

"Wait, I guess."

He punched Danny's shoulder. "*Wait?* What are we, pansies?"

"You asked what I thought."

"I can't do that, dude. I can't sit around and wait for fate to have its way."

He seemed emboldened, even by Charlie standards. His bad fortune earlier in the evening with Uncle Sal, Danny figured, had given him one more reason to be aggressive.

"Got to take action, got to do *some*thing."

"What are you going to do?"

"I don't know." He stood by the sink, studying himself in the mirror. "Get something going. Get our boy back in the swing of things." He noticed something on his cheek he didn't like, a blackhead or a tiny pimple, and he squeezed it. "Sweet girl," he said. "Sweet, sweet Lorraine. I don't know. Hasn't been a girl like her since—"

He didn't say Julianne's name. That was part of the pact, another ghost they had to keep at bay.

In the shadowy-yellow light he seemed to waver uncertainly before the mirror. He smoothed back his hair and stiffened his shoulders, then turned to yank open the door, striding into the bar to take charge of things again.

CHAPTER 14

Except for druggies passed out in doorways and hookers patrolling the shadows under the EL, Jerome was closed up this time of night. Every so often a no-name bar was tucked in among the auto-body shops, identifiable only by an orange or pink neon beer sign.

They cruised the avenue slowly in Charlie's aging Eldorado. At each traffic light, he slowed the car even more to evaluate the girls who would materialize suddenly out of a doorway or be slouched against one of the EL's stanchions, frozen in the headlights, eyes glittering, skin shiny with oil.

According to Charlie, Johnny needed some action, *someone to practice on* was his less than delicate way of putting it.

It was his theory that sentiment was killing Johnny. Emotion, he believed, was the enemy of good sex. The more you felt, the less effective your performance would be. Tenderness was all well and good, but there was plenty of time for that *afterward*. While you're doing it, it's all about how bad you want it, how bad *she* wants it. It's all about animal desire so you've got *to become* an animal. Sure, sure, a woman will tell you she wants sensitivity, vulnerability, all that kind of stuff. Try giving her vulnerability instead of a good, strong thump and see how happy she'll be.

Danny was thinking about Julianne. He'd never gotten that far where sexual performance was an issue. It was longing and need that had consumed him, longing and loss that consumed him now. "That's a little simplistic, isn't it?" he said.

"Some things are meant to be simple, Danny boy. Sex is one of them." He grinned in the dashboard light.

In the back seat, Johnny stared at the girls without expression and said nothing. He looked as if he didn't want to think about what he was about to do, that it was something he simply wanted to get over with, like a dentist's appointment he knew would be painful but, if he didn't follow through, the consequences would be even more painful.

"Maybe we should call it a night?" Danny said. It was already

The Bronx Kill

well past midnight and everyone's nerves were on edge. "He can call Lorraine in the morning to apologize."

Charlie shot him a hard look. "What are you, nuts? We've got to help this guy out."

"It's okay," Johnny said. "Really, it's okay—"

"It's *not* okay. If it was okay we wouldn't be in this car right now. We'd be at the Glow watching you put a ring on Lorraine's finger. It's definitely not okay."

"I don't know," Danny persisted. "I have a bad feeling about this. I don't think Johnny's up to it."

"Sure he is. Aren't you, Whales?"

In the back seat Johnny muttered, without conviction, a "Sure, why not?"

"You see?" Charlie said. "Our boy's a player." He looked at Johnny in the rear view. "All you have to do is be yourself. Women—even hookers—will like that shy, lost little boy thing about you."

"You don't have to do this, Whales," Danny tried one last time. "You know that, right?"

Charlie glared at him. "Back off, man, will you?"

Danny threw up his hands. "Fine. Have it your way."

"We're on a mission." Charlie's face was tight with grim resolve. "No time to waste. Can't you see that?"

It seemed to Danny that whatever the "mission" was, it had become as much about Charlie as helping Johnny out.

They rode in silence for several blocks before Charlie spoke again. "There's this place up ahead where everything's clean and simple. Well, maybe not so clean but I've got condoms in the glove box, so nobody need worry."

It would have been easy to miss. A small hand-painted black and white sign that read *Home Cookin'* hung above a metal door. Outside, a muscular black man offered them an impersonal nod as they filed past him.

"It's a place of last resort," Charlie confessed when they were inside, "but as a last resort it's never failed me."

Strippers danced on a platform above the bar. Farther back, in a dingy second room, dimly lit booths lined both sides of the dance floor. If you came in as a couple, Charlie explained, they brought you drinks but otherwise left you alone. If you came in alone, well, it wasn't long before company showed up, in the form of a woman bearing the expected over-priced magnum of champagne.

The light was scarce. What you saw, in the booths or on the dance floor, were shadows rather than people. A hostess appeared at their booth, a dark woman with a hard flat face.

"Three Buds," Charlie said. "And my friend here, Johnny, is celebrating—"

She walked away before he finished.

He told them not to take it personal. That's the way she was. A few seconds later, another dark-skinned woman, this one with dreadlocks, younger and more scantily clad than the hostess, came to the booth.

"Which a you's Johnny?"

CHAPTER 15

The hallway where Charlie and Danny waited, beer in hand, was cramped and smelled of urine. Every time the men's room door opened the smell grew stronger.

Charlie held his foot against the alley door to keep it open an inch or two: enough to hear Johnny if he was being mugged, but not enough to make him any more self-conscious than he was. Those were the options here: either do it in a booth, or take it into one of the cubicles that had been installed along one side of the canopied alley.

Pleasure Alley, Charlie called it.

The bare, dingy alley had been given a face lift of sorts with the addition of the roof and cubicles. Fortunately for Johnny, he said, it was a slow night. He'd been there when all the cubicles were taken and folks were lined up on both sides of the alley, humping assembly-line style in a stand-up position against the damp brick walls.

"How many times you been here?"

"A few," he said vaguely. Then added, by way of justification: "Beats beating off."

"I've never needed it that bad."

"So, what, you're too good for this, that what you're saying?"

"Why do you always have to twist what I say?"

"Well, don't say things that are so easy to twist."

"Whatever."

Charlie nodded toward the alley triumphantly. "See? I knew our boy had it in him."

The way he said it annoyed Danny. "Had *what* in him?"

"You know."

"No, I don't. What?"

"The guy thing."

"You mean the fuck-anything-that-moves thing."

"I didn't say that, did I?"

"But that's what you meant."

He gave Danny one of his gloating smiles as if he'd won again. "Now who's twisting things?"

"Well, don't say things that are so easy to twist."

"*Touché*, my man. *Touché*." He leaned toward the crack of the door as if he'd heard something. "I just want to know he's a normal guy, that's all."

"Why?"

"Why *what*?"

"Why does that matter so much to you?"

"He's our buddy. Of course it matters." He drained his beer and set it down on the floor. "What's bugging you, man?"

"The sooner we get out of here the better I'll feel."

A woman screamed in one of the cubicles. Charlie kicked open the door to find Johnny standing in the center of the alley, buckling his pants and looking frightened. Even more frightened was the dreadlocked girl he'd been with who was cowering along the wall, backing away from him and shouting, "Get away from me. Get away. Get away."

The hostess rushed through the hall and into the alley. "What's goin' on heah?"

"Keep him away from me," the girl said. She was sobbing, almost a wail. "He's a freak."

The hostess glared at Johnny. "What'd you do?"

"Nothing, I—"

"Trying to save me," the girl muttered. "Jesus talk. Crazy talk. Don't want to be saved by no white man."

Three large black men had come out through a door in the alley. The largest of them said, "You boys best be moving on."

"I didn't mean any harm." Reaching out in a stumbling trance-like gesture, Johnny lurched toward the girl but the bouncers moved quickly toward him, the largest of them grabbing him from behind and yanking him backwards. Charlie went after the man but the second bouncer, a stocky man with unusually thick biceps, swung at him, Charlie spinning back into the alley wall, the bouncer stepping behind him and pinning his arms.

"*Don't!*" the third bouncer, a dreadlocked Jamaican man who might have used the same hair-dresser as the girl, told Danny who had already taken a step toward him but stopped under his withering gaze.

They ran Charlie and Johnny to the end of the alley, through the metal doors and across the sidewalk, each of them flung hard against a parked car. The head bouncer, the largest of them, the name

Ernie stitched on his black shirt, kicked Charlie in the gut when he tried to get up. "That's for the other night."

With a groan, Charlie took a good look and recognized him as one of the two men he'd thrown out of the MoonGlow for packing. The second of the pair was the bouncer with the massive biceps, standing behind him. He came forward then and delivered a kick of his own. *Yusef* was the name stitched on his shirt.

Danny was rushed down the alley after them, shoved finally by the Jamaican who was escorting him so that he pitched forward, off-balance, and landed bruised and shaken on the curb.

"You're on my turf now, faggots. Don't come back, you heah?" Ernie said, before turning and heading for the alley door where his cohorts stood guard. "*Evah.*"

Charlie was on one knee, holding his stomach. Several feet away, Johnny leaned back against a car's bumper.

"What the hell did you do?" Charlie wanted to know.

Johnny shrugged. "Nothing."

"Nothing?"

"I said a few prayers."

"You said a few prayers?"

"Yes."

"You're supposed to be humping the girl."

"I know."

"You know?"

"Yes."

"What's wrong with you?"

"I felt sorry for her. She was just a kid. I asked the Lord to help her."

"She wanted to fuck you, Johnny. She didn't want help. She wanted your hundred twenty-five bucks."

"I know. I'm sorry."

He kept apologizing all the way back to the car, but inside the parked Caddy he was quiet. Charlie stared ahead at the street, both hands on the wheel, killing time it appeared until he figured out their next move.

"Didn't realize it was them," Danny said. "Your buddies, Ernie and Yusef."

"Me, neither."

"You know those guys?" Johnny said from the back seat.

Charlie laughed. "In a manner of speaking."

Danny had to laugh, too. "What are the odds, you figure? Running into them again?"

"I don't know. Nine zillion to one, maybe."

A train rumbled overhead on the EL, leaving behind its silver rain of sparks.

Finally, from the back seat, Johnny broke the silence. "I know I screwed up bad. If it wasn't for me, none of this would have happened."

"Don't worry about it." Charlie stared out the window at the shadows under the EL, his face grim as if he were being chased by ghosts of his own. Humiliation like this he wouldn't take lying down.

From the entrance to the alley, Ernie the bouncer drew on a cigar and watched them.

Charlie started the engine and gave him the finger.

CHAPTER 16

Not yet 2:30 but Uncle Sal had already closed the MoonGlow for the night. Charlie let them in through the back, turned on only the bar lights, kept the front door locked.

He poured shots for each of them, with beer chasers. His ribs still ached from the kick but it was his wounded pride that made him sulk. "Getting thrown out like that, man." He shook his head. "It's like you ask this girl out. You don't really like her. She's not even your type and she's way below your standards, you know, in looks *and* personality. But you've got nothing else going so you lower yourself. And what happens? She dumps you. You didn't even want her in the first place—and *she* dumps *you*."

"It was *your* idea," Danny said.

"Yeah, well, *some*body had to have an idea. Otherwise *what?* We would have all gone home defeated, especially Whales here. I couldn't let that happen."

"So how do we feel now? Like winners?"

Charlie glared at him across the bar.

Danny's hip bone hurt from where he hit the curb. He shifted his weight on the bar stool to favor it. But it was Johnny who seemed the most agitated. He had a gash below his right eye compliments of the car fender he was thrown against. His hair, always neatly in place, fell in jumbled reddish blonde strands across his forehead. And he couldn't sit still. He paced around the room punching his fist into his open palm. "It was wrong," he muttered. "It was just wrong."

Charlie groaned in exasperation. "Here we go with the moralizing again."

"It *was*, Charlie. It was wrong. Taking advantage of young women like that. Making them do that kind of work. Under those conditions. Putting up with every animalistic man who's got a hundred twenty-five dollars in his pocket."

"Like you, you mean?"

"I was trying to help her."

"If you'd have been more *animalistic* we wouldn't have gotten our asses thrown out."

"It wasn't right."

Charlie swallowed some beer, his eyes gone pensive, as if maybe he'd been through this before with himself. "It's the way of the world, man. What can I say? They're young, they're poor, they're uneducated. They've got no future, nothing but themselves to sell. Happens everywhere—Africa, Asia, Europe, *here*."

"That doesn't make it right."

"It doesn't make it right, but it doesn't make it wrong either. How they gonna survive if it wasn't for all the horny guys in the world? You'd rather have them starve, have no roof over their head, not be able to buy food and clothes for their kids? You look at it that way, we're helping them out. It's a mutual act of charity. They give us what we need, we give them what they need. It's a win-win situation."

"They'd find other options."

"Like what? You're in a hole that deep, what options you got?"

"I don't know. *Some*thing."

"I had this friend," Charlie went on. "Guy I knew from Fordham. Liberal politics, real progressive. He had this house cleaner comes in twice a week. She happens to be black. One day he decides it's demeaning for a black person to be cleaning dirty clothes and bathroom floors for a white person. He doesn't want to perpetuate the class system, the pre-civil war attitudes, whatever. So he lets her go. Never mind that she's the sole support of her family. Her husband's a disabled vet from 'Nam, one of her kids got some rare blood disease. Never mind that she really needs the money. He lets her go."

Charlie finished his shot and set the glass down hard on the bar.

"So what happened?"

"He couldn't stand going to the Laundromat and he sure as hell wasn't going to get on his knees himself to scrub the bathroom floor, so he re-hired her. But you see my point."

Johnny brooded over that, without saying anything.

"Whales would have been better off going to talk to Lorraine," Danny said.

"*Action's* what he needs now, not talk." He poured three

The Bronx Kill

more shots and set them on the bar. "Talk's useless. Biggest cop-out there is."

"Oh, God." Johnny stood at the window, looking into the street.

"What now?" Charlie wanted to know.

"Tommy Mooney. His car's outside."

"Where?"

"Down the street."

Danny joined him at the window. The black car, tinted windows hiding its secrets, was parked near the corner, facing their way.

"Don't stand there gawking at him, for god's sake." Charlie poured another shot and downed it.

Johnny stepped away from the window and looked at Danny as if he might cry. "We're under surveillance."

"He's busting balls," Charlie said. "That's all. Don't get hysterical."

"I'm not hysterical."

"You *look* it."

"I'm *not* hysterical."

"He look hysterical to you, Danny?"

"I just want to know what the hell he wants."

Charlie shrugged. "Who knows what he wants? I know he's not going to get it, whatever *it* is."

Johnny went back to the window, parted the curtain. "He's still there. Just sitting there."

"Fuck him," Charlie said. "Have a drink."

"It's 2:30 in the morning. What's he doing out there?"

"It's called the night shift."

"People are getting shot and mugged and raped all over the city and he's watching *us*."

Charlie laughed. "Don't take it personal."

"How else should I take it?" Johnny was pacing along the edge of the bar, eyes feverish and wild, as if he'd already been found guilty. "Isn't there a statute of limitations, or something?"

"Not on a homicide case," Charlie explained. "Not in New York."

Homicide. The word itself still terrified Danny, and by the look on Johnny's face it obviously had the same effect on him.

"Come on, man. Chill. We went through this how many

times back then?" Charlie pushed Johnny's shot glass across the bar in a gesture of encouragement. "In order for us to be charged with homicide, he has to prove first that we *caused* Timmy's death *and* that we did so with *criminal intent*. At the very least he has to prove *criminal negligence*. Which means, as you know, and I quote: 'that we engaged in blameworthy conduct so serious that it creates or contributes to a substantial and unjustifiable risk that another person's death will occur.'"

He studied Johnny's face to see how much of this he was recalling. "We all faced the same risk, right? Well, except maybe for me 'cause I'd been on the swim team. Besides, when we realized we made a mistake, we turned back, right? Is it our fault if Timmy didn't? It was a choice he made, free will. And even if we kind of coaxed him into the water, he was on his own after that. His choice *again*. No one made him keep swimming. You can lead a horse to water, but you can't make him drink, right? That's our story. So what's the problem?" The strain in his face suggested his patience had run out. They'd been through this too many times before. "What are we talking about?"

"I should have stayed in the seminary. I should have never—"

"What, priests can't get sent to jail? Come on, man. Get hold of yourself. It was an accident. We all know that. Nothing's going to happen."

Johnny stopped pacing. You could see by the way he looked at Charlie he was trying to let himself be reassured, trying really hard.

Then there was a loud knocking on the door.

Johnny's eyes went wide with terror, the way Danny remembered them looking when they all stood on the bank, scanning the river for some sign of Mooney. "Don't let him in."

Charlie laughed again, louder this time. "What are we gonna do, pretend? He knows we're here."

"*Don't*."

"You *act* guilty, he's gonna *think* you're guilty. And if he thinks *you're* guilty, he's gonna think *we're all* guilty." His eyes had turned hard as threats. "And I can't have that. You understand?"

Johnny shook his shoulders to loosen up. He ran his hands across his eyes to clear the anxiety from his face. "I'm okay."

"Good." And with that Charlie strode to the door and yanked it open, staring face to face with Tom Mooney.

"Mind if I come in?" He'd been to the barber. What was left of his hair had been brushed straight up in a crew-cut. He grinned like they were old buddies. "Hate to pass up a chance with the three of you together."

"Yeah, I do mind. We're tryin' to celebrate here. Private party."

"Only be a minute. I—"

"That case's been closed almost five years. I don't know what's buggin' your ass—"

"New information's turned up."

"Yeah? Like what?"

"Like I'd be happy to tell you, you don't keep me standing out in the street here."

"You're bullshitting me."

"No bullshit, man. It's pretty fucking amazing is what it is. I think you're gonna want to hear what I have to say."

Charlie hesitated, before stepping aside. "This better be good, Tommy. You got two minutes then you're outta here."

There was more than a little swagger in Tommy Mooney's walk. The extra weight he'd put on contributed to that; it made his presence more imposing in the dimly lit room. He nodded at Johnny and Danny. "Good to see you fellas again."

"So what's this amazing new info that's turned up?" Charlie said behind him.

For a moment the detective was caught between them, Charlie standing by the door, Johnny and Danny at the bar. The old street-fighting disadvantage, surrounded by the pack, and he smiled at the irony. He stepped back so that he could take them in at one glance. "We got a couple of mysteries in this case of yours I'm determined to clear up."

The phrase *this case of yours* hit Danny hard. A disease they'd been afflicted with. A terminal condition that wouldn't go away.

The detective stood there slightly out of breath, his shoulders heaving. He wiped a hanky across his forehead. "You know, you could offer a guy a drink."

"I could," Charlie said but stopped there.

Mooney smiled, shrugged. He folded the hanky and stuffed it in his suit jacket. He pulled a blue poker chip from his pocket and worried it with his fingers. "One of the still unanswered questions is why Julianne Regan's body never washed up. I mean, it does happen, bodies can take years for a river to spit them out. Sometimes they never surface, torn apart by fish, or snagged somewhere down deep. That coulda been the case with Regan. One of those bodies that never washes up. Coulda been what happened."

"What's your point?" Charlie said.

"I'm getting to it."

Steely-eyed, rubbing the chip between his fingers, he looked from one of them to the other. "Number two of the top ten unanswered questions is the condition of my brother's body when he washed up. He'd been banged up, as you know. Cuts and bruises about the head, which the M.E.'s report at the time said might have been caused by rocks or other sharp debris in the river. And there were contusions on his neck which the report said were consistent with your story, Danny, that you tried to stop him." He leveled his gaze directly at Danny. "Or maybe you weren't trying to stop him at all. Maybe you were holding him down—"

Danny stiffened at the accusation. "Why would I do that?"

"Yeah, why would he do that?" Charlie fired back.

"You tell me, hot shot." Mooney had turned his attention to Charlie now. "My source says one of you was fighting with Timmy right before you went for a swim. Johnny here's not much of a fighter, from what I can see. You ever been a fight, Johnny?" It was as much an aspersion as a question.

"No."

Mooney bobbed his head, confirming something. "Didn't think so."

"So it had to be one of you two, right?" He looked from Charlie to Danny. "Not exactly a fair fight, would you say, given my brother's size, given that he sure as hell was no fighter. So maybe you can enlighten me as to what was going down."

Danny swallowed hard but kept his eyes, unflinching, on the detective.

In stony silence, Charlie stood with his feet planted squarely in front of the door, his shoulders pulled back like a bouncer's.

The clock over the bar hummed into the silence.

Mooney turned to Johnny. "What about you, holy man? The maybe not-so-innocent bystander. What's your part in this?"

Johnny looked away but kept his mouth shut.

The distant rumble of the EL broke the stillness of the night outside.

Mooney popped a square of bubble gum in his mouth, chewed with his mouth open. The sweet sugary smell of the gum mingled with the room's decades-old stench of sour beer.

The Bronx Kill

"I'm on you guys," he said, "like a fly on you-know-what." He stepped closer to the bar where a braided basket held complimentary books of matches. He lifted one from the cluster: the cover a black starry sky with a moon in the center, the word *GLOW* printed beneath it. "The moon ain't glowing so bright these days, is it now? Far as you all are concerned."

He flipped the matchbook back into the basket and moved past Charlie to the door. "Oh, and one more thing you guys might want to know. About Julianne. The reason her body never washed up's a simple one. The most logical one in the world. She didn't drown that night. Somehow, current or no current, she made it across."

CHAPTER 17

It was Danny who broke the silence that followed in the detective's wake. He downed the third round of whiskey Charlie had poured and said to no one, "If it's true—"

He left the thought unfinished. It seemed unimaginable that she was alive. Life and death were the unbridgeable extremes. Once fixed in our consciousness, they couldn't be altered.

Yet hadn't he at one time, in the days and weeks following that night, considered the possibility of, *hoped* for, *begged* the Almighty for, her safe passage across the river. Something sparked into being inside him with an excitement he thought had been lost for good. "If it's true—"

"How can it be true?" Charlie wanted to know. "She wasn't a better swimmer than me, was she? If I couldn't make it, how could she?"

"I don't know," Danny conceded.

"And if she *had* made it, where did she go? Why didn't she contact one of us?"

"That's right," Johnny agreed. "No way she could have survived. The water was too rough, too cold. The distance was too far." He looked to Danny for reassurance. "She couldn't be alive."

Danny let go of the fantasy, felt the rush of blood in his veins go still. "Right."

"He's scamming us," Charlie said bitterly. "Playing with our heads."

Johnny's head bobbed too vigorously in assent. "Right. Right. He's always hated us."

Charlie poured himself another shot, this time sipping it thoughtfully. "Of course, if it's true, if she's alive by some miracle, we may have to alter our story."

"How?" Johnny looked as if he'd been slapped. His face had flushed. He pressed against the bar, staring hard at Charlie. "*How*?"

"I don't *know* how. Depends on what she tells the cops. *If* she tells the cops anything. *If* she's alive. *If* this isn't some cockamamie story Mooney's concocting—"

"You said he was bluffing. You said cops do that all the time." It was an accusation Johnny thrust at him.

"I know what I said."

"So why you even bringing that up? Why are you changing your mind?"

"I'm not changing my mind. I said *if*—"

Johnny leaned away from the bar as if he'd been betrayed. A frantic determination had taken root in his eyes. "It can't be true." In the presence of doubt, he took up the cause himself. "It's not possible."

Danny's hopes were hammering at him again. *What if? What if? What if—?*

"Say something, Charlie," Johnny demanded. But Charlie stood behind the bar in silence, one hand on the bottle of scotch as if about to pour another shot.

In the stillness, the old jukebox hummed against the clock's relentless ticking.

The bar phone rang into the silence with the fury of a sniper's bullet.

Once.

Twice.

A third time.

Johnny looked at the others as if bad news had already been delivered.

"Yes?" Charlie said into the mouthpiece. "Yes." He listened for a few moments, said, "All right, thanks," then hung up.

Here it comes, Danny thought, though he couldn't have said what *it* was.

Charlie looked at them across the bar. "Mooney wasn't lying about one thing, at least. His source is real."

He lifted the bottle of Cutty, poured each of them another round. "My man at the 43rd. Says the guy's name is Ellis."

A dim memory flashed in the recesses of Danny's mind. "That homeless guy we used to see sometimes at the Kill?"

Charlie nodded. "Lives there now. In the railroad yard. Must have been watching us that night."

CHAPTER 18

Through vacant lots.

Past bent and twisted remnants of chain-link fence.

Under a railroad trestle.

The familiar route of their youth. What they had called the "Old Renegade Trail."

There were a number of ways of entering the Kill, but this was the one they had used most often. Easy access from the street. Fences with holes or gaps they could squeeze through. Weeds grown tall as a man. A path, well-worn, that led through dirt lots pockmarked with tangled bushes and refuse, the detritus of the city's poorest borough: wrecked and abandoned cars, TVs, crushed beer cans, the glittering shells of broken bottles.

Here it was difficult to measure the progress of urban blight, Danny thought, except to say the weeds had grown taller and the landscape, especially in the dark, seemed dingier than he'd remembered, more threatening.

They stopped at the edge of the abandoned rail yards.

Rusting boxcars, sections of track that vanished into thickets of overgrown weeds. A maze of broken or defunct things lit only dimly by the distant lights of the bridge.

"Kill the flashlights," Charlie said.

From the far end of the yard the railroad bridge arced eastward and beyond that the vegetation grew thicker, clots of trees and vines, impenetrable in places, through which the long channel of the Kill with its sludge-like flow stretched river to river.

At one point the Kill meandered between the Tri-Borough bridge's cement trunk-like supports which formed a tunnel of sorts. If you walked east, past an area of dry man-sized stalks they had in their youth named the *Skeleton Zone*, you came to the promontory where they had left their clothes that night nearly five years ago, before plunging into the river.

Where they stood at the edge of the yards, they couldn't see the river but its sour breath came faintly on the wind. It seemed to

The Bronx Kill

Danny the place was still alive with the heat and fury of that August night. If he'd had any doubts about the existence of spirits, returning here certainly put them to rest. For him, at least, Timmy Moon and Julianne had become indistinguishable from the salt-sour air, the decaying metal around them, the endless weeds, the low distant hum of traffic on the bridge.

"No lights from here on," Charlie was saying. "We move slow and quiet. We don't want to scare this guy off."

It was nearly four in the morning but Danny felt a fierce energy throbbing inside him. Later he would attribute what was about to happen to the long night, its bizarre and unexpected events, the whisky they'd put away, a fear they all shared that Mooney was out to destroy their lives. And especially to Charlie's anger, unnamed and unanchored, always on the verge of breaking through his take charge, take-control-of-the-situation manner.

At the bar, Charlie had insisted they come to the Kill right then, find this guy Ellis. I've got too much at stake, he said—it was obvious what he meant: if Uncle Sal was ever going to give him the chance he'd been begging for, that he felt he so deserved then something like this, the resurrection of the accident re-cast now as a possible homicide, would be enough for him to put Charlie on permanent hold. I can't take the chance, he'd said. I've got too much at stake here. *We all have* too much at stake.

Nobody disagreed. He didn't have to elaborate.

They crouched now behind a vine-draped section of chain-link fence. "Johnny, stay on the left side. Danny, take the right. I'll go up the middle." Charlie doled out instructions in his usual brusque, this-is-the-way-it-has-to-be mode. "Yell if you see the guy."

"No way," Johnny protested. "You're the only one with a weapon."

Charlie had tucked the .38 in his belt before leaving the Glow. At the time Danny had thought it a bad idea, carrying a gun seemed to him as much a way of attracting and escalating trouble as protecting oneself, but here in the warm sinister dark he was glad to have it along.

As a back-up.

In case.

The Kill, by virtue of its isolation, had always held the potential for danger and in the years he'd been away the neighborhood had grown even more violent.

"All right, we'll stay together," Charlie was saying. "We'll circle the perimeter, then we'll move into the center."

Like a game they played as kids, Danny was thinking as they moved single-file along the fence: Charlie in the lead, Danny close behind, and Johnny bringing up the rear. But the rush of excitement he'd felt back then was tinged now with dread. For all they knew there might be a colony of homeless living here, they might be easily outnumbered and overwhelmed. Or Ellis himself might be armed and dangerous.

What could he remember about the man?

Not much.

Occasionally, in their wanderings, they would see him here. A dark strip of a man with a slight build, a round quizzical face that always seemed to be squinting. He liked to sit in one or another of the boxcars, his feet dangling from the open door, his thin cracked voice calling out, "What you boys lookin' for?"

They'd ignored him. They wouldn't have been able to answer his question, even if they'd wanted to. They had no words for the kind of adventure they were seeking.

He didn't remember seeing him the night in question, but the man could have been watching them unseen from any number of locations: the thick weeds along the Kill, from between the bridge supports, or from one of the wooded thickets that dotted the marshland near the promontory, maybe even from the Skeleton Zone itself.

What had he seen? What had he told Tom Mooney?

When they reached the end of the fence, Charlie led them stealthily into the yard.

It seemed to Danny they were too exposed a target, their moving shadows too conspicuous. He scanned the expanse of track and abandoned freight cars. No movement anywhere. Nothing but deathly silence and heavy, stationary shadows.

Yet the quarter moon's light put them on display.

You're in an abandoned train yard, it's four in the morning, he had to remind himself. Even homeless people have to sleep sometime.

But still he felt apprehensive. Who could predict the schedule, the behavior, of someone who lived like this, cut off from the world? The man had been odd five years ago. He would most likely be even crazier now.

Behind him came the sound of Johnny's breathing, the faint crunch of his feet on gravel.

They followed a section of track to the first of the abandoned cars. As they moved along the car, still single-file, Charlie reached to pull the .38 from his belt but Danny squelched his own fears enough to grip his arm to stop him. "We don't need it yet."

The sight of it made him nervous. He liked knowing it was there, but he didn't want to see it—unless it was absolutely necessary. Truth be told, he admitted to himself, the sight of Charlie waving a gun unnerved him as much as their being in the train yard in the dead of night.

Charlie pushed the gun back into his belt and peered into the black interior of the boxcar. "Hold this."

He handed Danny his flashlight and pulled himself up onto the car's floor. He reached for the flashlight and thrust the beam into the thick darkness.

Even from outside Danny could smell urine and the fetid stench of excrement.

Charlie jumped to the ground, said "Somebody's shithouse" and led the way to the second car, a hundred or so feet ahead.

This one had signs of life. A crude yellow sun had been spray-painted on one end. The sliding door had been pulled nearly closed, and a towel had been hung like a curtain to cover the open crack. Beneath the car, rats crawled over small garbage heaps of Styrofoam fried chicken boxes, beer and whisky bottles, the rotting remains of orange rinds, banana peels and melons.

They listened for sound inside the car but Charlie was too impatient to dawdle. He gripped the metal ladder and pulled himself up until he could slide open the door. He shined the light through the opening then stepped onto the floor and slid the door open wider.

For a time, Danny could see only the circle of the light's beam jumping wall to wall.

"What's he doing?" Johnny wanted to know.

Then Charlie appeared in the doorway. "You've got to see this."

Inside, a sleeping bag and some blankets lay in the center of the floor. At one end of the car there were boxes with clothes stored in them, and a pile of random household items: an ancient TV, an iron, four toasters, various pots and pans.

Charlie flashed the light on a black garbage bag behind the

TV, then leaned forward to pull the bag out. Setting it on the floor, he tugged at the drawstrings to expose its contents: hundreds of loose bills of all denominations, large and small.

Danny jerked back in amazement.

Johnny said, "Wow!"

Charlie flashed the light into the corner where two more stuffed bags sat. "Plenty more in those."

A rat crawled out from behind one of the bags and scurried across the toasters in the direction of the door.

Danny raised the question for all of them: "Where does a homeless guy get this kind of money?"

CHAPTER 19

" 'Course we don't know that's Ellis living there," Charlie said as they followed the set of tracks toward the south end of the yards. "Who knows what's happened to this place since we were here."

"It's what it always was, a place to get away from people for a while," Danny said. "What *we* used it for."

Charlie grimaced at the comparison. "'Least we weren't shooting up like these assholes." Needles and empty glassine bags lay scattered along the tracks. He kicked one of the needles. It *pinged* against the metal rail.

"Same objective, different route," Danny said.

Charlie shook his head. "Not the same thing at all, man."

Danny let it go. No way Charlie wouldn't insist on having the last word.

Johnny said, "Imagine leaving all that money lying around like that."

Charlie gave him a look. "You get high enough, you're not thinking about money."

"I guess."

"They have drugs in the Sem?"

Johnny looked offended. "No. Of course not."

"Just askin', man, that's all. Can't take anything for granted these days."

After considering it, Johnny said with less certainty, "At least I never saw it. Some guys did act funny, though, sometimes."

"Funny, how?"

"I don't know. Just funny."

"Like the mystics of old. Those guys had to be toking up on *some*thing."

"That's nothing to joke about," Johnny said.

"Lighten up, man. Religion's only another game we invented. You, of all people, should know that by now."

Johnny, about to speak, bit his lip instead. He looked at Danny and shrugged as if to say, who am I to argue?

Two flatbed cars in tandem lay directly ahead of them. They had been piled to overflowing with all manner of junk: tires, appliances, wooden pallets, old boxes. Behind the cars the garbage heap continued, a mound of refuse high as a hill. Charlie turned away in disgust. "Our own shit's going to bury us."

They were on the far side of the yard when Danny caught a flicker of movement.

Or thought he did.

He blinked, stared hard into the yard's center, across the lines of track and the scattered abandoned behemoths of rust.

"What?" Charlie wanted to know. "What'd you see?"

There it was again. A moving thing. A grey shadow flitting between the cars.

They began running toward it.

It was gone again, reappearing moments later in the open space between cars.

Then briefly it was directly ahead of them, no longer a shadow but a thin slightly built man jumping the rails, then he was lost to sight once more, a flitter of motion zigzagging between the cars until finally he was on open ground again running toward the boxcar with the money inside.

Charlie caught him climbing into the boxcar. In his ratty grey sweatshirt and black work pants, Ellis tried to pull himself up. Like a scared kid, Danny thought, clambering for the safety of home.

By this time, Charlie had him by the shoulders and swung him around so that the wizened brown face, gone grey with fear, was turned toward them in supplication. Charlie held him pinned against the car's rusted metal.

"What? What'd I do? What you chasin' me for?"

"This your crib?"

"Who wants to know?"

Charlie raised his hand but didn't swing. "Don't back-talk me, man. I asked you a question."

"Yeah, it's my crib. So what? What you buggin' me for?"

"You recognize us?"

"Can't hardly see ya's."

Charlie held the flashlight under his chin, then turned it on his two friends standing close behind him, keeping it on each of them briefly, the beam just below their eyes.

"Can't hardly see." The man blinked several times. His eyes

were covered in a hazy film and he seemed to have a hard time focusing. "Never seen you before."

"Take a closer look."

The man squinted at each of them. He had aged considerably, Danny thought, his hair greyer, his face gnarled and withered from too much sun. His eyes had a washed-out look but his face had retained its façade of ornery defiance. "Never seen y'all."

"That's funny," Charlie said, "seeing that you've been telling stories about us."

"What stories? What you talkin' about?"

"A summer night. Five years ago. You watch some people go swimming?"

The old man's eyes seemed to roll back in his head. He was lost somewhere in the murky recesses of memory. "Five jump in the river, three come out."

"That's right. Now you remember us?"

The jittery eyes struggled for focus. "You them boys? The ones come out?"

"That's right. We them boys."

"Ask him what he saw," Johnny shouted. "Ask him what he saw that night."

Charlie nodded in agreement. "He's gonna tell us that. Aren't you, old man?"

"I ain't seen nothin'. Five jump in the river, three come out. Next day, one more come out. Drown-ded."

"What'd you tell the police?"

"No police. What police?" His head jerked side to side as if to free itself from Charlie's hand which had collared his neck.

"A Narc. Named Mooney. What'd you tell him?"

"Nothin'. Didn't tell him nothin'."

"That's not what he says."

Ellis twisted his body hard, side to side, trying to rock himself out of Charlie's grip. "What he say? What he say I say?"

"*I'm* asking the questions." Charlie was half-pushing, half-dragging him along the side of the car. "*I'm* asking the questions."

Danny said, "Take it easy, man," but Charlie's focus was on Ellis alone.

He was pushing the man into the metal flank of the car. "What'd you tell him?"

"He tendin' his brother, that's all. He feelin' bad for his kin."

Shoving him hard against the rusted metal, Charlie spit the words: "That's not what I asked you."

The old man choked on what he was trying to say, then began again. "Told him what I seen, that's all. Two guys fighting. Then three guys in the river, fourth guy not wanta go in. Three guys come out, pull him in. Girl comes by. Takes off her clothes. She jumps in the river, too."

"The girl." Charlie was shouting now. "You ever see her again?"

"Everybody think she dead."

"That's right. She drowned."

The old man shook his head. "Not dead."

"What's that mean? Not dead. 'Course she's dead." Charlie was shouting now, pulling the man away from the car, swinging him in an odd, dance-like lilt toward the track beyond.

"One day she come back. Stand by the river." The words came choking out of him.

"You're lying. She's dead. She's dead." Charlie was squeezing the man's throat, shaking him hard.

But the man kept insisting. "Sometimes she come back. Say nothin' to nobody. Stand by the river."

Charlie struck him then, a blow to the side of the head, and the old man reeled away from him, stumbling on the cross-ties. "You lying bastard. You coked-up old fool."

"Back off, Charlie." Danny started after them, knowing Charlie was gone now, out of control and that he had to be stopped before the old man had a heart attack.

Before he could reach them Charlie had grabbed Ellis again, throttling him in an effort to shut him up but the old man kept muttering something, a non-stop indecipherable babble.

Charlie must have tripped on the rail, or the old man did, and they plunged forward onto the track bed, Charlie landing on top of the old man whose head struck the rail with a dull *thunngg*.

When Danny and Johnny pulled him off, Charlie was still shouting, "She's dead, she's dead, she's dead."

The old man lay crumpled on the track, his head twisted against the rail at an unnatural angle.

CHAPTER 20

They stood frozen, saying nothing, staring at the fallen man on the tracks.

It was Danny who knelt beside him, felt his wrist for a pulse. Sweat dampened the old man's flesh which was clammy to the touch.

"He's dead, isn't he." It wasn't a question Johnny asked, but a statement delivered with the certainty that a judgment had been levied against them.

Danny, crouched over the body in disbelief, said nothing.

"I knew it," Johnny said with finality.

Charlie, still breathing hard, still looking to take on whatever got in his way, glared at him. "Knew *what*?"

"Bad things—" Johnny's voice trailed off.

"Talk sense, man."

"Bad things were going to happen."

"Don't give me your mystical mumbo-jumbo. I don't need it right now, all right." He stood there, his shoulders heaving, his face broken out in sweat from the exertion, from the warm night which had grown warmer. He pushed Danny aside and pulled the old man up with two hands, shaking him hard. "Wake up, you loser. Wake the hell up."

The old man shook in his grip like a rag doll, loose and lifeless. Charlie stared at the face which had lost its defiance, seemed now calm and untroubled. "Jesus!"

The man's smell seemed stronger than before, a mix of unwashed body parts, urine and fear. In disgust, he dropped the heap of bones and soggy flesh, saying "No. No." He raised his eyes and looked for something down the line of track.

"What do we do now?" Johnny said.

It was a question addressed to himself as much as to his friends.

Danny stood up and moved away from the body, as if those few steps would give him the distance he needed to understand what had happened, how they could be involved in yet another death in this shabby wasteland. Anger pulsed like venom in his veins.

It was Charlie who was destroying them.

The revelation, buried for years, shocked him senseless. More than Tom Mooney's vengeance, more than old man Ellis' babbling rants, it was Charlie who had bullied them into this hell.

"We bury him," Charlie was saying behind him.

Johnny brushed the hair from his face, kept his hand pressed to his head as if easing some pain. "That's it?"

"You have a better suggestion?"

"We call the police."

"And tell them what? We killed Mooney's star witness?"

"It was an accident."

"You think that's how *they're* gonna see it? Same guys involved in two *accidents* in the same place, five years apart? Mooney doesn't believe his brother's death was an accident, why's he gonna believe this one was?"

Johnny was pacing in a loose circle, running his hand constantly through his hair. He stopped and shook his head. Something didn't sit right. He stared at the broken figure on the tracks. "He's a man, a human being."

"A *homeless* man."

"A man. With an immortal soul."

"What kind of burial you think a guy like him's gonna get, soul or no soul? Potter's Field. They'll haul him out to Hart Island, throw him into a mass grave."

"Maybe he has family."

"We don't know that."

"We don't know that he doesn't, either."

"Think straight, man." Something desperate had crept into Charlie's voice. "We can't let the police in on this. Mooney's already after our ass. This gives him more ammo. We're goners, they link us to this."

In the moon's tinny light, he stood silhouetted against the long line of track behind him. "Matter of survival. Whose life is worth more, his or ours? Think about that. Three lives, three futures versus one dead man. What's worth more?" His face softened then. "I'm not trying to be hard ass. I'm sorry the guy's dead. But it helps us out. It really does. Mooney's got nothing now."

"Unless it's true about Julianne," Danny said.

Charlie looked as if he'd been betrayed. "Don't you go soft on me, too. This Ellis guy was a wacko, a hophead. He was crazy back then, he's crazier now. Hallucinations, man. That's all that Julianne nonsense is."

"Yeah," Danny said. That's what it had to be. Hallucinations. Like his feeling the presence of ghosts. Like Johnny's seeing Timmy Moon in Times Square.

"It's not right," Johnny was saying. "There's got to be something else we can do." He looked to Danny for help.

"Charlie's right." He said it begrudgingly. The rage inside him didn't want to give the man credit for anything but getting them deeper into trouble. There was no other way out, though, that he could see. "We don't have a choice."

CHAPTER 21

They carried the body toward the most remote section of the Kill, more than a mile from the yards, an area of tangled vines and clotted trees and bushes. Several times Johnny complained about the distance, the weight of the old man, but Charlie insisted they keep going.

For emergencies, he kept a shovel in the trunk of the Caddy. "Who would have thought—?" he said. He used it now to clear a space beneath the low-hanging vines.

The ground was soft but even so, each of them taking a turn, it took nearly an hour to dig a hole they thought was deep enough.

Charlie, bare-chested, his arms and shoulders glistening with sweat, began and ended the process. He stood finally leaning on the shovel's handle, staring into the pit. "This should keep him from the animals."

They held the body over the hole before letting it drop. Somehow the man landed with one arm raised as if reaching for something.

Johnny insisted on saying a prayer.

"Just make it snappy," Charlie said. "It's gonna be light soon. Standing over an open grave like this isn't exactly the smartest thing we could be doing."

Johnny stood at the edge of the pit, head bowed, hands clasped. "Lord, deliver his soul from the pains of hell and from the bottomless pit; deliver him from the lion's mouth, that hell not swallow him up, that he fall not into darkness. Eternal rest grant unto him." He made the sign of the cross in the air.

"Amen," Danny said.

"Amen," Charlie muttered.

In the time before the first shovel-full of dirt struck the dead man, Danny thought despite his fury at Charlie that maybe the guy was right about the respect thing. However barbaric and unlawful this burial was, it beat being thrown into Potter's Field. At least here Ellis had his own plot. At least here he was buried near his home, such as it was.

With his next breath, though, he questioned that line of reasoning. Maybe he was simply trying to ease his part in this, his guilt by association.

For camouflage, they collected branches and twigs and loose rocks to scatter over the newly churned earth.

When they finished, Charlie said: "If they ever find him, if we ever get tied to this through DNA or whatever, we say we found him already dead and buried him out of courtesy."

"What about all that money?" Johnny asked.

"What about it?" Charlie said.

"We just going to leave it there? We could give it to charity."

"I'm not going anywhere near that boxcar, man."

"Me, neither," Danny said.

Johnny let it drop.

Charlie slung the shovel like a rifle onto his shoulder. "We're finished here. Let's get the hell out."

Danny started walking in the direction of the Kill.

"Wrong way, man," Charlie called after him. "We're finished here. Where you going?"

"*I'm* not finished here." Danny didn't bother to look back at them. He simply kept walking.

Maybe it was the ghosts that were to blame, Danny thought later. Maybe it was the presence of Julianne and Timmy Moon that he'd felt from the time they entered the Kill. Maybe that was why he needed to return to the place where he'd last seen them alive. Maybe, like Charlie, he'd simply been worn down by all that had transpired that night—that he'd been pushed to the breaking point, that he needed some release from the anger that was choking him.

He knew it was foolish to linger here, to increase the chances of someone seeing them, to make it easier for Tom Mooney to link them to Ellis' death. But that wasn't enough to stop him. He crossed a weedy lot, moving eastward in a steady line toward open water. Behind him, a reluctant Charlie kept muttering to himself—or to Johnny who followed dutifully, as if he had no will of his own.

They passed through the arched openings of the supports for the Tri-Borough, the rush of traffic steady and insistent, then fading as they followed the Kill's dark sluggish flow to the river, Danny deep in thought.

It was their last night together he was remembering. The hour before they came here for their fateful swim.

Standing with Charlie at the dance, Charlie already heavy into bad-mouthing Timmy Moon, an assault that's been building all day, all summer.

"Look at him. Look at the fucker. The way he stands there."

They watch him from across the church basement. The Moon standing alone, near one of the columns. Not far from him Julianne dances with some guy none of them know. If Timmy's the least bit jealous, you can't tell it from his expression. His face, at rest, wears a dreamy, slightly detached look.

"Look at him." Charlie's sneer more pronounced this time.

"Look at *what*?"

"Nothing bothers him."

"So?"

"The building could be falling down around him. He wouldn't care."

"He's easy-going."

"Julianne could be balling that guy right in front of him. He wouldn't blink."

"She's not balling him. She's dancing."

"The guy's got his crotch plugged into her like a socket, for god's sake."

"She does what she wants. Besides, everybody dances like that now."

"Not with my girl, they don't." He turns his anger on Danny. "That doesn't bother you? Her dancing like that?"

Everything she does with other guys bothers me, Danny thinks. "Yeah, it bothers me."

"Not Mooney, though."

"He's not the jealous type."

"There's something wrong with him."

"Like what?"

"Dunno. But something. Some *thing*."

"He's a nice guy. Let's face it, he's the nicest guy we know."

"There's something wrong being *that* nice."

"Says who?"

Charlie frowns, considering the situation. "Man without some meanness in him isn't a man."

The Bronx Kill

"You ever think, maybe you're way too jealous of him?"

"Not me. No way. What do I have to be jealous of?"

"Julianne likes him." It's the first time he's ever said that out loud and it hurts.

"I have plenty of girls. I don't need her."

"You don't act like it."

"Like what?"

"Like you don't need her."

He jerks his head, squints at Danny. "Fuck you, man."

He walks to the concession stand, orders a large Coke, ducks behind one of the columns to spike the Coke, then reappears beside Danny.

He picks up where he left off, evil-eying Mooney from across the room. "Look at the way he stands there. Like he doesn't have to make any effort. Like he *knows* the world will come to him. Like he *expects* it."

A short-haired girl, boyish and tough-looking, comes up and asks Timmy to dance. He, of course, obliges. He never turns anyone down.

"Jesus!" Charlie snarls in disgust.

"He's got universal appeal."

He's the only guy they know who doesn't have to ask anyone to dance. Girls ask *him*. Not only white girls, either. Puerto Rican girls, Black girls, Dominicans, Asians.

"Is he screwing *any* of them?" Charlie wants to know.

Danny shrugs. "Moon never talks about it, never says a word."

"I don't think so. I sure as hell don't think so." Charlie drinks from the large plastic container. "I don't get that guy. I really don't." He gulps down more rum and Coke. "I don't need this." He walks to the back door where his girlfriend, Mona, has just come in.

At least she *used to be* his girlfriend. He never calls her that when Julianne's around, referring to her only as "she" or "her" or if he's feeling really kindly toward her, "Lady M."

Minutes later, Danny's dancing with Julianne. She moves into his arms and, holding her, he's thinking how *some* things, *some*times, happen so easily, how the dream you dreamed becomes the life you're living. If only for a moment.

Her softness against him. The faint wild-berry smell of her hair. The heat where his cheek touches her head, and the stronger heat where their bodies join below the waist. How, he's wondering, can he feel so hard and so soft at the same time—when Charlie cuts in. He stands there, large and imposing, a smile barely concealing his anger.

He swings his arm around her, pulling her close, away from Danny. He rubs her shoulders and nuzzles her. Leaning away, she tilts her head from him but he laughs and holds her tighter. "Come on. You know you like it."

She strains against his grip. "Charlie, stop."

He puckers his lips and pushes his face against hers. "I'm your man, aren't I?"

Danny tries to step between them. "Cut it out, Charlie."

"Ooo, jealous, are we?" Charlie pulls her tighter, rocking side to side. "I'm your boyfriend, right? I gave you the night of your life, didn't I? I mean, Danny's pathetic attempt to impress you, showing you some art works at the Kill, I mean, what kind of night on the town is *that*, how can *that* compare to what I gave you, right? I'm the one knows what women like. I'm your man, honey. So why not make it official? Here, in front of everybody."

She's still trying to free herself. "You're hurting me."

Danny shoves Charlie to get his attention but the man of muscle's having too good a time to respond.

Danny shoves him again, harder this time. Charlie stops what he's doing, pushes back at Danny. "Chill out, man. It's all cool. Isn't that right, J-honey?"

"Sure, Charlie," Julianne says coldly. "Whatever you say."

Danny thinks about punching him out. But he doesn't. You don't do that to a friend. Instead he takes up a position next to Timmy near the columns and watches with a solemn eye what follows.

Charlie, having pulled Julianne close again in his take-charge manner, chatters in her ear. She seems to be paying him little attention, though. Her gaze is directed at Timmy. With unbearable longing in her eyes.

The Moon, though, seems immune to such looks, no matter the source, and Danny feels so jealous he thinks it's him he should be fighting, not Charlie. *If only Timmy Moon wasn't here, if only he hadn't become a Renegade. If only he would disappear.*

It takes a minute or more before Charlie, noticing at last that her interest is elsewhere, stops talking and throws a threatening glance at Timmy. Mona, meanwhile, has been watching Charlie

The Bronx Kill

dancing close with Julianne and doesn't like it. She comes over to Timmy and asks him to dance. No platonic dance, either. They've barely taken a step before she throws her arms around his neck, presses herself against him and begins a slow grind.

Next thing, Charlie's yanking her from Timmy with one hand and swinging at Timmy with the other. Two security guys come running over to intervene.

Timmy's been knocked down. He sits on the floor with a dazed look. "I didn't even want to dance with her," he's saying as he rubs his jaw. There's a red bruise on his chin. Julianne kneels beside him and turns his face side to side to see where else he's hurt. "I'm okay," he says. "I really am."

Danny helps her pull him up. "I'm okay," Timmy repeats. "I'm okay."

Charlie's being ushered out the back doors when Johnny and Lorraine come over. "What happened?" Johnny wants to know.

Timmy stands on his own then, a bit unsteady, red-faced at all the attention. "Nothing. It was nothing."

Danny suggests they go outside to check on Charlie.

In front of the church the security guys stand by the basement door, laughing about something. Charlie leans against a parked car talking to Mona. Or rather *listening* to Mona. She's giving him an earful, none of which Danny can hear because of the downtown express passing overhead on the EL.

Mona's shoulders stiffen and she walks away without looking at any of them.

Charlie shrugs, says, "Let's get out of here."

Outside the playground they sit on benches under the maple trees. Silver-blue lights dot the trails of the park but the light from a pole inside the fence is yellow and dappled, falling through thick clusters of leaves, staining the ground with ragged shadows.

Johnny is staring at Timmy in his dream-like, distant way but Danny's focus is on Charlie whose face in the dark seems calmer, not so restless. He passes his flask around, urging everyone to drink up. He's the host again, trying to get the party going. When the first flask is finished he produces a second, full to the brim with the same throat-burning whiskey.

Danny waits for him to apologize but that doesn't come. Instead he stays mostly quiet, sitting hunched forward and staring through the playground fence as if looking for something there.

On the opposite end of the bench Mooney sits with Julianne. If he's expecting an apology, he doesn't show it. And Danny thinks that's another reason why Timmy Moon is nobler than the rest of them. Anybody else would have *demanded* an apology or simply walked away. But Timmy hangs in there. These are his friends and this is where he'll stay, no matter what. Without doubt, he's the most faithful of the Renegades. Or maybe, Danny would think later, he was only the neediest. Nothing, not even his pride or dignity, was worth more than his need to belong.

Before they took him in, he'd been a loner, target of the punks in the neighborhood, because of his pretty-boy looks, his mild and easy-going manner. But after he became one of them, nobody bothered him. Charlie made sure of that. So *he* owed Charlie, too. And maybe, Danny figured, after having been roughed up for so long by the hood's tough guys, a few punches from a friend were nothing to worry about.

"Drink up, Timmo." Charlie passes him the flask again. It's his way of apologizing.

Timmy takes the flask, raises it in a salute, then drinks heartily. He's one of the boys again.

And for a moment, before Charlie suggests they all go down to the Kill, Danny thinks this angry night might turn out all right, after all.

Now, near the narrow promontory that stretched from the bank of the river, they stood in silence. It seemed they had suddenly become strangers, afraid to stand too close to one another as they stared across the river toward Queens. This was the first time any of them had been back.

The sour smell of the river was so much stronger here. Danny held his nose against it. Across the dark water the lights of the Con Ed plant illuminated a section of the Queens shoreline; and farther east were the softer blue runway lights of the airport.

He wondered why he had come back to this place, what he hoped to accomplish.

But even as these questions competed for his attention, his mind was reaching elsewhere, like a hand brushing away the soil on the surface to find what was buried beneath. He became aware of their positions on the shore: Charlie was closest to the promontory, *he* was farthest from it, and Johnny stood midway between them. Unconsciously, they had taken their positions from that night.

"Timmy Moon stood on the bank, twenty feet maybe from where Charlie is," he said. "And Julianne came over that rise, surprising us all."

"Why you doing this?" Charlie wanted to know.

"We weren't supposed to come back here." Johnny's voice quivered. He shifted his position, turning to Charlie for support. "We aren't supposed to talk about it."

"Our friend seems to have forgotten that."

"The bank there," Danny continued. "That's where you started—"

"What is this?" Charlie's face had tightened. He stood with his head raised, lifted into the breeze off the water. "You forgot our agreement?"

Johnny, his hair blown back wild, stood between them like a mediator. "It was an accident. I mean, no matter what anybody says, it was an accident, right?"

"'Course it was an accident," Charlie said. "Unless our friend here knows more about that night than he's telling us."

"No matter what Mooney's brother thinks," Johnny said.

"What does he know? He wasn't there."

"*We* were there," Johnny said dumbly.

"Of course we were there. We were the only ones there, the only ones who could know."

"What do we know?" Danny asked.

Charlie shot him a malevolent look. "We *know* we couldn't have done anything. That's what we know. The guy was crazy. I told him to go back. I told Julianne, too. I told all of you. You listened, they didn't. Simple as that."

Danny looked at him doubtfully. "Is it?"

"Is it what?"

"Simple. Is it that simple?"

"'Course it is. That's what we agreed, remember." He glared at Danny. "You saying it isn't?"

"Whose idea was it to come here that night?"

"Hey, we all were a part of that."

"But whose idea was it?"

"We needed a break. We needed to get our minds off things. So what if this time it was my idea?"

"You think you got it all figured. You're always so damned sure of yourself."

"Why shouldn't I be?"

"You're always right."

"I'm confident, if that's what you mean."

"Always the big shot. Pushing people around."

"Who do I push around?"

"Everybody. Johnny. Me. Mooney. The guy we just buried."

Charlie shook his head in recognition. "So that's what's setting you off. Well, man, you saw what happened. I had no intention of icing the guy. I was roughing him up, that's all. Things got out of hand—"

"You mean you went too far. The way you did with Timmy that night."

"That's not true." Johnny had taken to pacing along the bank, looking from one of them to the other. "Charlie's all right. He didn't mean to—he—"

"He's been pulling our strings since we were kids. You know that as well as I do. Whatever Charlie wanted, we did."

"He was protecting us, that's all."

"From what?"

"I don't know. The neighborhood, ourselves maybe—"

"Maybe we didn't need protection. Maybe we just needed to figure things out in our own way. Make our own mistakes."

"You were only trying to help us, right Charlie? Trying to keep the Renegades together, keep us strong."

But Charlie ignored the question. He had moved closer to Danny, as if to back him toward the water, though Danny stood his ground. "So you blaming me for Timmy's death. Maybe Julianne's too, right? Even though she went into the water on her own. Is that what this is about?"

"If we hadn't come down here. If we hadn't gone into the river—"

"If, if, if—"

They stood close now, breathing hard, glaring at each other.

Johnny tried to wedge himself between them. "It wasn't anybody's fault. That's what we decided. What we agreed on—"

"That's right," Charlie said. "But our friend here seems to have forgotten the pact we made."

"No, he didn't." Johnny took Danny's side now, ever the

The Bronx Kill

peace-maker trying to dampen the fires of discontent. "He's just a little confused. It's been a long night. A hell of a—"

"Is that all it is, Danny? You're a little confused? Is that the problem? Or you got something else to say?"

Johnny had weaseled his way between them. "No, no, he doesn't—"

Charlie pushed him aside. "This is between me and Danny. Ain't that right, Dan-o? You've been pissing about something ever since you came back. This what it is? *I'm* the one responsible for Timmy drowning?"

"You're the one came up with the idea of swimming to Queens. Test of our manhood. All that bullshit."

"Bullshit, huh? I don't remember you putting up any protest."

"You egged us on. You wouldn't let up."

"So what's your point?"

"You got us drunk and way too overheated."

"That's crazy. Charlie didn't—"

"Sure he did. The son-of-a-bitch—"

Charlie came at him then, swinging hard, knocking him back against the hard rim of the bank, his hands around Danny's throat, thick fingers squeezing hard, Danny coughing and choking, turning red in the face as he was forced to his knees, Charlie letting go then, Charlie raising his fist and driving it against Danny's face, one, two and three times, Johnny shouting for him to stop.

Charlie, breathing hard, wheezing, finally did stop, standing over Danny's swaying torso, Danny's head bowed now, blood spilling from his lip, his shoulders drooping until he fell forward onto all fours as he sucked air, staring into the oily mud of the river bank.

Johnny knelt beside him, arm around him, asking, "You all right? You all right?"

Without lifting his head, Danny nodded that he was.

Charlie hunkered over them, shoulders heaving, clenching and unclenching his fists. With great effort Danny struggled to his feet, shaking off Johnny, standing unsteadily at the river's edge.

"No more fighting. *Please.*" Johnny's eyes darted from one of them to the other. "It was an accident. That's all it was—"

"Tell yourself that the next time you have one of your nightmares," Danny said. "See if it helps."

"Get a grip, man." Charlie turned away and started back along the Kill.

Johnny hurried after him.

Only Danny lingered, brushing the mud from his shirt and pants, thinking nothing had changed, nothing had been settled.

When they reached the Caddy, a line of grey light stretched like a crack in the horizon. Nobody had spoken on the walk back. Danny glanced at Charlie but the man was lost in thought, his face dark and closed. He opened the trunk and threw the shovel in.

None of them noticed the car parked farther down the street, or the two men inside watching them.

PART TWO

CHAPTER 22

Half past two in the morning.

Parked at the end of the block, Mooney had a straight-on view of the tavern door. He'd come directly from the Kill, from the latest piece of evidence he'd found, because this was where his search for Ellis had taken him.

The MoonGlow.

What frustrated him, what drove his blood pressure sky high, was that he still didn't have enough hard evidence to make his case in court. But he already had enough to convince *himself* of the link between the Renegades and the homeless man's disappearance and—he'd bet his life on this—more evidence would be forthcoming soon.

Maybe tonight.

Getting rid of Ellis was a sure sign of their desperation, and the desperate—he knew from experience—would always do themselves in. Sure as hell, he wanted to be there to see it. He wanted to watch the three of them go down *in flames*.

Ellis had been missing now far too long for it to be coincidence, *fifty-eight hours and counting*, and he'd spent the first twelve hours of that time cruising the streets of the southeast Bronx in search of him: St. Mary's Park, an occasional haunt of Ellis' where he'd apparently taken a long-standing protective interest in a flock of pigeons; a cemetery he sometimes visited—God knew why—near Westchester Square; and a fast food barbeque joint off the Bruckner Expressway where the old guy's one known friend, a fellow homeless man named Jocko, hung out.

Jocko, as it turned out, had no idea where Ellis had gone. So because Ellis rarely strayed from the Kill—for a homeless man, he was a home-body: an irony that offered the detective a modicum of grim amusement—he'd spent the remaining hours at the Kill in the company of a cadaver dog, a black and brown Belgian Shepherd named Hunter.

He'd been unable to convince his precinct commander to

call in the NYPD's Human Remains Detection team, a specialized unit of the K-9 division.

"HRD? For *what*? the Captain had wanted to know. Some half-nuts homeless freak? Who may or may not even be dead? Who could have wandered off somewhere, *any*where in this friggin' city? Who more than likely'll show up tomorrow like nothing happened? For God's sake, Tommy. No way I can justify that. Those guys are way too busy. They'd laugh me outta my job."

So, on his own dime, he'd called in Walter Applegate, a retired dog handler who wearing his trademark western hat and boots had grunted, not looking at all happy, when the detective showed him the area around the train yards he wanted to search. "God knows how many possibilities of disarticulated human remains we got out here. *Got* to be one of the best damn places in the city to dump a body."

The dog had taken off, scampering left then right, bolting from the shadow of the bridge onto a dirt and rubble-pocked patch of ground along the yard's southern edge. It took only several minutes before it was circling a small section of earth near a clump of trees, finally dropping to the ground, head raised, mouth open and panting, tongue lolling.

Turned out, after ninety minutes of back-breaking excavation, it was only a recently buried cat he found.

"Cadaver dogs are supposed to know the difference, aren't they?" he'd groused to Applegate. "Animal or human, they're supposed to know, aren't they?"

"The smell of death can bounce off a tree or some other object. It can come from a distance, and confuse a dog," was all Applegate had offered by way of defense.

He'd known from experience this wasn't the best way of excavating. Better to use probing rods to establish a grid around the gravesite, better to screen the soil, better still to use ground-penetrating radar. But he had neither the time nor the money nor the patience for that.

Out of desperation he'd called *Home Cookin'* for help and two members of the crew showed up: young, strapping boys he'd seen working around the club but didn't know well. The next time the dog stopped her circling and lay down in a copse of trees closer to the Kill itself, the detective and the two boys got to work again.

This time the smell of death was unmistakable.

Shirtless, stopping only to wipe his face and neck and arms

with a hanky, he had dug at the walls of the pit till he thought his heart might burst from his chest. He was sore in his shoulders and lower back, and his arms had gone numb and rubbery. After three hours in the pit, finally, finally, they'd hit pay dirt.

Bones.

Recent bones.

Bloodied flesh still clinging to them.

The stench was gut-wrenching.

What they had, though, was not Ellis at all, but the dismembered corpse of what appeared to be a short Hispanic man.

By flashlight, they excavated three more potential sites. Skeletal remains in each. In the last one, only a skull. The detective had wiped his face in disgust. The place was a damn killing field, all right. If they kept going, who knew, even Jimmy Hoffa's bones might turn up.

When they finally quit for the night, when they were walking back through the train yard, his flashlight had picked out something in the crevice of the tracks, not far from the boxcar Ellis called home. He bent to retrieve it.

A matchbook.

A black starry sky with a small white moon in its center, the word *GLOW* printed across the bottom of the flap.

Now, in his car outside the MoonGlow, he fingered the matchbook with reverence, with awe. It was his holy grail. It was what cemented, in his mind at least, this newest angle in his case against the Renegades.

Not only had his crew witnessed them leaving the Kill in the early morning hours—after which Ellis had not been seen again, *this* put them right where the old guy lived. They had the motive, and they had the means, cowards that they were: three of them against a frail old man.

No way they hadn't done him in. They'd simply hidden the body well, that's all.

The door to the tavern opened. Holding it was Charlie Romano, who stood talking to the two neighborhood old-timers he was ushering out.

They stood on the sidewalk, apparently deep in conversation, Romano the one doing all the talking. It might have been a rant he was delivering, judging from the passion in his face, the wild gesticulation of his arms. And seeing him like that, pumped-up, dominating the conversation, acting like he was king of the street, like his was the only opinion worth airing, set the detective's blood to boiling. Again.

He thought about his brother, how Timmy continually idolized all of the Renegades but particularly this guy—a fact that Tom Mooney could never understand, how it was always Charlie *this* and Charlie *that*. Charlie saved me from getting beaten up after school today. Charlie threw three touchdown passes at the game on Saturday. Charlie gave me his baseball mitt because he's getting a new one, Charlie buys beer for us whenever we go into the Kill. Charlie showed me how to . . . Charlie, Charlie, Charlie.

Got so he couldn't bear to hear the guy's name. The sound of it made him want to punch something. The guy was a show-off, a braggart, a control freak, a manipulator. Couldn't his brother see that?

He uses people, he's using *you*, he'd told Timmy how many times.

But Timmy *couldn't* see it. No, no, he's a good guy, a terrific guy.

He pushes you around.

No, he doesn't.

I've seen it. I've seen him do it.

He's just kidding around. He doesn't mean anything by it.

He makes fun of you, he disrespects you.

It's a game, that's all. It's a game we play sometimes.

You're his lackey.

I'm *not*.

Do this, do that. Get me this, get me that. Get down on your knees, so I can kick you in the ass.

No, it's not like that.

You're a punching bag, kid. Face it. You're a doormat.

It's not like that at all. He's my friend. He's my friend.

Yeah? Try telling him off some time. Tell him *no* when he asks you to do something. See how much of a friend he is then.

But his brother wouldn't listen.

And one night, in the days he was still a beat cop, he was coming home—off-duty, in street clothes—when he saw them, the Renegades, in this very park he was facing, between the EL and the

Expressway. Charlie Romano was trying to goad Timmy into boxing with him, and Timmy who never fought back for anything in his life was trying to talk his way out of it, trying to make a joke of it, but Romano wouldn't back off. He kept coming at Timmy, slapping at his face, his shoulders, poking at his ribs.

Seeing that, had set something off in him. He couldn't control himself, couldn't hold himself back and he came at Romano swinging, saying you want to fight somebody, fight *me*, big shot, let's see how much of a big shot you are now.

With one punch he knocked Romano over a bench and he thought he'd finished him off, but the son of a bitch climbed back over the bench looking like he wanted to kill somebody and he'd said, come on, you think you can, come on, come on. But before the kid could lunge at him, a patrol car stopped at the corner, seeing the commotion, and the fight ended in a stalemate. To be continued . . .

Now the two old-timers moved off down the street and Charlie Romano went back inside.

The detective lit a cigarette, tried to ignore the ache in his bones, the stench of the day's sweat that still clung to him.

The bar would be closing soon.

The vultures would be coming home to roost.

Then it would be time.

CHAPTER 23

Charlie called from the bar with bad news. "Mooney wants to see us. Here. In an hour."

"Why?" Danny asked.

"I asked him what it was about. He said we *knew* what it was about."

In the wake of silence, Danny could hear the faint clink of glasses, the low moan of the jukebox.

"He was pissing mad, I'll tell you that."

Another silence followed. Danny waited for him to say something about their fight. They hadn't seen each other since then; Danny had stayed away from the MoonGlow. It wasn't an apology he expected now, he knew Charlie better than that, but some mention of the fight, some acknowledgment that it happened.

What Charlie did finally say was: "Not cool your keeping yourself isolated like this. We don't wanna give the bloodhound any more ideas than he already has."

"Yeah, well, I'll take my chances."

"*Our* chances," Charlie corrected him. "We've all got a stake in this."

"Sure. Whatever."

"Hey, man. We've been through a lot together. Don't forget that."

Danny understood the implication. Charlie meant the night they lost Moon and Julianne, the night with Ellis in the rail yards, the times he fought to protect their asses, their years together going all the way back to grade school. But the hard, penetrating tone of his friend's voice meant something more, too, made sure he didn't forget the most important thing of all: *I saved your life, man. You owe me.*

It happened when Danny was in eighth grade—their first attempt to swim in the river, before Timmy Moon or Julianne had moved into the neighborhood. In the cold, swirling water Danny flailed to stay afloat. He wasn't a good swimmer then, he tired easily, and that day he was too exhausted to swim free of the current that had locked around him, too exhausted to make it back to shore even if he could escape the water's icy grip. It was Charlie who'd swum back out for him, dragged him in, choking and sputtering and hysterical with panic.

He could feel the sensations even now: the strangle-hold of water in his nose and throat, the current's downward pull, the blur of shoreline ever-receding, the swirl of sky and clouds and the darkening shadow of the bridge. Then Charlie's arms stronger than the current, wrapped across his chest, holding him above the waterline, pulling him toward the rocky finger of the promontory.

Danny had taken an oath of allegiance that day. All three of them had taken the oath. They would cover each other's back, no matter what.

He'd been paying his debt of loyalty ever since.

"I needed a break," was what he said now in his defense. "I needed some time."

"To do *what*, man?"

"I don't know—think, worry. I've been reading the papers. Watching the news."

"No one gives a damn about some whacked-out homeless guy gone missing."

Charlie's words echoed in Danny's mind. *He was pissing mad, I'll tell you that.*

He snapped shut the phone and sank into the couch next to his father who was up, later than usual, reading a brochure he'd sent for.

"I've been thinking," his father said. He waited until Danny looked as if he was listening. "Maybe I should get out more. Do things, you know?"

"Sure." Danny struggled to push aside the after-effects of Charlie's phone call. He wasn't sure where his father was going with this. "Why not?"

"I'm thinking about taking a class. Ballroom dancing, maybe. I used to be quite a dancer, you know, in my time."

Danny was surprised. He'd never seen that side of his father. In fact, he knew little of his father's life *before* he became a father.

"Sounds like fun," he said tentatively because he thought that's what his father wanted to hear.

His father seemed even more tentative, leaning forward as he was, looking to Danny for some kind of approval. "Your mother and I, we were pretty good together on the dance floor. I've always thought that's why she fell for me. I could dance better than the other guys in the neighborhood."

"I didn't know that, Dad. I didn't know you and Mom liked to dance."

He seemed invigorated by the memory, his eyes bright, his face red with blush. "That's what we did. On our dates, I mean. Before you were born. We went from club to club. Different one every week. The Bronx, Brooklyn, Queens. We went all over." Abruptly his face turned thoughtful. "That's the problem, I guess. It was *our* thing, what *we* did together. It doesn't feel right to do it with someone else. You see what I mean?"

And Danny *did* see. Because it was the way he felt about Julianne, the things they'd done together. He wouldn't even *think* of bringing someone else to see the artwork under the bridge. Or even such a simple thing as walking under the EL, holding hands. That belonged to her, too. It would seem a betrayal to do it with someone else.

On the other hand, he knew, though he himself had failed at it, you had to go on with your life. He didn't like it that his father spent so much time alone, nights and weekends. Sometimes he'd go out with his friends for a beer, they'd play poker at someone's house, or maybe catch a night game at the Stadium. But much of the time, when he wasn't working, he was on his own and Danny sure as hell knew, from his own experience in Florida, that too much time alone brought you down, got you nowhere.

"I *do* see," Danny said. "But it's not really the same thing, is it? I mean, you're not going to clubs or dating or anything. It's only a class. It's just about having some fun for a few hours a week."

His father settled back in the chair, folded his hands, and thought about it. "Maybe you're right. Maybe it's not the same thing."

Danny checked the time and got up from the couch.

"You going out?" his father asked. "I'm kinda getting used to you being home at night."

"Yeah," Danny said, patting his old man's knee. "Charlie

wants to have a beer."

"That detective fella—what's his name, Mooney—ever get a hold of you?"

"Yeah. He did."

"And?"

"He had some questions about the night his brother drowned."

His father gave him a disapproving look. "He's like you then."

"What do you mean?"

"He doesn't know when to let a thing go."

CHAPTER 24

The street outside the MoonGlow was deserted this time of night, Mooney's black Merc—driver-less—the only car parked there. From a distance, the bar with its darkened windows looked as if it had long since been abandoned. Up close, though, through the smoky glass, Danny saw a shadow move across the soft yellow bar lights.

It was Johnny who opened the door, his eyes grim with worry. "We're all here," he said.

Danny had already taken in the room: Mooney slouched on a bar stool, Charlie with both hands on the bar as if waiting to serve someone. With a nervous flutter of his arm, Johnny ushered Danny in as if he were the guest of honor.

"You fuckers never cease to amaze me." Mooney pulled himself from the stool and swung his massive weight to face them. His body ached terribly from the day's activity but that did nothing to make him less of an imposing figure.

"How's that?" Charlie said but with much less bite than in their previous encounters.

The detective went on as if he hadn't been interrupted. "You must think you can get away with anything."

Charlie kept his hands firmly on the bar as Tom Mooney executed an unwieldy half-pirouette to include them all in his unflinching glare. "What are we being accused of now?"

"Kill a man, dispose of his body, go on your merry way like nothing happened."

Johnny said, "We don't know what—"

"Shut the fuck up. I'm not finished." Mooney's roar filled the room.

Johnny's eyes fluttered closed as if against a strong wind.

"You're like a pack of coyotes, you know that? Lowly, skulking, cowardly dogs. Gang up on the weak and defenseless, the easy prey, then tear it to shreds. Who better than a kid who didn't have a mean bone in his body? Or a frail, homeless old man?" He kept his right fist in his pocket, balled tight and as he lurched between them Danny could see its outline clenched against the cloth of the raincoat. Inside the fist, he'd lay odds, was the blue poker chip taking the brunt of the man's rage.

"I'm not even gonna ask you where you were late Saturday night." His face had gone white with rage. The bile that had been building inside him swelled his cheeks, enlarged his neck. "And you know why I'm not gonna ask? Because I *know* where you were. And when I find a certain man's body—and I will find it, you can bet your cheesy lives on that."

He left the threat unfinished and reconsidered his options. "But even if I don't, let's say for argument's sake, even if you slime bags are so slick and ruthless you broke the guy into a million pieces and deposited those pieces in every foul-smelling sewer you could find in every corner of the five boroughs, even if he never shows up again in any shape or form, even then I'm gonna hang your asses. I swear on my brother's grave. One way or another I'm gonna finish you guys."

In the silence that followed, he turned his harrowing glare on each of them in turn. A fearsome look, Danny had to admit, a look of grim determination that had intensified since their first meeting, that went now beyond all reason, the look of a vigilante, for whom punishment was the goal, not justice. Poor Johnny seemed visibly affected, his face clenched, his teeth gritted as if about to ward off a blow.

The detective moved toward him. "You got something to tell me, *Father*?" The word, heavy with contempt, hung in the silence.

Johnny stammered something unintelligible and Charlie cut him off. "What's it gonna take, Tommy, to get you off our backs?"

Tom Mooney grinned malevolently. "You can show me that shovel you carry in your trunk."

Charlie stood his ground, hands still on the bar, and didn't flinch. "Why would I do that?"

"You do it voluntarily, or I get a warrant. Simple as that."

If it was that simple, Danny wondered, why hadn't he gotten the warrant *already*? A bluff, it had to be. One more reason to think the case had no official sanction, that it was a private cause, and Mooney its lone crusader. So he was shocked when Charlie said sure, the detective could look all he wanted.

"The car's out back."

"I know where it is."

"Make him get a warrant," Danny said.

"Why? He's gonna look sooner or later. Right, Detective? So might as well be now."

Danny thought it was a mistake. Even if Charlie had gotten rid of the shovel, there might be traces of dirt, *some*thing that could link them to the Kill.

But if Charlie was nervous about it, he hid it well. He led them out through the back into the alley where the Caddy was parked. His apartment above the bar was dark, curtains drawn across the windows.

While Charlie fumbled with the keys, Danny felt a wave of nausea rising in his stomach.

Standing beside him, Johnny had broken out in a sweat, despite the night's cool. When the trunk popped open, he emitted a low moan, close to a whimper and bit his lip to stop it from quivering.

There was no shovel. Only a spare tire, a partly rusted lug wrench, a can of Valvoline motor oil and a few rags. Mooney shined his pocket light into the corners of the cavernous trunk. "You'd have to have been a retard not to have gotten rid of the thing."

Charlie grinned. "I take that as a compliment then."

The detective pushed aside the lug wrench and the Valvoline and lifted the rags. "Looks like you cleaned up things pretty good."

"I keep a clean car. Always have."

Mooney wiped his finger along the bottom of the trunk, held it up to the light, then smelled it.

"Satisfied?" Charlie asked.

"Listen, asshole. I'll be satisfied when I see you three roasting in hell. You got the blood of two people on your hands now." He raised his hand and slammed down the trunk.

"Easy, man, that's my baby you're roughing up."

Tom Mooney took a slow walk around the car, flashing his light at the wheels, then inside the cab. He came around to where they stood and slashed the high-intensity light across their eyes. "I may never find out what really happened the night my brother died, but you guys are gonna pay for his death. I guarantee you that."

And then he added again in the same threatening tone he'd used earlier: "One way or another." He pulled his hand from his pocket and instead of the blue poker chip he held the matchbook. "One a you dropped this in the train yard the night Ellis disappeared."

He walked down the alley, his head hunched in against his massive shoulders, his coat flapping around his legs.

Johnny paced feverishly along the wall of the alley, watching him turn the corner. "He knows. He *knows*."

"Anybody could have dropped those matches," Charlie said. "Anybody."

"He knew about the shovel. How'd he know that? Tell me. How'd he know?"

CHAPTER 25

Two nights later, Danny accompanied his father to the Vanderhill dance studio on Westchester Ave. His father was having lingering doubts so, afraid his old man would chicken out, Danny offered to go with him. "Not to dance, though," he made clear. "I'm no dancer. I'm coming strictly as support staff."

The studio was a converted pool hall, Danny had played there often after he'd turned sixteen, located on the second floor, its tall wide windows facing directly out on the EL. The large room had been broken up into three smaller ones: the first hosting a class in salsa dancing, the second some sort of Afro-Caribbean dance marathon, and the third housed the ballroom dancing class where some fifteen or so people, more women than men, stood inside in a loose circle waiting for the class to begin. They were an older and more genteel group than the dancers in the adjoining rooms. More formally dressed, as well.

In the open doorway, Danny stood beside his father who had prepared himself carefully for the occasion: three piece suit, white shirt and tie, new haircut. But the man was clearly nervous. His hands were clasped tightly in front of him though he couldn't keep them still; his eyes darted impatiently around the room as if searching for all the possible exits. It reminded Danny—the roles reversed now—of when his father had taken *him* to his first dance at St. Cecilia's.

It seemed his father might bolt but one of the two instructors, a perky blond with a bright smile and a too heavily made-up face that made more obvious the fact she wished she were younger, approached him with her hand outstretched. "Mr. Baker," she said. "Wonderful. I'm Marina Vanderhill." Her wide, expectant eyes swept the room and returned to him. "We're all here now. Time to give ourselves over to Herr Strauss. Tonight we'll be concentrating on the Waltz."

"I'll be right outside, Dad." He patted his father's shoulder. A moment's desperation flashed in his father's eyes before Marina Vanderhill took his arm. Danny mouthed the words, *Loosen up*, and watched her whisk him into the center of the room.

In the small lobby, Danny sat on a vinyl couch assaulted by a barrage of sound. The walls shook with Latin rhythms and hip-hop clashing with the more melodic strains of the Blue Danube. Every so often the elevated train came crashing through the musical jumble adding a rhythm of its own. The mix created a dizzying effect and for a while he had to clasp his hands to his ears to hold the racket at bay.

From time to time he cracked open the door to glimpse his father in action, his tall elegant frame gliding smoothly across the hall with the various partners he was paired with. At break time his father came out for a drink at the water cooler. "It's all coming back to me," he said. "It's funny how it's all still there, inside you."

Once during the hour a young woman Danny's age came out of the salsa class. At the water cooler she glanced at him, asked if he wanted to come in and dance with her. "I'll teach you," she said. "It's real easy."

She was a pretty girl and there was something about her—her hair maybe or the shape of her face—that reminded him of Julianne. Briefly he was tempted to say yes. "Not right now, thanks. Another time maybe."

"I'll be here till nine," she said with a smile, before returning to the room.

When the ballroom class was over, his father came out flushed and out of breath and looking guilty.

"It's only a dance class," Danny reminded him

Later that night, after he closed up the MoonGlow, Charlie was walking along Westchester Ave on his way to an all-night diner. A downtown local clattered above so he didn't hear the truck coming up the street. In the moment before the flash of light, he caught sight of the SUV keeping pace with him.

Large. Black.

The passenger window opening. An arm thrust through it.

Two shots.

A plate glass window shattering.

Charlie hit the ground as the truck sped off, flickering in the spaces between the stanchions. Behind the ruptured window of *Exotic Nature's Wild World Pet Store* came the sound of whining puppies, shrieking parrots.

Charlie had barely gotten to his feet and dusted himself off when the police arrived.

"For once they were *almost* there on time," he joked on the phone with Danny in the morning.

"It's Mooney," Danny said.

"I don't think so."

"*One way or another*, remember?"

"This was a black guy."

"What about the driver?"

"Couldn't see him."

"Somebody Mooney hired. Had to be."

"My guess is it was a random thing. A drive-by. Maybe a gang initiation. Or a vendetta with the pet store owner. That's what the cops think. Rumor has it he's a shady guy. Does business in the black market. Animal smuggling. Exotic and endangered species, that sort of thing."

"And you just *happened* to be walking by?"

"Wrong place, wrong time."

"I don't buy it."

"Hey, it's the Bronx, remember? These things happen."

"Not in our neighborhood."

"No, not right here. But all around us."

Danny said nothing.

"You still there?" Charlie wanted to know.

"Yeah, I'm still here."

"So what are you thinking?"

"You haven't convinced me."

"Don't sweat it, man."

"You going to open the bar tonight?"

" 'Course I am. It's *my* bar. Or it's gonna be, one day." Then he added: "Bad coincidence. That's all it was."

Bad coincidence. Danny hoped that's all it was.

But the next night, after the bar closed, they came after Charlie again. This time in the back alley. He was climbing the stairs to his apartment when the truck came roaring in, nearly slamming into the Caddy. A gunman, wearing a Santa Claus mask, rose through the sun roof holding an assault rifle. So incongruous was the image it took Charlie a second to process it.

The first shot struck him above the left ankle, the second struck higher on the same leg. More shots were fired but he was already down, turning on the stairs, gripping the rail for support. There hadn't been time to reach for his .38.

He pulled himself up on the rail and watched the SUV, this one silver grey, go screeching backward down the alley. The front plate had been taped over and once the truck reached the street, all he saw was its profile as it turned toward Westchester Ave.

Before blacking out, he managed to pull his cell phone from his pocket and push the buttons for 9-1-1.

CHAPTER 26

A cop frisked Danny outside Charlie's hospital room.

Inside, while a nurse attended Charlie, Danny stood by the window that overlooked a subway yard: acres of tracks on which sat trains, or parts of trains, waiting for repair. Beyond the yard he could see the blue-black water of Westchester Creek threading between a row of warehouses and gas storage tanks. The fields of marsh grass, one of the places they played as kids, had been paved over, divided by a grid of chain-link fences.

"He's all yours," a nurse said behind him.

He turned from the window as she pushed her cart toward the door. She had a slim body and a perky way of walking, qualities that Charlie despite his groggy state had noticed as well. The appreciative gleam in his eyes gave him away. His bandaged left leg rested on pillows. Danny pulled a chair close and seated himself.

Behind the curtains of the second bed a man was saying, "No, no. No more of that—"

"You were right," Charlie said begrudgingly. It was an admission of defeat, as if he'd lost a wager.

"I was hoping I wouldn't be."

"The prick. I didn't think he had the balls—"

"He warned us." Danny remembered the clenched mouth when he'd said it, the venom in the way he spit the words. *One way or another—*

"Question is, were they lousy shots or were they just sending a message?"

"Pretty deadly message."

"Happened so fast. Like the last one. I had no time—"

"You were packing?"

"Yeah, I was packing. In case you were right."

"I should have been there."

"To do what? Get shot alongside me?"

"I don't know. *Some*thing."

Charlie pressed his palms against the mattress to shift his

position. "It's like my leg's on fire. It's hell if I have to move."

"Ask them for more drugs."

He grimaced as he settled himself against the pillows. "I'd rather feel pain than nothing at all."

"Pain brings the heroism out in some people."

"What the hell does that mean?"

Danny shrugged. "I read it somewhere."

"Yeah, well, I don't feel like much of a hero. More like a guinea pig. Or an asshole."

"What do the doctors say?"

"I won't be quarterbacking the Renegades any time soon. No permanent damage, though. They tell me I'll need crutches first, then a cane." He laughed at the prospect. "Imagine me with a cane."

"How long are we talking about?"

"For the cane? They didn't say."

Danny gave him an appraising look. He'd been shaved, his hair combed back. Despite his condition, his squared face bristled with impatience—Danny had felt it soon as he'd entered the room—as if he wanted nothing more than to get out of bed and get back into his life.

"You look pretty good, considering."

"Do I?"

Same drive, less execution, Danny was thinking. With the traces of fatigue in his eyes and the sluggishness in his movements, he seemed like a slower-motion version of his old self.

"Did you see anything? Were they the same guys?"

"Different car. Silver, this time. An Escalade."

"The other one was a what—?"

"Caddy or a Lincoln. I can't be sure."

"Same shooter?"

"Didn't see him, really. This guy wore a Santa mask. Didn't see the driver, either. Same deal. Tinted windows all around."

"The police—do they have anything?"

"Nobody's told me, if they do."

" 'Least they put a guard out there."

Charlie grunted. "And I had to beg them for that. You know the extent of their interrogation?" His eyes widened with indignation. "One question. *Did I have any enemies?* That was it. One lousy question."

"Maybe they'll come up with something."

"I'm not holding my breath." Charlie turned toward the window where the greying sky stretched south and east across the

Bronx. A moment's despair rose in his eyes. He wasn't the kind of man to depend on someone else, or some outside agency, to guarantee his survival. And for now, bed-ridden, that was the only option left open to him.

Danny regretted the dumb comment he'd made: *maybe they'll come up with something*. Even if they found the shooters, which was a long shot, it was unlikely they'd be traced back to Mooney. The guy was too smart for that. If, of course, they were right in their assumption that this was the detective's doing.

"Just when we all get back together. Just when I'm feeling like my old self again," Charlie was saying. "Fate paints a bulls-eye on my ass."

The real issue, Danny thought, was the things *we* do to create our fate. But now wasn't the time to bring that up, so what he said was he'd be willing to cover for him at the bar until Charlie got back on his feet.

"Thanks, man." He looked genuinely moved by the offer. "But you'd best be laying low for a while. Till this thing gets straightened out."

Danny wondered how that would happen. With Charlie laid up like this. Without him fighting to make things right.

Charlie was saying, "You guys are gonna have to watch your ass," when Johnny came in.

He was flushed, breathless, close to frantic: never having been frisked before, never having had to deal with a friend being shot, and the implications of that for his own safety.

Danny got up, gave him his seat. The guy looked too unsteady to be left standing.

"How are you feeling?" he asked Charlie. "I've been praying for you. I went to Mass this morning, I—"

"I'm okay, man. I'm okay."

Johnny still hadn't caught his breath. Wide-eyed he studied Charlie like a son looking at a father who'd exhibited the first signs of mortality. His own father had died when Johnny was a child. It was a loss he couldn't bear a second time. "Your leg? Does it hurt? Is it bad?"

"They tell me it's gonna heal up fine."

"You're sure?"

"That's what they tell me."

But Johnny's concerns seemed unassuaged. He looked from Charlie to Danny. "What are we going to do now?"

Outside the room, as he walked with Danny to the elevator, he seemed no less agitated. "Are we next?"

"I don't know. Maybe getting Charlie was enough. Or maybe he wants all three of us."

"Maybe we're wrong. Maybe it's got nothing to do with Mooney. Maybe it's the two guys Charlie threw out of the Glow, the guys who threw us out of the club. Maybe it's a racial thing." Johnny raced on, not waiting to catch his breath. "Or maybe it's some other vendetta against him. You know how Charlie can be sometimes. He can irritate people. He could have enemies we don't know about. What do you think? You think we're wrong about Mooney?"

"Maybe."

"But you don't really think so?"

"No."

"What do we do?" They were in the elevator, alone. Under the fluorescent light, Johnny's face seemed even more blanched, sickly. His hair looked a washed-out orange.

"Wait."

"For what?"

"See if they come after us."

Johnny's eyes turned inward, as if he was already running from something. "Too dangerous. Maybe we should—"

"—What? Go to the police?"

"Yes."

"They're going to tell us they can't do anything until a crime has been committed. You know that. It's their favorite line."

"It'll be too late then."

"Course it will. But that's how the system works."

"We could be dead. Or maimed. Or—" The horror of possibilities stopped him. "We could explain—"

"Explain what? We think one of their undercover narcs is trying to kill us because he thinks we rubbed out his chief witness against us? You think that's gonna get them on our side?"

They were on the street then. Johnny, flat-eyed with despair, glanced up and down the lanes of traffic, squinting at each passing car as if it was the enemy. "So—what? We're on our own?"

"We're on our own."

The reality set upon him like a judgment. His pale blue eyes

The Bronx Kill 123

looked frozen, dead. "It's a web, isn't it?" He was looking through Danny to some inner place, searching for something—a reason, a belief, a shred of philosophy, anything—to hold onto.

"What is?"

"What we've gotten ourselves into. Beginning with the night we lost Timmy. It's been spinning itself around us. Tighter and tighter."

"Come on. I'll walk you home." Danny clamped his shoulders, pushed him toward the corner. He wanted to give the guy a breather, some relief from their present danger. "So tell me what happened with Lorraine. You talk to her yet?"

Johnny slowed his step, caught his breath. "I did. I did talk to her."

"So what happened?"

"It wasn't easy." He had his hands shoved in his pockets and he chewed on his lip, calculating something. "I thought it was over. I really did. She wouldn't say anything at first. Just stared at me like I was some kind of freak she couldn't figure out."

"So what'd she say?"

"She thinks we should go away—a weekend someplace. Maybe even a week. A vacation, sort of. Talk things over some place quiet, no distractions. But she's not ready to do that yet. She's still too hurt. She wants some time. She wants me to take some time, too. Figure things out. Decide what it is I really want." He pushed his hair back from his face. His eyes had a faraway look. "I almost blew it. I almost blew it for good this time."

"At least she still wants to talk. She hasn't closed the door."

"I caught a break, I guess. I didn't think she was going to forgive me." His eyes drifted away again. In the distance, a train's rattle grew louder. They had reached the corner where he lived. The silence between them was filled with their anxiety. "So what now?" Johnny asked.

Danny grinned to ease the tension. "If we go down, at least we'll go down together."

"That's no comfort."

"Of course it isn't."

"Why'd you say it then?" Johnny looked genuinely disappointed, as if he'd been betrayed, having been offered nothing to serve as a buffer against his fear. "You shouldn't joke at a time like this."

"What else you gonna do when you're caught like we are? *In a web*."

Philip Cioffari

CHAPTER 27

"Your move," his father said. He'd taken the afternoon off to spend time with Danny who shook himself free of his reverie and stared down at the board.

His father's kings had him barricaded. Whether he moved to the left or the right, he'd get jumped. "Some choice," he muttered. Instead he pushed his only other remaining piece, a king, in what he thought was a safe move.

His father cackled. "How many times I got to tell you? Think ahead, boy. Think ahead." He moved his hand to execute a triple-jump, the third leg of which eliminated Danny's king.

"You boxed me in," Danny complained.

"You're not concentrating. You boxed yourself in."

His father had always been an aggressive checkers player, willing to sacrifice his advance guard in order to get his back pieces into position. Sacrifice early on, win later. It was a system Danny had refused to adopt, preferring his own more laid-back approach, slowly and methodically moving his men forward, protecting each of them as if they were indispensable. He'd lost, playing this way as a child; he was losing again now.

No point making his last move. Either way he'd lose. Besides, as his father had said, he wasn't concentrating.

"Concentration, the name of the game—how many times I got to tell you."

"Doesn't matter whether I concentrate or not—I still lose to you." He laughed and rested his elbows on the dining room table, staring at the red and black squares without seeing them.

His father had moved to the end of the table and, adjusting his glasses, began entering numbers into his notebook. His debit book, he called it, though it was nothing like the thick debit books of old. The company he worked for, Metro City Insurance, had some time ago computerized its operations, but his father clung to the old ways. He liked to say he had more important things to do than stare at a screen all day. So rather than learn to use a computer he entered his accounts by hand in a spiral notebook, then at the end of each week paid one of the secretaries at the office to log in the figures on the company spread sheet.

Watching him work, Danny was reminded of the times as a child he'd accompanied his father on his daily rounds, standing beside him as he rang doorbells, made sales pitches about the value of life insurance, collected monthly payments to save his clients having to mail them in. Even after his fellow salesmen cut back or even eliminated house calls altogether, relying instead on phone calls and emails, his father insisted on the personal touch. "So, *what*," he would say whenever Danny's mother had suggested he not work so hard, "We're not supposed to look into each other's eyes anymore, we're not supposed to shake hands?"

But Danny knew his mother was as proud of her husband's concern for his clients as he, Danny, was. Once Danny had told her when he grew up he wanted to be an insurance agent just like his dad. "They'll be a better life for you," she had replied. "Your father and I both want a better life for you. But you can be the same kind of man he is. That's the way you *can* be just like him."

Now, watching him bend over his notebook as he meticulously double-checked his figures, Danny said: "Remember how Mom would say all the time how much she hated baseball, how ridiculous it was for grown men to be spending their lives playing a child's game? And remember the time we finally got her to go to a Yankee game with us? That Sunday doubleheader against the Sox? And how much she loved it? How excited she got when Mattingly hit that ninth inning, walk-off homer? How she couldn't stop talking about it on the way home?"

His father removed his glasses and leaned away from the table, the wooden chair creaking beneath him as he shifted position. "What made you think of that?"

"I don't know. It just popped into my head."

He chuckled. "You never used to be this nostalgic."

"Tragedy, I guess. It makes you value your memories." And sitting there at the dining room table, uncertain of the days ahead, other memories crowded his consciousness: their Sunday dinners together, his mother preparing her most elaborate meal of the week, two meals really, a first course of pasta and sauce meat, a second course of roast lamb or veal; his mother taking him to midnight mass at Christmas, the Easter parade in Springtime; his father taking him on walks in Pelham Bay Park, telling him stories of how the Bronx *used* to be, the Indians who once lived here, the early settlers like Anne Hutchinson and Thomas Pell, and Gouverneur Morris, for whom the area around the Kill was named.

The room felt heavy with silence and loss.

"You're worried about your buddy," his father said. "You've got a lot on your mind."

"Charlie. Our point man."

"Damn shame is what it is. The streets aren't ours anymore."

He patted down the thin strands of hair on his head. Under the dining room's yellow overhead light, his eyes looked pensive and concerned. He'd missed the reference to being on point. Danny hadn't filled him in on the larger picture. His father thought the crime against Charlie might have been random. "Only a matter of time," he said. "One neighborhood goes, the ones around it go, too. On and on it goes. Why shouldn't ours be included in the package?"

"Violence begets violence." Danny had read that somewhere. It was as contagious as any epidemic, addictive as any drug, as unstoppable and enduring as love. He said it now as a way of agreeing with his father but he was thinking of it in a more personal sense: their violence against Timmy Moon, against Ellis, had come full circle.

His old man was looking toward the grey light of the living room window. It had rained earlier and the sky still looked threatening. "Maybe I should think about going to Florida with you when you go back."

"You have a job here. Your life's here. Isn't that what you're always telling me?"

"Lives can change."

Danny laughed. "That mean you're going to keep on with the dance lessons?"

"I'm thinking about it, yeah."

"Anyway," Danny said, turning serious again, "I'm not sure I'm going back."

His father raised his eyebrows. "No?"

"*My* life's here, too. My memories. You can't really run away from them. I see that now. Too many things to—"

His father waited for an explanation but Danny looked at him without finishing his thought.

The Bronx Kill 127

"You want some more coffee?"

Danny waved his hand in dismissal. "No. No. I'm too wired as it is."

"Some water then?"

"Sure."

His father gathered their cups and brought them into the kitchen. Over the sound of running water, he said, "You didn't go out at all today."

"I'm staying close to home," was all Danny would say.

His father brought two glasses of water to the table. "This—this Charlie business—wouldn't have anything to do with that detective coming around asking questions, would it?"

Danny tried to put on a shocked face. "Why would you think that?"

His father gave him a long, probing look then turned away, shaking his head. "Don't mind me. Rambling thoughts, that's all."

"Be sure to take the garbage out now, Johnny, will ye?" his mother called from the bedroom.

She was getting ready for her mid-afternoon nap, a habit she'd developed since her knee surgery. Normally she was a woman of high energy, always on the go. By day she worked as parish secretary at St. Cecilia's; by night she was active in various church social functions. But now, during her recuperation period, she was forced to do her book-keeping at home, a few hours each morning, a few each afternoon—followed by her doctor-prescribed forty-five minutes of rest.

First, she would brew herself a cup of Irish Rose decaffeinated tea, blowing on it constantly as she sipped it at the kitchen table. Between sips she would bite delicately into a scone—raspberry or strawberry-filled—that Johnny purchased at the corner bakery. Next she would spend ten minutes in the bathroom, washing her face, brushing her teeth, as if preparing for a long night's sleep.

After she closed her bedroom door, he would hear the low sound of violin music coming from her Panasonic clock radio, then exactly three-quarters of an hour later, at 4:30, she would emerge from her room, walking with determination despite having to use a cane, to begin preparations for dinner. Tonight, Tuesday: lamb chops, mashed potatoes, peas and carrots.

While he'd been in the seminary, she had become a creature of minute and scrupulous habits.

"Ye hear me, John? The trash—it needs to go out."

"Okay, Ma. Will do," he called from the living room.

"Ye won't forget now, will ye?" She had developed a morbid fear of vermin. Garbage—even in a plastic bag, even in a waste basket with the top securely fastened—had to be removed from the apartment at least twice daily.

"No, Ma. I'll do it." He stood by the window, staring down three flights into the alley with its long row of trash cans, lids askew. The light was always dulled here, a reflection of the grey brick wall across the alley, but today the rain drained away even more light. A rainy grey sky, he was thinking, set loose the bleakest of thoughts.

"Johnny?"

"Okay, Ma. I said I'd do it. You can go to sleep now."

Still, he lingered there like a man under house arrest gazing longingly at the world that had been denied him—even if it was only an alley.

He'd been running errands for her all afternoon. He thought he was safe traveling in daylight on crowded streets. He had thought it safe, also, to stop at St. Cecilia's on the way back from the Food Mart. So far as he knew, no one had been gunned down in a church. Life in the Bronx hadn't degenerated *that* far.

He had knelt in the first pew, closest to the altar, because he thought the presence of the Lord could be felt most strongly there. Mostly, though, what he felt was only the comfort of undisturbed space: the shadowed stillness of high ceilings, the rain-muted colors of stained glass, the barely-heard murmur of elderly women scattered across the empty pews behind him, reciting their rosaries.

Dear Lord, please grant Charlie a speedy recovery. Lift the evil hanging over us. Keep Danny and myself safe from . . .

He stopped his prayer and thought how pathetic we must sound to a Supreme Being, begging as we did constantly for safety and protection, to be spared from the world's dangers. Surely we were capable of more than that, weren't we, of bringing to the altar of God some gift other than dependency.

Yet, he asked himself, what other choice did we have? To whom or to what else could we turn to in our need?

And so he had placed his head in his hands and finished his prayer: *Keep violence from our lives. Allow me to survive this ordeal that I might live to serve my mother in her needs, as well as my beloved, Lorraine . . .*

Beyond the window, though the rain had let up, water dripped from the railings of fire escapes into the dismal alley. He thought about calling Lorraine, asking how she was doing, when they might talk again. She'd still be at work, he reminded himself, she would most likely be annoyed at the intrusion. He would call later after dinner, in the evening hours when, like himself, she would be more susceptible to the torments of loneliness. Now he would do as his mother had asked: take out the garbage.

In the kitchen, lifting the bag from the waste container, twisting its neck and securing it with a plastic tie, he felt almost saintly. The way, he imagined, St. Therese the Little Flower must have felt tucked away in her convent, anonymous and unheralded, performing the most menial of chores. For what task was more menial than this: disposing of garbage? An insignificant act made significant because it was offered, in private, for the greater glory of God.

Immediately, though, he felt ashamed of himself. St. Therese would have never indulged herself with such smug satisfaction. Her virtue was that she was truly ingenuous. She wanted only to serve in the most humble of ways, without earthly reward of any kind, with no sense of her own holiness.

Johnny Whales, humble servant of his mother and the Lord—he mocked himself as he stepped out into the hallway, dragging the bag. Theirs was an old building, built almost a century ago—complete with marble staircases and even dumbwaiters, though those were no longer functional.

A sign, in broken English, was taped over the wall chute: *No working*.

Over the years it had been a frequent occurrence, the trash compactor breaking down. You had to bring the garbage out to the alley yourself.

Instead of waiting for the elevator—the slowest ride on earth, as Charlie and Danny liked to call it—he slung the bag over his shoulder and took the stairs.

In the lobby he crossed to the side door which opened directly into the alley. He stepped out into the damp air that smelled of wet stone and decay.

At the rear of the alley, the trash cans lined both walls. As he moved toward them he thought of Timmy Moon—maybe it was the cold grey light and the dampness that resurrected the memory of him, the dampness of the alley recalling the damp sour smell of the river that night.

He was thinking, too, about the boy he had mistaken for Moon in the rain at Times Square, and something disturbing began to uncover itself inside him.

He clenched his body as if to lock it down and force it to submit to his will. Like a despot, he wanted to impose martial law upon his senses. His mind would determine which feelings would be allowed to surface, which would not. To that end he shifted the focus from himself, concentrated instead upon the weight of the bag draped over his shoulder, the row of cans along the wall ahead of him.

He began lifting lids until he found an empty container. Holding the lid aloft, he hoisted the bag with his right hand and deposited it.

Before it touched bottom something exploded in the alley.

A great weight struck the lid, almost ripping it from his hand, but he held onto it as the force spun him backward against the line of cans. The barrage of sound continued, seconds or microseconds he couldn't be sure, before he realized it wasn't one unbroken sound but individual bursts of gunfire, sharp cracking sounds amplified by the alley's vault-like stone and the metallic ringing of the lid which served as a shield as he stumbled, raising a clamor of his own, against the last of the cans.

In one flashing instant, falling, he glimpsed—from behind—a man carrying an assault rifle, running from the alley.

The Bronx Kill

CHAPTER 28

One thing seemed clear to Danny: *he was next.*
Today or tonight or tomorrow.
This week or next.
It was coming.
He paced in the room where he'd left his innocence behind, where pennants still decorated the walls: the Yankees, the Giants, St. Cecelia Elementary School, Cardinal Hayes—his high school. But it was the photo of the Renegades on his dresser that his gaze kept returning to.
They had started out in laughter, as the photo indicated. But they'd ended up in tears.
Time now to take matters into his own hands.
Sacrifice early, win later.

He stood in the doorway of the living room and watched ballplayers move across the screen.
"Have a seat. Watch the game with me," his father said from his chair. His face, turned away from the window, was in shadow. "The damn Sox. I need someone to commiserate with."
"The Yanks'll come back. They always do."
"Not always." There was a rueful note in his voice. "But that's what we love about them. They make us believe victory is possible. Even if our own lives aren't the success we want them to be."
"Dad—?" But he wasn't sure what he wanted to ask, and said nothing.
His father had turned off the sound on the TV. He looked at Danny a long while before speaking. "How you think it makes me feel?"
"What, Dad?"
"You know what." He leaned from the chair, his thin and lined face heavy with shadow. "Being in the dark like this. Knowing you boys are in some terrible trouble but not knowing what it is. Not

knowing why you won't talk about it, why you don't go to the police."

"The police can't help us."

"How you know that?"

"I just know it."

His father shook his head sadly. "And you can't tell me why?"

"Someday, Dad. Someday I will."

"Someday," his father nearly snorted the word. "The history of the world could be written from what fathers and sons refuse to talk about." He glanced at the TV but it wasn't a ballgame he was seeing there. "And meanwhile, what? I sit here wondering if one of these days or nights I'm going to get a call saying you're lying dead in some alley? What the hell did you three do to bring this on?"

"It's not completely our fault."

"What the hell does *that* mean?"

"It's complicated. It's a long story."

His father laughed. "I've got all night."

"I'm not sure I even understand it myself." He disliked himself for the lame excuse, for the lie behind it. He looked beyond his father at the window, the sky grey with clouds above the rooftops. His father had always been able to see through him, but he hoped his shame was buried deep enough to avoid detection.

"You're old enough to fight your own battles, God knows. But this, this—it makes me feel so useless."

"It's not you, Dad. It's me."

"Someday, when you have kids of your own, you'll realize there's no difference."

Danny felt a sense of gratitude swell within him. "You've always been a good father to me."

"I wish I could have protected you more from what's out there."

"There are things I had to deal with on my own. Still have to."

"But in a situation like this—I don't know. I don't have a clue how to help you."

"If there was something you could do, I'd tell you."

"I hope so." His father sounded unconvinced, unsatisfied. "I sure as hell hope so."

Danny watched him sink back in his chair, a lonelier and thinner version of the man whose hand he'd held as a child. The room felt heavy with grey light. From the kitchen came the low hum of the refrigerator motor clicking on. From the street came the thumping sound of a basketball on pavement.

"Remember you told me once friends can be like family, that you thought my friends were the brothers I never had—" But Danny didn't finish the thought.

He left it hanging, like a promise, in the silence of the room.

CHAPTER 28

He left phone messages for Tom Mooney, three of them, at the 43rd Precinct. He even stopped by the precinct in person. The desk sergeant didn't know when the detective would be in, *if* he would be in. "It's not like an office job," he told Danny. "It's not like you punch in at nine, out at five. He's a detective, for Chrissakes."

When Danny persisted, the sergeant slid a pad across the desk. "Leave him a message."

"I already did."

"What can I tell you, guy? You wanna leave another one, I'll see he gets it."

So Danny scrawled the words *Call me* on the pad and left his number.

He asked Charlie if he knew where the guy lived. "The Mooneys are gone," Charlie said. "From what I hear the wicked witch of an aunt is dead. And Tom's been out of here for years, supposedly somewhere in Yonkers. Nobody'll say where. Not even my contact at the 43rd. Some cops, they're sacred, man. Like the Feds or the C.I.A. They live a secret life."

They were in his hospital room: Johnny sitting on one side of the bed, Danny on the other. A late afternoon strategy meeting. They spoke in low voices, even though the other bed was unoccupied, even though there was no longer a cop outside the door.

"That's all you can tell me?"

"That's it. Nada."

"So what do you think?" Danny asked. "You figure these were assassination attempts that failed? Or you think Mooney's toying with us, maybe. Scaring the shit out of us. Either we give him the confession he wants, or he delivers the final blow."

"Wish I knew, man. Wish I knew." Charlie was looking stronger. His face had some color, his deep brown eyes had regained their focus and intensity. He would have been released already, he said, except his upper wound—the one on his thigh—had become infected. The doctors wanted to keep him a few more days.

But the infection in no way dampened his energy. "What

The Bronx Kill 135

you should do is this." He pushed himself up on the bed so that he was almost in a sitting position. "There's these four Albanian guys. They come into the bar sometimes. Huge mothers. Tough as iron."

"What about them?" Danny wanted to know.

"Next time Mooney comes into the neighborhood, tail him. Pick your spot, then go after him."

Johnny looked horrified. "Kill him, you mean?"

"Knock hell out of him, that's all. Put him in the hospital. Let him know we mean business, too. You gotta give back what you get. Street rules, you know that. You can't flinch. He's got to see he's in as much danger as we are."

"I—I don't know," Johnny stammered, his face turning red. "He's a cop. We can't just—"

"He's trying to kill us, man. Cop or no cop."

"But still—"

"Danny," Charlie said, cutting him off. "*You* get what I'm saying, right? You won't have to do anything but set it up. The Albanians will take care of it. I've already told them you'd be in touch. If you wear hoods, Mooney won't be able to prove anything. But he'll *know*. Just like we *know* he's behind the attacks, even though we can't prove it."

Danny thought it over. "I want to try my way first."

"What's *your* way?" Charlie couldn't hide the sneer in his voice.

"I'm working on it."

"Yeah, while you're *working* on it we're getting shot to shit. "I'm trying to help you out, man, before you end up like me, or worse. I'm trying to help us *all* out."

Danny ignored the sarcasm, the look of betrayal on his friend's face. "I need more information," he said. "What can you tell me about the shooters? I need something, *any*thing." He looked from Johnny to Charlie. "You've got to give me *some*thing."

"What can I tell you?" Charlie said, losing interest. Time was running out and here they were playing Twenty Questions. "The guy wore a Santa mask. I already told you that."

"Like what, though? What kind of a mask?"

"What difference does it make?"

"I don't know. That's what I'm trying to figure out."

Charlie looked toward the window where the sky had finally cleared. Grey sky and heavy clouds had released their hold on the city. "Plastic, I think. Curly white hair, rosy cheeks. The usual."

"What else?"

"I don't know. Jolly St. Nick. Big red smile. Like he was laughing *at* me, not *with* me."

"How tall was the guy—assuming it was a guy?"

"Hard to say. He was in a window the first time. Shooting from a sunroof the second time."

"Did he *fill* the window—height-wise or width-wise? When he stood up through the sun roof, how much of him could you see?"

Charlie grimaced in dismay. "Geez, you're worse than the cops with these questions."

"I'm what we have *instead* of the cops."

Charlie dropped his head back against the pillow and closed his eyes. "Tall—I'd say he was definitely on the tall side. Thin to medium build."

"And the driver? Can you tell me anything about the driver?"

"Not really."

Danny leaned close to the bed. "Think, man."

Charlie closed his eyes again, squinting as if trying to see in a room without light. "He was just a blur the first time. The second time—tinted glass, you know—I got nothing."

"A big blur. Or a small blur?"

"What are you talking about?"

"The first time. How much of the window was filled with the blur?"

"I have no idea."

"Guess then. A lot or a little? Wide or narrow?"

"A lot, I guess. Wider more than narrow. Geez, I don't know."

"The shooter was black, right? You saw his hands."

"Black, dark brown—yeah."

Danny looked across the bed at Johnny who raised his shoulders and stiffened his back, as if about to give a formal presentation.

"Like I told you. All I saw was his back. I don't even know if he wore a mask or not."

"You thought he was tall, though, right?"

"Tall, yes. Athletic—the way he ran. Something dark on his head."

"A hat? Hair?"

"I don't know. It was only a blur." Johnny nodded, as if

The Bronx Kill 137

agreeing with himself. There was a serenity about him Danny hadn't seen since he came back. As if he'd been transformed. The near-death experience, rather than pushing him over the edge and making him a basket case, had acted like a sedative. Things had been put in perspective, he said. He'd learned what mattered, what didn't. Rarely, though, did he leave the apartment. Not even for church. He communicated with the Lord at home, trying to pray his way—as was his custom—out of his problems. As for the supermarket? Now he used their home delivery service.

"When something like that happens," he said in a soft, even voice, "everything, all the parts of it—sights, sounds, every little sensation—merge into one. One thing, one moment. I don't know—it's hard to separate the details."

Charlie said, "You got that right."

"I went to the police, asked them for protection." Johnny looked sheepishly at them, as if he'd done something wrong. "For all of us, I mean. But they said they couldn't do anything, other than what they were already doing. Their investigation."

Charlie smirked. "That's why we need the Albanians." He gave Danny a cutting look. "I'm telling you. It's our best shot."

Danny pushed his chair back and paced in front of the window. "I'm the one on point out there. I get to choose."

A nurse came in, gave Charlie some pills in a plastic cup. Danny stared at the long, stalled line of subway cars in the yard below. When she left, he turned to them, his shadow falling across the bed like a divider. "Here's what I think we should do. Johnny, you and Lorraine want some time alone. I think now's the time. Take her some place for a few days. Don't tell anyone where you're going."

Johnny nodded obediently. He might have been a grade school boy accepting his penance from a priest in confession. "I'll have to see if she can get some time off."

"Go as soon as you can."

"What are *you* going to do?" Johnny asked the question tentatively, as if the implications of what might take place had only begun to dawn on him.

"I'm working on it," was all Danny would say.

Charlie said, "Hell, man, if I wasn't laid up, I'd be out there with you, running the show."

"You've done enough." Danny meant it in every sense of the word. "My turn now."

"The Albanians, man. You're making a big mistake. You're gonna regret—"

Danny raised his hand to silence him. "It's all right. It's all right. Worry about yourself. But I figure you should be relatively safe here. You've got the hospital guards down in the lobby. They know the situation."

Charlie laughed. "I'd feel a hell of a lot safer if I had my .38 under the pillow. But hell, man, you're gonna need it more than me."

"No, thanks. Not going to carry a gun. I'm no criminal."

"Depends on who you ask."

None of them thought that was funny enough to laugh.

PART THREE

CHAPTER 30

After midnight, armed with only a flashlight, Danny went back to the railroad yards.

He didn't know where else to begin, and he thought he would be safer coming this late, under cover of darkness. Near a makeshift walkway over the Kill, he spotted a gang of kids who had taken up residence on the bank. He passed close enough to hear their loud voices and laughter, to smell the weed they were smoking; but other than turning their gazes in his direction, no one responded to the shadow passing by.

When he slipped through the break in the chain-link fence, he was struck again by the almost unreal stillness of the yard. No sound, no movement, only the dark hulking shapes of rail cars going nowhere.

For several minutes he stood against the fence, watching. When he ventured into the yard he kept as much as possible to the shadows of the cars, making his way to the south end where Ellis had lived. He stopped a distance away, before approaching the old boxcar. It stood as still and undisturbed in its solitude as the other cars in the yard. No sound came from it, no sign of occupation. Only from a distance, beyond the Kill and the woods where they'd buried Ellis, came the low hum of traffic on the bridge.

He moved along the track toward the lone boxcar, approaching it from behind, walking softly around it until he came to the section of track where Ellis' life had ended. He stopped short, seeing again the small twisted body coiled in the space between the rails, feeling the shock and horror of it once more.

In the hushed silence, he swore he could feel the presence of spirits again but he shook away the sensation and walked to the open door of the car. He flashed his light briefly into the interior before pulling himself up. Inside he stood still to steady himself and flashed the light into the corners to be sure he was alone. The smell of rust and decay was as strong as he remembered it, the collection of household goods and random junk had been undisturbed, but the garbage bags of money stored behind it were gone.

Which made sense, of course. You didn't leave money lying around in the open, if you wanted it to be there when you got back. Unless you had some screws loose. Or—unless your place was protected by someone or some thing.

He was mulling that over, crouched in the space where the bags had been, when he heard voices outside. They were at a distance, coming from the south end of the yard, coming closer. Male voices, two of them. He straightened up and flattened himself against the wall, straining to hear.

"Ellis," one of them said.

Danny couldn't hear what came next. Their footsteps drew closer. The same voice, more clearly Hispanic now, said, "Liked it a helluva lot better, man. . . ." The rest was lost.

The second voice, older, deeper, with a hint of a rasp said, "Yeah. Yeah. I can dig it, but. . . ." The voice shifted, changed direction perhaps, took the words with it.

The footsteps stopped right outside the car. There was a metallic click, a short hiss, and the smell of tobacco smoke drifted into the car. He wondered what he would do if they discovered him. Play dumb, he told himself. Just say you're wandering around, getting material for a story. You like urban blight. You grew up around here. Whatever. Hope you don't get your ass kicked. Or worse.

"Fuck this nickel and dime stuff, man. Got no use for it," the younger voice said.

"Nickel and dime? You're kiddin', right? You know how much they pull down?"

"Nickels and dimes."

"Bullshit." It was the older one with a cigarette. His words were thick with smoke. "Over. . . ." Whatever number he gave was lost in the exhalation of breath. ". . . a month."

"No shit?" the younger one said.

"No shit."

"Yeah, well—"

"Yeah, well, *what?*"

"Nothin'."

"And that don't count what comes in . . ." The voice had turned away again.

Danny edged along the wall, closer to the door, to hear better.

144   *Philip Cioffari*

"Still ain't what I had in mind," the younger one said.

"So, what, you're too good for this?"

"Yeah, maybe I am."

"Hey, you don't want this gig, say so."

"It's all right—for now."

"You an asshole, you know that?"

"I know what I know." A moment passed when neither of them spoke then the younger one was saying, "Imagine living in this shithole."

"Hey, for a homeless guy he didn't have it bad. The boss took care of him."

"You and me got different values, man."

"So you want to see the inside? See how the guy lived?"

Danny stiffened, felt his hands go clammy where they touched the wall. He gripped the heavy flashlight in case he had to fight his way out of here. Maybe Charlie was right: packing the .38 was the only way to negotiate the world he was moving into.

"Nah," the Hispanic voice was saying. "The cat was crazy, man. Who cares how the fuck he lived?"

"Thought you wanted to see it. It's why we walked all the way the hell over here, for fuck's sake."

"Can smell the stink from here, man. Close enough for me."

"Break's over then, ass-wipe. Let's get back to work." There was another insuck of breath, and the footsteps moved away. "You think you some kind of King snake but you jest a dumb shit don't know shit. You . . ."

The rest was lost.

Danny felt his body relax, the tension draining like liquid from his muscles. His heart stopped its hammering. He waited a moment before taking a position at the door where he could see the backs of the two men, moving toward the north end of the yard: one of them short and wide, his gait more a waddle than a walk, the other taller and wiry, a step or two ahead. They stopped once and stood face to face, as if they might be arguing again, which afforded Danny a good look at their profiles. Then they moved on again. The heavy-set one had trouble negotiating the fence, having to turn his body sideways in a crouch, then wriggle in order to fit through the opening.

Their dark forms struck out across the first of the vacant lots, in the direction of the street.

The Bronx Kill

So at least one of his questions had been answered, Danny thought. Ellis got away with leaving his money around because apparently this area *was* being monitored.

Someone had been protecting the old man, except at the time he needed it most.

CHAPTER 31

Danny waited until they were out of sight before crossing the yard.

He found a place where the fence had been trampled, as if a truck had rammed it, and followed a path through the western edge of the lot. The grass grew taller as he neared the street, blocking it from view.

Not far ahead, beyond the wall of grass stationary in the windless air, he could hear a car motor idling. From a radio came the heavy strains of a symphony, intense and dramatic. Something out of Wagner.

The path spurred off onto a small rise, home to a dead tree and some large rocks, barely high enough to offer him a view above the grass. The street was empty save for a lone car, a restored '76 silver-grey Camaro parked along the curb not more than a hundred feet from where he stood. The music was coming from the car which, from what he could see, had only one occupant. An arm dangled out of the passenger side window, the fingers of the hand tapping a beat on the door's metal.

A moment later two figures emerged from the lot just beyond the front of the car. One of them was the Hispanic kid who had stood outside the boxcar. The other wore baggy pants and, despite the mild evening, a hoodie pulled all the way up so at first it wasn't possible to know if it was a man or a woman.

A man, Danny guessed, by the way the hooded being moved up the street. The hunched over figure headed toward a row of abandoned two-story brick buildings that might, in better times, have been small factories or machine shops.

No sooner had the figure turned the corner and vanished when another figure appeared out of the same cross street, this one clearly an old black man, grey-haired, hands in his pockets, a shuffling gait as he crossed to the car. It was the heavy-set dark-skinned man, the other half of the pair outside the boxcar, who hoisted himself now from the Camaro to accompany the old man into the lot. The

The Bronx Kill

heavy-set man looked familiar to Danny and it was then, as the man crossed the sidewalk, that he realized he was one of the bouncers he'd seen that night in the alleyway at Home Cookin'.

As soon as the Hispanic kid got into the car, the music changed to a dry, thumping hip-hop beat.

From where he stood, Danny watched the two black men as they left the street and moved along a path rimmed by cottony-tipped reeds and the thin spiked blades of tall grass. Within minutes the pair re-emerged: the old black man trudging toward the street that had brought him here, the heavy-set man returning to the car, where he abruptly changed the radio station. Once more the symphony reigned over the quiet street.

Over the next quarter hour there was a steady stream of traffic that made its way to the waiting Camaro. They came on foot, mostly alone but occasionally in pairs, materializing out of nothing it seemed on the abandoned side streets that fed into the avenue. Down and out types mostly, men and women, young and old, black and Hispanic and occasionally a white man. The better dressed types came in cars, cruising warily down one side of the avenue and up the other, before pulling over.

You came in here, you were on your own.

You came in here the last thing you wanted to see was a cop.

The heavy-set man and the Hispanic kid took turns, escorting each new arrival into the lot and then out again. The soundtrack shifted from classical to hip-hop, accordingly. From what Danny could tell, judging by the handshakes and high-fives, the big smiles and the banter, these were mostly repeat customers.

He walked to the far edge of the rise where he had a clear view of the object of these trips into the lot: the windowless hulk of an abandoned '59 Chevy Biscayne, its color faded to the lifeless grey of the undercoating.

The Chevy's trunk lid appeared to have been permanently sprung. Inside the trunk a large cooler occupied most of the space, the spent contents of which—beer cans, soda bottles, dented Burger King Styrofoam containers—apparently had been discarded right there in the dirt around the car.

A rat ate from the one of the Styrofoam containers. Another one—or some other animal—made a flickering dash beneath the car.

The voices grew louder on the path in from the street. The heavy-set man—Short Fat Fannie, Danny had named him, because of his wide butt and his waddle—led two young white boys, high school age, to the dead Chevy. The first of the boys counted out some bills into the thick, black palm. The hand that took the money reached through the car's side window and came out with two glassine packets, distributed one to each of the boys.

The black man said, "Go back to wherever it is you come from. Don't be doing this shit down here, you heah?"

"You got it, man," one of the boys said. It came out sounding unnatural and forced, not cool, the way it had been intended.

The boys hurried back toward the street. Short Fat Fannie checked his watch, then reached into the cooler for a can of beer. In a surprisingly tender way he tapped the plastic lid back into place, before pulling the pop-top and raising the can to his lips.

In the moon's faint light the Chevy, sunk on its air-less tires into the dirt, loomed as an unglamorous treasure cache for the damned. He wondered if that was Ellis' function, to serve as caretaker of this dispensary and the area around it. An eccentric old man simple-minded enough not to know the complexity of the operation he was involved in. A low-risk liability if the cops showed up. Someone, in short, to take the fall.

That, at least, offered an explanation for the bags of cash stowed away in the old man's boxcar.

He was thinking about what Short Fat Fannie had said to the Hispanic kid in the train yard: *you don't want this gig, say so.* Was the Hispanic kid Ellis' disgruntled replacement?

Some blocks away a car engine revved, the sound echoing off the hard brick and macadam, rising as it drew nearer. A black SUV appeared at the end of the street, turned the corner hard and came at street-racing speed down the three blocks where it jerked to a halt and double-parked beside the Camaro. A tall man wearing a bandanna around his neck stepped out and opened the rear door for two young black men, barely out of their teens.

Danny thought he could identify the man with the bandanna: it looked like the Jamaican bouncer who'd dragged him down the alley of Home Cookin'.

When the man began pushing the two young men into the lot, Danny was sure of it. The sculpted face, the dreadlocks, the large hands, the long loping stride.

At the sunken Chevy, Short Fat Fannie waited for them. Words were exchanged, muffled and inaudible, and in the next

The Bronx Kill

moment the Jamaican had drawn a gun, jabbing it at each of the young men, shouting at them to "Get the fuck on your knees. Get the fuck on your knees."

Short Fat Fannie began the assault, hammering at each of the young men in turn, battering their faces with his club-like fists. Then it was the Jamaican's turn. He used a bat he took from inside the Chevy, applying his home-run swing to chest and back and legs, then wielding the bat like an axe as the men squirmed curled and broken on the ground, their wails of agony filling the night. Never had Danny heard a man's scream before, a sound more high-pitched and jagged—*unearthly*—than he would have thought humanly possible, horrible in such a different way than a woman's scream, the two men's screams locked into one tortured, unending cry of despair. He pressed his hands to his ears, turned away.

When the bodies went inert, the night's calm settled once more. Briefly. The only disturbance came from the Camaro's radio, and the summer's first crickets rousing themselves in the grass.

The beaten men were dragged out to the street and loaded into the SUV's cargo space.

The Jamaican climbed into the driver's seat and the black SUV leapt forward, sprinting the three remaining blocks to the point where the avenue dead-ended against a barbed wire fence. It took the turn with its tires screaming and was lost behind a wall of buildings.

The tire noise lingered, though, a howl of defiance hanging above the vacant streets and the dark dismal symphony coming from the Camaro.

On the way to the club, on a deserted side street, Danny came upon the bodies dumped mid-block at the mouth of an alley. Two blocks west, on Jerome, he found a working phone booth and made an anonymous call to 9-1-1.

CHAPTER 32

The Home Cookin' sign was still flashing in the window of the two-story building under the EL.

It was past two in the morning and yet Jerome Ave offered no sign of shutting down. Voices called to Danny from shadowed doorways, offering joints or sex or both.

What gave him pause before entering the club was whether he would be recognized as one of the "troublemakers" from last week. The small number of whites among the clientele would argue in favor of that happening. But he had been the quiet one of the three. It was Johnny first and then Charlie who had caused the commotion. So he was counting on that small amount of circumstantial anonymity to get him through the door, past the oversized man who sat on a bar stool at the entrance, eying those who came in and out.

To his dismay it was Ernie, the bouncer who'd been particularly rough that night on Charlie as they were ram-rodded like cattle in a chute into the street. The man's hard, penetrating stare descended with equal intensity on everyone in line, but he showed no sign of recognition as Danny approached and he was waved on through. Once inside, Danny breathed easier. He found a place at the bar, ordered a beer and sipped it with his shoulders hunched to keep a low profile.

The men around him were drinking heavily, their voices at an unusually loud level to compete with the thumping, piped-in dance music. The girls on the runways, in the true spirit of diversity, were drawn from various backgrounds. In addition to the black and Hispanic girls, there was a white one, an Asian, an Indian and a Middle-Eastern beauty who wore a Muslim head scarf along with her bikini.

Apparently, there was a contest going on. The voice over the P.A. system was saying something about which of them could do the down and dirtiest hip swivel. The winner, as determined by the level of applause from the crowd, would be the recipient of a two hundred dollar gift certificate, compliments of the house.

Danny scanned the room in search of—what? He wasn't sure. He caught sight of the waitress who had brought them drinks last week. Again, she was serving the booths and tables in back, gliding sleek as a dancer through the crowded aisles, her face stone-cold and joyless. Charlie had been right. Her attitude wasn't to be taken personal.

Other than for Ernie at the door, he didn't recognize the other bouncers with their yellow arm bands who moved through the crowded room. One of them stood by the door to the infamous alleyway. He was monitoring the flow: when one man came out, he sent another one in. A non-stop process. Like planes taking off and landing at an airport. You could depend on it.

And something else he hadn't noticed last time: the constant line to get into the men's room. Either the club drew an exceptionally high percentage of men with bad prostates, or you got something there that improved your frame of mind.

"What's available?" he asked one of the bouncers standing near him. He nodded in the direction of the men's room.

"What you need?" the man responded in a way that suggested the choices were limitless.

So maybe, Danny figured, that explained the activity at the Kill. It made sense that there'd be a satellite operation there, six blocks to the south, given both its isolation and its proximity to the ramps of the Tri-Borough, ideally situated to serve not only the South Bronx but Manhattan and Queens, as well. Easy on, easy off.

He drank his beer and watched the scene before him, reminded once again how awash the world was in needy loveless men. Like himself, he conceded. The mere residue of a man. What had become of him when Julianne had been taken out of his life: a man without desire. But he'd never been interested in the kind of solutions places like this offered. Drugs and booze had never been a refuge for him, and the thought of sex with strangers depressed him rather than tempted him.

That he refused to worship here didn't make him a better man, only different, he told himself. His preferred indulgence was memory: the regret and guilt it carried, his fixation with it as an emblem of his still-young but failed life. His existence might have been so much easier though, he sometimes thought, if he simply joined the majority of his brethren, like those around him now, and camouflaged the void within him with these simple, if temporary, acts of pleasure and release.

He laughed at the improbability of that, given who he was. And yet, looking at the packed house around him, he wondered: could so many men be wrong? Because even here, in what was the poorest urban county in the nation, there was money enough for the basics: sex and drugs and booze: pleasure and release, pleasure and release.

And then his thoughts descended to where he needed them to be—the matter at hand. He was thinking this place had to be operating with the blessing of the NYPD—it was too flagrant, too brazen an operation not to be.

Suddenly a loud cheer went up for the winner of the contest—the Middle-Eastern dancer with the head scarf—and he couldn't tell if the cheer was mocking or sincere.

In the past few minutes, there seemed to have been a surge of late-night activity. The voices around him had grown louder, more aggressive and he found himself being jostled more often than he cared for. The large room seemed to have grown even more crowded than when he'd first arrived. As Charlie had said, this was a place of last resort, and these were the hours of last resort, when your options—even in a city like this—were limited.

And then, through the confusion of motion and noise around him, the exposed flesh of the dancers, the unrelenting thumping beat of the music, the ceaseless movement of waitresses and bouncers and impatient men forcing their way through the aisles, he did recognize a familiar face: the Jamaican with his signature red bandanna.

He was against the far wall, leaning close to Ernie, saying something fast and, judging by the fixed expression on his face, something urgent into the big man's ear.

They were looking in his direction, or so it seemed to Danny, but whether they were looking at *him* or at something else in the sea of activity that churned like a breaking tide in the room between them, he couldn't be sure.

Time to leave.

The night breeze came at him as a relief from the thick, sweat-filled air of the club. At the entrance, the bouncer who had replaced Ernie paid him scant attention as he turned south along the EL. That put Danny at ease. Now the only gauntlet he had to negotiate were the six short blocks to the car, past the restless shadows slouching in doorways.

He reached the end of the first block before he sensed he was being followed. Glancing back, he saw two men walking behind him: the bouncer at the door who had seemed oblivious to his exit, and the Jamaican.

He picked up his pace.

When he glanced again from the next block, they were still behind him, gaining on him.

Take off, the voice of panic urged, *flat out run for it.*

But the old caveat about never showing fear had a stronger hold on him. He waited until he reached the corner where he turned onto a street that led away from the EL, *then* he ran. All out, middle of the street, arms flailing, legs working like pistons.

His breath came hard, his footsteps echoing off the metal gates of the locked and vacant shops. When he reached the end of the block he looked behind and saw the two men had stopped at the corner. They were talking to the driver of a dark SUV. Several seconds went by before the two men continued down the street following the EL, as the SUV came slowly up the street toward him.

Coincidence? He didn't think so.

He veered off the street onto the sidewalk, running hard, thinking he was safer here closer to the buildings, in case the SUV turned into an assault vehicle.

Which it did, once he rounded the block.

The EL loomed at the end of the street and he sprinted for it, the SUV's engine revving hard before it shot forward in a bee-line for him.

At the same time, a second SUV—this one a steel-grey— seemed to come out of nowhere from the opposite end of the street.

There was an alley somewhere along here, he knew, somewhere up ahead on the north side of the street. Too narrow for a car. They had used it as a hide-out in their Renegade games. Past the long brick façade of the defunct linoleum factory up ahead. Right past it.

At any moment he expected to be crushed between the two vehicles, engines breathing hot and furious and bearing down on him, front and back.

With a final burst of speed, he zig-zagged between them and reached the alley that turned out to be more a gap between buildings than any kind of full-fledged alley. It ran between the factory and two warehouses. A storage area—empty now, the size of a basketball court—opened into a large parking lot, home to hundreds of empty spaces and a few abandoned school buses rusted and lopsided, their windows smashed, their ancient and graffiti-scrawled bodies sunken on tire-less rims.

When he crossed the lot he arrived at Jerome, mid-block, in the shadow of the EL. Neither the SUVs nor the bouncers were in sight so he thought he might make it to the car, after all. He made it another block before he saw the Jamaican coming up the avenue toward him.

Oh God, no.

In the distance he heard the rising clatter of a train—uptown or downtown, he wasn't sure.

Only a matter of time, he knew, before the SUVs would emerge from the side street behind him and he would be trapped again. Fortunately though, the station lay directly ahead at the end of the block.

So close.

Without hesitation, he sprinted for the stairs. He could get there before the Jamaican, he was sure of it, he was that much closer.

Taking the stairs two at a time, he had climbed halfway up when he heard the train pulling in above him on the downtown side. Below him, on the street, he saw the black SUV double-parked now at the corner. The Jamaican yelled something to it and the truck took off—most likely, Danny figured, to follow the train and meet him at the next station, or at whatever stop he decided to make a run for it.

At the foot of the stairs, the tall black man had his hand on the railing and began climbing.

Danny heard the train's airbrakes squeal as it came to a stop, then came the whooshing sound of the doors opening. He passed the token booth on the fly and in one fluid motion jumped the turnstile—a feat he'd practiced to perfection as a kid.

A voice was raised sharply in anger behind him. "Hey! Hey you!"

One more flight of stairs to the track level. *He wasn't going to make it.* He had barely begun his climb and already he could hear the electronic voice saying, "Stand clear of the closing doors."

Too late. Too late. The doors were sliding closed.

Reversing direction, he came past the token booth again as

The Bronx Kill

he crossed to the uptown side.

"Hey you!" the voice shouted again from the token booth. "We got you on camera. We got you—"

Sometimes the local trains arrived at a station at the same time: one going downtown, one uptown. Right now that was his only hope, albeit a slim one. When he reached the uptown stairs, he caught the red flash of the Jamaican's bandanna as the man became the second person in the past sixty seconds to jump the turnstile.

Which provoked another outcry from the token booth. "What the f—?"

On the platform Danny looked south toward the city. The red tail-lights of the downtown local moved slowly away, growing dimmer. On the uptown side he could see the lights of a local two stations away.

Too far for him to wait.

Much too far.

He cursed the bad timing and hurried to the north end of the platform as the Jamaican appeared behind him, now accompanied by his fellow bouncer. It took them no time to spot him.

Out of necessity Danny jumped onto the track. Like the old days. A game they played called Racing the Uptown Express. Only this time it was the local, not the express. Same game, same rules. Same stakes, too: if you weren't fast enough, you died.

Charlie had taught them how to do it. The idea was to wait at the north end of a station platform until the uptown express came into view. Then you ran along a narrow strip of metal between the track and the railing. You had to reach the platform of the next station before the express did, or else you'd be slammed into oblivion by the oncoming rush. You had, depending upon the station, between four and four and a half minutes from the time you first spotted the train.

They'd played this game any number of times, at any number of stations, Johnny and Timmy Moon the slowest of them, the ones most likely not to make it. But they *had* made it. Yet one more Renegade victory, Charlie liked to proclaim each time they all reached the platform safely, panting and exhilarated. And they all agreed, it was the thrill of a lifetime.

Danny wasn't as agile now. His body took up more of that narrow space between the track and the railing and he had to watch his footing, so he was forced to run at a slower pace. His only consolation: his pursuers had stopped on the platform: they didn't follow him onto the track. The Jamaican was on his cell phone, walking in circles, waving his arm. His cohort glared down the track at Danny who turned away from them now to concentrate on the matter at hand.

He held onto the railing and placed his feet carefully, moving as fast as he dared. Charlie's rules rang in his head like an alarm: look straight ahead, never turn around, never look down, use the handrail only if you need it. And, his last harrowing piece of advice: *run like your life depended on it.* Which, of course, it did.

The breeze was stronger here, tearing his eyes. He kept blinking constantly to clear them, to check his footing, to look up occasionally at the curve of track and the lighted station ahead.

He was three-quarters of the way there when the train horn sounded behind him.

He had to let go of the rail and increase his pace.

Everything came at him in blurred form—the seemingly endless line of track ahead, the wavering station lights, the rooftops that climbed away like hills beyond the reach of the railing—and all the while the train horn at his back, screaming its warning into the night. He forced out one final burst of speed and grabbed for the rail to pull himself onto the platform as the local came roaring into the station.

He was already headed down the stairs before the train came to a stop and opened its doors. Fearing the SUV would be waiting for him, he scanned the street below as he descended. Beyond the row of shops and taverns, the cemetery stretched away for as far as he could see, the grey stone of mausoleums luminescent in the moonlight.

He had come nearly halfway down the steps before he spotted the black SUV parked at the next corner, pointed in his direction. Right then, though, across the street from the SUV, a police cruiser pulled into a space in front of an all-night diner.

A break. Danny sighed with relief. *A break at last.*

Above him, the Jamaican and his sidekick had appeared at the head of the stairs. But Danny came unhurried the rest of the way down the steps and walked directly toward the patrol car, glancing once in the direction of the SUV to make sure those inside understood his intention. Before he reached the car, the SUV had gathered up his two pursuers. In the next moment it pulled out into traffic and sped away.

He stood there on the street until he could no longer see the black truck's tail lights, before crossing to the next corner where he hailed a livery cab. He would have to leave his father's car where he parked it, until tomorrow. Right now all he wanted was the safety of his apartment and a beer.

In the aging Town Car, he rested his head against the cracked leather seat that smelled of smoke and cheap perfume. He'd learned something this night at least. It was the Home Cookin' crowd that was out to get them.

And why would that be, unless they were carrying out Tom Mooney's orders?

CHAPTER 33

So it came as no surprise the following night when Mooney himself showed up at the club.

Danny watched from across the street, in his father's car. He sat low in the seat, sheltered by the cars parked in front and behind him, as well as by the over-arching shadow of the EL. He'd been watching the club for almost two hours before the detective suddenly appeared. Shortly past midnight. Near the alley alongside the club, talking to Ernie.

And that's what it was like: an *apparition*.

Danny had turned away for something, blinking to clear his vision. When he looked again, the alley door that had been a blank slate now had two men standing before it. The detective in a grey windbreaker and jeans leaned close to the bouncer, talking fast and hard. Explaining something, or chewing out the barrel-chested man, Danny couldn't be sure. The detective's balding scalp reflected the light above the door. He moved forward and back as he talked, a slow rocking motion that brought him in and out of shadow. Ernie kept nodding, in agreement it seemed with whatever was being said to him.

Holding out his cell phone, Danny clicked a picture of them.

At that point Mooney stopped talking and stared out toward the street. Danny lowered the phone, slunk down lower in the seat. *As if he knew*, Danny thought. *As if he had a sixth sense.*

When the detective turned back to the bouncer he said something short and abrupt. The two men walked over to the club entrance and went inside.

Danny didn't think he'd been spotted. Too much distance between them. Too many shadows cast by the EL.

An hour passed with no sign of the detective.

Restless and cramped within the confines of the car, he wondered what he should do next. If only—

Before he had time to finish the thought, Mooney came strolling out from the alley door. Alone this time. Head down, he

The Bronx Kill 159

walked to the end of the block where his Merc was parked.

If his theory was correct that the club couldn't be operating without the protective indulgence of the police, there was now at least the possibility Mooney was that protection.

Tom Mooney did a U-turn under the EL and drove south.
Several cars behind, Danny followed.
Past the automotive shops—mufflers, tires, brakes, transmissions—their graffiti-stained grates lowered for the night. Past darkened doorways with their usual inhabitants. He felt unsafe traveling this street, even in a locked car; he kept his eye on the rear view mirror to be sure he wasn't being tailed.

They were south of the expressway where it was less commercial, more industrial. One by one, cars turned off left or right, until only empty space separated his vehicle from the detective's. He slowed down, leaving as much as a half-mile between them. There wasn't much chance he would lose the Merc here.

The EL veered off in a long sweeping curve to the west, to Manhattan, and they were left to the deserted warehouse streets adjacent to the Kill. Finally the Merc turned onto the marginal road, moving slowly toward the restored Camaro, its symphonic music barely audible tonight. It was parked as it had been last night, midway down the street.

The Merc pulled in behind it. Mooney got out, and walked briskly to the Camaro's driver side, bending to speak through the window.

It appeared to Danny who watched from the corner, afraid of being spotted if he made the turn, that Mooney reached through the window for something. Then his hand withdrew and went to his pocket. Danny could now see it was Short Fat Fannie in the driver's seat. The two men spoke briefly before Mooney returned to his car and drove off.

Danny had taken another picture—Mooney leaning into the window of the Camaro—but at such a distance it was difficult to make out his face. He thought again about trying to talk to Mooney, one on one, in hopes he might get him to call off his vendetta. This wasn't the time or place, though. No way he wanted to venture, unarmed, into the maze of these streets and put himself at the detective's mercy.

Besides, it seemed even more unlikely now than ever that the detective would meet him face to face, for *a talk*. The man had already played his hand.

And there was that other troubling complication, as well. Whatever Tom Mooney was involved in, it seemed to go far beyond exacting vengeance for his brother's death.

CHAPTER 34

Tom Mooney couldn't say exactly when his priorities had changed. It was, he thought, sometime after he made detective, sometime in this past year, when he came to believe he might really be capable of making a case against the Renegades. Like many of the turning points in his life, it had passed without notice, the effects of the change realized only in retrospect.

That was what he was mulling over as he drove across 149th to his meeting with the Nunez brothers from Miami. What he *should* be thinking about, what he *should* be feeling, he knew, what would be normal to feel under the circumstances, was fear pure and simple. Because tonight his life would be on the line, *again*. Tonight he would be walking the edge, *again*.

So, yes, he should be feeling terrified. He should be shaking in his boots as they used to say in cowboy movies. But he was the man with steel balls—that's what the crew at Home Cookin' liked to call him. And men with steel balls didn't flinch in the face of danger. Which was the best explanation he could come up with why, only minutes before his meeting with two temperamental drug lords, he felt nostalgia rather than terror.

What filled him was a sadness, heavy with grief and loss, that carried with it memories he couldn't dispel. He was thinking of himself as a younger man, the ideals that had made him want to become a cop. Simply this: he had wanted to serve and protect the city he loved. He believed in justice for all, and he wanted to do his part to insure the law was upheld for every resident of the five boroughs, black or white, rich or poor.

That was the cop's life he had wanted to live.

What caused him to drop out of law school, shortly after Timmy's death, was the belief his ideals would be best realized on the streets rather than in some law office. He would be one of those who kept the city safe from all things threatening.

At least that had been the plan.

Until his sense of justice had been whittled down to one

thing that had only a tangential reference to his youthful dreams: punishing those responsible for his brother's death.

And that had made the next step so much easier: accepting the fact that *the end justified the means.*

This section of the city that he covered, this job working with the crew at Home Cookin'—helped make his transformation complete.

Stopped now for a light, at the corner of 149th and Southern Boulevard, he watched a group of men loitering outside a bodega. Inside, despite the fully-stocked shelves containing bread and chips and beer and salsa, drugs were the primary items for sale.

This was true, too, of the bodega on the opposite corner. And the one two blocks over. And the one on—the list was endless. And if it wasn't a bodega, it was a liquor store, or a bar or a convenience store or an auto body shop.

And a few blocks ahead, in the Hunts Point Section where he was heading, coke and meth and smack were sold openly on the street, and hookers stood in twos and threes along the curb, offering bargain-priced, drive-up service.

Over the years the scum of the earth had risen like a tidal wave around him. And it was drowning him. He could feel the weight of it pushing him deeper, so far beneath the surface at times that he thought he might never see the light of the heavens or breathe pure air again. Yes, he was drowning. Because this was *his* world now. And the hard truth of undercover work, he'd learned, was that you had to live in one world or the other. *You couldn't live in both.* This was his: the world of drug lords like the Nunez brothers, of smaller-time dealers like Ernie and the crew at Home Cookin'. These were his associates, his colleagues, his pals, his buddies. Friends who were not his friends. An inverted world where wrong was right, and right was wrong.

Where the end justified the means.

Avenging his brother's death was the moral principle he clung to like a life raft.

The "office" the Nunez brothers used whenever they were in New York stood on a street of mostly abandoned buildings, six blocks from the Hunts Point Market. No difficulty finding a parking space. Not even the hookers or pushers worked this street.

Three cars, all of them black Mercedes, were parked side by side in the vacant lot adjacent to the building. Tom Mooney left *his* on the street. Safer that way, he figured. Faster getaway, if it came to that, though he didn't think it would come to that. If they were going to come after him, it would be *inside* the building. If he made it to the street unharmed, he'd be home free.

He stood outside the three-story building, its brick the color of mud. No lights in any of the front windows. Nunez and Company would be in the rear of the building. Third floor, left hand side of the hall. He knew the drill.

Antiquated though it was, the place had a buzzer system. A sour-faced Mexican wearing a shoulder holster let him in, frisked him, then motioned to the stairs. "*Tres.*"

"*Sì, sì.*" The detective waved his hand dismissively and mounted the steps. The building smelled of stale air and dust. Beneath him the stairs creaked.

It was only when he reached the third floor that the first tremors of panic made themselves felt. Nothing disruptive. Just enough to remind him he was human. Hand on the banister, he steadied himself.

A door opened down the narrow hall and two guards with assault rifles appeared, watching him flat-eyed as he approached. One of them frisked him a second time while the other stood by, rifle at the ready. The room they allowed him to enter had been altered since he'd last seen it.

Familiar were the high ceilings, blank unpainted walls, the curtains on the windows to erase the view of the rubble-strewn lot behind the building. But a desk had been added in the far right corner. Behind it sat a thin man with thick, black-rimmed glasses, typing on a laptop. Across the room, in an area that had been newly decorated to resemble a living room—a plush sectional, two matching plush armchairs, a glass-topped coffee table, an oriental throw rug—the Nunez brothers lounged at opposite ends of the luxurious sofa.

It looked to Mooney like an unfinished movie set. "Real sweet. Real homey. Makes me warm and tingly inside."

"Ah, Mistah Mooney," Manuel, the heavier of the two brothers said. "You were always the joker, *sì?*"

A lingering trace of perfume hung in the air, though no women were present.

Manuel heaved his weight forward to light a cigar. He wore a black jogging suit with a red stripe on the sleeve, though by the looks of him it was clear the outfit had never been used for its intended purpose. Eduardo, by contrast, the trim athletic half of the pair, was dressed in a dark suit, complete with white shirt and tie. He stood up, his smile slick and brief, then gone. "You forget your briefcase, amigo?"

"I didn't forget."

Eduardo's smile returned, without sincerity. "You left it in the hallway, perhaps."

"No briefcase tonight."

"*Non comprender.*" Eduardo's face had hardened. "You're confusing me, and I'm not a man who likes to be confused."

"Seems simple enough to me."

Manuel, who had been puffing steadily on his cigar, waved his hand to disperse the smoke he exhaled. His big grin lit only the lower half of his face. "Where are your manners, bro? Offer our guest a seat."

Eduardo, hands jammed into his pockets, stood there sulking in silence.

"Forgive my brother," Manuel said, "sometimes his temper, like a *puta*, it gets the better of his good manners." His grin revealed yellow, uneven teeth. "Won't you have a seat, Mistah Mooney? I'm sure you can explain the absence of the briefcase."

"I'd rather stand."

Manuel drew deeply on the cigar, his eyes hard to read. "In my country when a guest is extended an invitation, it is considered *insulto* if the invitation is declined."

"Well, this is *my* country. We cut the bullshit here. We get right to the point." The detective remained standing, enjoying the stalemate, the tension it created in the large, mostly barren room.

Manuel broke into a deep-throated laugh. "Our friend here is joking with us. He makes fun. Is that not right, Mistah Mooney?"

"No joke. No briefcase and no joke. I'm here empty-handed, except for the news I bring."

"Tell us, please. We are most anxious to know. Aren't we, Eddie?" He exchanged glances with his brother.

Something passed between them that the detective couldn't read.

Manuel offered again his gratuitous grin. "We are always interested in what our partners have to say to us."

Tom Mooney nodded to the man at the desk. "Who's he?"

"Our new accountant," Manuel said. "No one for you to be concerned about. *Insignificante*."

But changes, new additions or alterations, in situations like this were always of concern, the detective knew. For the time being, though, he'd have to accept Manuel's word.

Eduardo had moved behind the sofa, leaning forward with his hands pressed to the rim. "So what's the deal?"

"Yes, Mistah Mooney," Manuel said in a more conciliatory voice, "tell us please why you have failed to bring the briefcase."

"We're doing business with the Venezuelans now. We don't need you anymore."

The accountant stopped typing into the computer. Eduardo straightened his body stiffly to its full height. Expressionless, Manuel puffed without pause on his cigar. All eyes were on the detective, the silence in the room ticking like a timer.

"Just like that?" All traces of a grin were gone from the fat man's face. In fact, Mooney thought, it looked like the man had never grinned in his life.

No apology. No concession. No explanation. That was the way Tom Mooney handled situations like this. "Just like that."

"We've done business with your *compañeros* six years. *Seis* years. We give them their start." The rage was building inside the fat man, adding visibly it seemed to both his complexion and his bulk. "Without us they'd be dung, *estiercol*, shit. They'd be shining shoes on Jerome Avenue. Without the Nunez brothers they'd be living on welfare checks. Without the Nunez brothers they'd have nada, nothing, nothing, nothing." His voice rose to a crescendo, filling the room's high, shadowy spaces. "Nada! You hear me? You hear me? Nada!"

Eduardo, whose hands on the fabric looked as if he might tear the sofa apart, spoke through clenched lips, a hiss more than a voice. "You have some *cojones* coming here like this."

"That's what they pay me for."

"You think you can just walk out—?"

"We want a clean break, Eddie. We don't want a war." There *would* be a war. He knew that. He just didn't want it to begin here, now.

"Someone's gotta pay," Manuel said. "For this, someone's *gonna* pay."

Mooney said nothing. He'd said everything he'd come to say.

"So who's gonna pay, you *señor*?"

"I'm only the postman."

"You know," Manuel said, grinning again, "in ancient times they cut the head off the man who brought bad news."

Mooney smiled. "They weren't as advanced as we are." He turned then and started for the door.

He wasn't sure who was more likely to blow his head off, the sulky Eduardo or the extroverted Manuel. Either of them was impulsive enough, furious enough to do it. A bullet to the back? A machete chop to the neck? The Nunez brothers were renowned for both.

Walk tall and straight. Show no weakness, no hesitation. The man with the steel balls always makes it through.

In the narrow hallway he passed the guards. As he walked away, it was as if he moved in slow motion, each lift of his leg an effort, each step a small eternity. He could feel the heat of their eyes boring into his back. In the barren hall, the sound of his footsteps rang like thunder. Would that be the sound that carried him into the next world?

Walk tall and straight.

He was on the stairs, going down. His footsteps even louder as he descended. On the ground floor the sour-faced guard lounged against the banister, shifting his body begrudgingly to let him pass. Then he was on the street, breathing in the warm fetid air of the June night, like a man released from death row.

Changed priorities or not, he thought, he could still take pride in his work.

No one could say he wasn't one determined son-of-a-bitch. No one.

CHAPTER 35

"This *is* self-defense, right?" Danny was asking.

They were in Charlie's hospital room. The shriveled old man in the next bed was ninety years old and hard of hearing, but Danny wasn't taking any chances. He lowered his voice to a whisper. "If I have to shoot Mooney or one of his goons, it's not murder or homicide, is it? It's self-defense, right?"

"Legally or morally?"

"Both."

Charlie considered the question. He shifted on the bed, favoring his injured leg. The thigh wound infection had worsened and he pressed his fingertips into the bandage to ease the soreness. "Morally I'd say, yeah, it's self-defense. They tried to chase you down, for God's sake. They tried to make Swiss cheese outta Johnny and me. Me, *twice*. So, yeah, no doubt about it." He pressed his fingers gingerly around the edges of the bandage. "Legally, I don't know. First of all, we don't know who the shooters are or, in your case, who the drivers of the SUVs were. You sure it was a Caddy?"

"An Escalade, yeah. And the second one might have been, too."

"So, most likely the same guys who came after me. But we don't know what they look like. We've got no plates. No witnesses. No proof of anything really. Nothing to stand up in court."

"We're still in the same place then, right? Sitting ducks."

"What did the police say?"

"Pretty much what they said to you. They need something more to go on."

"You told them about the club?"

"As much as I could, without bringing Mooney into it."

"And—?"

"They said they'd check it out." He remembered the weary look on the sergeant's face, the man's response weighed down by the same weariness: *You know how many black Escalades there are in this city?* And the question he was probably thinking but didn't ask: *You know how many clubs sell dope?*

" 'Least you tried," Charlie was saying. "You can say so to the judge, if it ever comes down to that. You can say you tried to let the police handle it."

"Some consolation."

"Like you said, man. We're sitting ducks. Waiting to be picked off." A second later he added angrily: "Don't know why the hell you don't take my advice. Cripple the bastard. You're in over your head, can't you see that? You're no match for a guy like Mooney."

Danny held up his hand to stop him. "Let's not go there."

"You turned out to be a stubborn son-of-a-bitch, you know that?"

"I didn't come here to fight." Danny glared back at him. "This isn't one of your damn competitions."

Charlie winced at that. "Who said it was?"

"You're acting like it is.'

"Like *what*? Like what'd I do?"

"Like it's your way or no way. Charlie *knows*, everyone else *blows*. I can't tell you how sick to death I am of that."

Charlie gave him a stricken look, as if he'd been kicked when he was down. "You got this hate thing for me. Ever since you came back."

"I don't hate you. I don't."

"You sure act like you do. I'm only trying to help."

"Then help me, don't lecture me. Don't tell me how damned incapable I am."

"All right. All right."

His pale, empty face looked defeated in a way Danny hadn't seen before. He'd come here looking for help, a way out of the dead end street where they were cornered. But what else could he expect from the man but his usual solution to all things troublesome: brute, swaggering force. Coming to him like this was like coming in search of a miracle. Charlie, the man who always had the answer, had nothing Danny wanted to hear. He was just an ordinary guy with an extraordinary amount of rage, helpless now, laid up with a bad leg. No more father of the street.

Again Danny realized how alone he was. Either he figured a way out of this mess himself, or he went down. They *all* went down.

He came back to the question he was debating, the morality of what he might have to do, whether he could justify it according to his own conscience. If only he could believe what Tom Mooney thought about them wasn't true, *that they were all killers at heart.*

A nurse came into the room, told Charlie it was time for his walk.

"All right, all right," he grumbled. He waved her away when she came toward the bed to assist him. "We can do it. My buddy here will help me."

When she'd gone he asked Danny to get the crutches propped against the window sill. "Don't know which I hate worse. Lying in this damn bed, or hobbling around like a broke-down old man."

"You gotta do it, man. You gotta keep the muscles loose."

"I know. I know. Pisses me off, that's all." He adjusted the crutches under his arms, then straightened the gown which came to his knees. "I feel like a fruitcake."

In the hallway he walked with a plodding determination, lifting his crutches and plunging them hard at the floor as if *it* was the reason he was so incapacitated. "Johnny leave yet?"

"Don't think so. Told him to call me before he left."

"Poor guy. He doesn't know shit about women."

"Hey, if you're gonna feel sorry for anyone, *I'm* the one out there with the sharks." He laughed then at the bizarre set of circumstances that had descended upon him, *them*. He would have nudged Charlie if the guy hadn't needed all the balance he could get. "Who would've thought, huh?"

"You the man."

Charlie kept moving in a straight line, forcing an orderly with a cart to wheel it around him. His face was locked so tight Danny wanted to find a way to cheer him up. After all, this was a hospital visit, a corporal work of mercy as the nuns at St. Cecilia's had taught. He hadn't come here to make the guy feel worse than he already did. "I stopped in at the Glow last night. On the way home."

A spark of energy fired in his eyes. "Yeah?"

"Didn't stay long, though. The place isn't the same without you."

"Jimmy's doing all right, though, isn't he? Keeping the place afloat?"

"Jimmy's doing fine."
"Decent crowd?"
"Decent crowd."

"I miss the place something awful."

"It's a special place. One of a kind."

"The *last* of its kind." Charlie ruminated on the overwhelming truth of that. "You know, I never really figured why people looked forward so much to the weekend, their precious two days off, their holidays, their vacations. Work is what holds us together. Used to think it was women, the whole chase thing, you know. But women come and go. Work is what you can rely on. The only constant thing. It's always there, waiting for you, keeping you focused."

"You're lucky. Feeling that way, I mean."

"I'd feel a hell of a lot luckier if I was standing behind a bar."

"You will be. Soon."

"Yeah, yeah."

Charlie grunted as he pushed himself forward. From the pain or the exertion or simply from exasperation, Danny couldn't tell which.

"You're lucky, too, man. You've got your writing."

Danny laughed. "Yeah, when I get back to it."

"You'll have one hell of a story, if we live through this."

Danny lowered his voice as they passed the nurses' station. "On the walk home from the Glow last night, I had my disguise on. Yankees' hat pulled low. Wrap around shades. Every time a car went by on the street, my heart felt like it was gonna jump out of my skin."

"It worked," Charlie said. "The disguise, I mean."

"So far."

Charlie shook his head sadly. "It kills me, man, not being at the Glow. It kills me not being out there on the streets with you."

The sun room, with its plants and green leather chairs and white tiled floors, was flooded with light. Beyond the windows blue skies, no clouds. Charlie stopped at the hemisphere of windows that provided an expansive view of the subway yards and the river beyond it with its low-rent marinas sandwiched between rows of warehouses and oil storage tanks.

There was no one around them so he didn't have to lower his voice. "Back of my closet," he said. "Under some old work shirts." His lips held the barest hint of a smile, as if he'd gotten away with something. "Same model as the one I kept in the bar, the one the cops confiscated the night I got hit." His grin spread wider. "Actually, I've got a third one, too. You can never have too much of a good thing, right?"

The Bronx Kill

He regarded the palms and other potted plants spaced out along the curve of windows and said nothing for a long while. "We're like these plants here. Things of nature trying to survive in an unnatural world." He turned his gaze on Danny with a begrudging admiration. "You don't know it yet but you, man, you've gotten to be a hell of a lot tougher son-of-a-bitch than me, than anybody I know. You got balls, real balls. Or else you're just the craziest son-of-a-bitch I ever met. I woulda been, and *was*, packing from the first time they came after me. I woulda never waited this long."

"Had to be sure, I guess."

"Of what?"

"The self-defense thing."

Charlie shifted on his crutches, gave him a questioning look. "What self-defense thing?"

"The morality question. I mean, it's one thing going to jail. But having to live with another unjustified death on my hands, that's more than I can handle."

An hour later he was standing in one of the firing lanes at Gus's Gun Shop and Shooting Range on 149th Street. His feet spread apart, his body in a slight crouch, he held Charlie's .38 in both hands. He extended his arms, took in a deep breath, held it and fired down range. The paper silhouette shuddered but the face and torso remained unscarred.

Danny took a deep breath and raised his arms again. This time he let his shoulders relax. He kept his arms steady and remembered to squeeze off the round slowly. The silhouette shook again, the bullet striking high on the right shoulder.

Way to go. Way to go. He heard Charlie's encouragement from long ago. *Way to go, shooter.*

He had been here once before, years back, with the Renegades. Charlie had decided a true Renegade should know how to handle a gun. *Never know when a man's gonna have to defend himself, or his woman,* had been his reasoning. *You never know.* So he had rented a lane for an hour. Fifteen minutes for each of them.

First he showed them how to do it. Feet spread apart at a comfortable distance, a slight bend at the knees, arms and shoulders relaxed but firm, both hands supporting the weapon and most important, *squeeze the trigger, don't jerk it.* He himself had been shooting at the range since he was ten. His old man was a gun nut, believed having a weapon was not only a man's right but a man's duty. *Trust nobody or no thing*, was his advice to Charlie. *Nobody gonna save you but yourself. Not the government, not the police, not the army, not the Church. Nobody at all.*

"I don't think that's true," Johnny had protested at the time.

Charlie laughed at that. "Wait till some mugger's got the barrel of a gun shoved into your face, then tell me how true it is or not."

"It's not Christian," was Johnny's reply.

"Christianity's got nothing to do with it."

"I'm not a fighter, that's all," Johnny said.

"But you can *act* like one."

Johnny took his turn at the firing line, even though he never hit the target, not even once.

Timmy Moon was the only one who didn't shoot that day. When it was his turn, he held the .38 in his hand as if it was a dirty rag he didn't want to touch. His eyes had a glazed-over look. After a few seconds of holding the gun like that he handed it back to Charlie. "I can't," he said.

" 'Course you can. Take the damn thing and hold it like a man."

"I can't." There was no apology in his eyes. Nothing in his voice except the flat, simple statement. Looking neither contrite nor regretful, he walked to the back of the range and took a seat on one of the folding chairs for visitors.

It was as if someone had slapped Charlie, insulted him to his face, but he shook it off, said, "So what? Big deal. He doesn't want to learn how to protect himself, what do I care?"

But Danny knew it was one of the things Charlie never forgave him for. *One* of the things.

He stepped to the firing line again now and raised the pistol.

He squeezed off a round but the bullet went wide, missing the paper altogether. He stepped back and lowered the gun. That was the Timmy Moon part of him, he thought. The part that didn't even want to *touch* the gun, much less fire it. The part of him that wanted to walk back to the folding chairs and be an observer.

But these were different times. His sideline days were over. That wasn't an option.

He moved into position again. This time it wasn't a nameless, faceless silhouette he aimed at. It was Tom Mooney charging at him with a gun. He saw the broad, flat face, the receding hairline, the dark brooding eyes, the cynical ripple of his lips, the careless heaving shoulders—and fired.

The paper shuddered from the impact.

He fired again and again.

It was Tom Mooney still coming at him, still on his feet, still firing his weapon. Then it was the truck, the black SUV, bearing down at him. It was Mooney driving, his face distorted with rage behind the tinted glass. It was Mooney shooting from the sun roof at Charlie, shooting from the mouth of the alley at Johnny Whales.

It's him or me, him or me.

It's him or *us*.

This was self-defense. It *had* to be.

Danny fired until the chamber was empty. When he examined the paper silhouette afterward, he saw that bullets had slashed the torso in a diagonal line from right shoulder to left hip.

One had struck what would have been the heart.

CHAPTER 36

She was already fifteen minutes late.

The Merc's engine idling, Tom Mooney waited for her on the marginal road outside the Kill.

She'd insisted on meeting him here, rather than him picking her up at her apartment like old times. "Don't be late," he'd warned her. It was his way of retaliating, of showing his displeasure. "Don't keep me waiting."

"I'll be there," she said.

"And be there on time."

"I keep my promises."

"Not all of them."

"Most of them."

"Yeah," he said. "*Most* of them."

Through the phone wires, she had sounded weary. "We've been through that, what, a thousand times?"

"Yeah, sure, a thousand times. Doesn't mean it's settled."

"Nothing's ever settled with you."

"Some things are." It was a statement of bravado rather than truth. In his view, all promises, big and small, *had* to be kept. That's what he expected of people: to follow through on what they promised. Especially the women he went out with. Especially them.

Which meant, of course, that he lived in a constant state of disappointment, so many things remaining forever unresolved.

"Do *you* keep *all* of your promises?" she had asked.

"The ones that count." Again, he was giving himself the benefit of the doubt. Or simply deluding himself. So often these days he couldn't tell the difference.

In exasperation, now, he turned off the car engine. It was late afternoon and the sky above the desolate Kill had turned grey and sullen. What had it been, twenty minutes already that he'd been waiting? He glared at the wall of tall grass that abutted the road and forced back the urge to go in there and pull her out. He wouldn't do that; he couldn't do that. After all, it was a *vigil*—as she liked to

The Bronx Kill

call it—to commemorate his brother. It was her way of honoring his memory.

But even *that* caused him torment.

What about *his* memory? She'd been in love with *him*, too, hadn't she? At least she had said she was, she'd acted like she was. And now she wasn't. She had gotten over him so easily, it seemed, and yet she still had such strong feeling for a dead man. So in honoring the memory of his brother she was dishonoring *him*. That's how he saw it.

Immediately he felt besieged by guilt. To be jealous of a dead man, to be jealous of his poor dead brother, that was pathetic, wasn't it?

But the fact of the matter was she'd stolen from him, and he couldn't forgive her for that. One by one she'd withdrawn the promises she'd made. She'd gotten what she wanted from him and now she didn't need him. Which made her *what?* A bitch like so many of the women he'd been with. In his less bitter moments, though, he told himself she was simply confused, she needed help, guidance. She needed *him* to show her she'd been wrong. She needed *his* help to undo the mistakes.

That was why he was seeing her tonight. To convince her she'd been wrong. To prove to her once and for all that testifying against the Renegades was absolutely the right thing to do. If he had to exterminate all three of them himself, he would do it. But if he could get outside vindication as well, from the courts, the legal system, how much sweeter would his vengeance be.

He checked his watch. Twenty-five minutes. She was *twenty-five* minutes overdue. He couldn't sit still any longer so he paced outside the car. What the hell took her so long? What did she *do* on these vigils of hers? She wasn't the praying kind, that much he knew. Did she simply sit there and stare at the water, the last place she'd seen Timmy alive? Whatever she did, she wouldn't talk about it. "It's personal," she'd said whenever he pressed her about it. "It's between me and Timmy."

That was the difference between them. She could brood and brood and brood, but sitting around obsessing about something wasn't his style, at all. Not anymore, at least. A man with steel balls has to take the initiative, has to find the path of action as a way out of all the moodiness and grief and despair and whatever the hell else was holding him down.

He had to laugh at himself. The man with steel balls, *right*. Not when it involved a woman he had feelings for. Easy enough on the outside to play it tough and indifferent. Inside, though he'd learned how to keep it hidden, he became amorphous, a panicky kid with nothing to hold onto.

And he did have real feelings for her. No matter what she thought. No matter how much he'd concealed it from himself.

He checked his watch again and looked down the long street. The silver Camaro hadn't yet arrived for its nightly ritual. Just as well. He was in no mood to deal with the crew. So he started walking away from where it would eventually be parked, walking aimlessly, killing time.

"Tom," a voice said behind him.

She stood at the curb where a path led out from the tall grass.

" 'Bout time."

"Sorry."

"No, you're not."

She bit her lip. Her eyes held the leftover look of tears. "You're right, I'm not. I have a life too, you know."

"You used to be so much nicer." He took her arm and pushed her toward the Merc.

"So did you."

In the car, driving away from the Kill, he tried to get her to focus on what was about to happen. "You've got to remember. This is one of the guys who killed Timmy. Don't forget that. He's the reason your life turned out the way it did. He's the reason you have to come here to cry your eyes out."

CHAPTER 37

It was not yet dark when Danny happened to glance out the living room window and saw the black Merc parked directly across the street. In his bedroom he strapped the shoulder holster in place and pulled on a jacket to cover it.

His father was still at the dining room table, finishing his coffee and working on his account book, as Danny moved past him to the door. "Gotta go, Dad."

"You gonna be out all night again?" It was a straightforward question for the most part, with only the slightest hint of disapproval.

"I don't know. Maybe. I hope not." He still hadn't explained the trouble he was in. His justification was that he didn't want his old man to worry. Which meant, as his father had pointed out, that if anything happened to him, if he died on the streets, it would come as an unexplained jolt. He felt bad about that, he truly did, but he couldn't talk about it now. He just couldn't.

One day, though, one day.

He promised himself again he'd tell the old man everything: about Timmy Moon and Julianne, about that night and all that it spawned.

One day.

Not waiting for the elevator, he took the stairs, his steps heavy and thudding as he hit each landing. Running across the lobby he saw through the windows the Merc in the middle of a U-turn. When he reached the door, the car was moving past him, accelerating with an angry snarl as it traveled down the block. He saw the detective's grim face at the wheel and his passenger beside him.

A woman.

She sat stiffly facing forward.

What he could see of her face was not so much expressionless as vacant, eyes fixed on the street ahead.

It took him a moment to realize it was Julianne.

Under the EL on Westchester Ave, he followed in his father's car. It had taken him several minutes to catch up with them—sixteen blocks, to be exact—before he spotted the dark sedan moving in the line of traffic beneath the tracks. His hands were sweating on the wheel and his heart thundered in the hollows of his chest. What he felt was not so much disbelief as the raw shock of recognition, of seeing her again in the flesh, of *knowing* she had survived the river's cold black churning waters.

Julianne.

Not as she appeared in his memories where she was youthful and radiant, not the Julianne who once walked with him hand in hand under the EL, but as some distant offspring of that image. Her hair had lost its golden shine; it hung lifeless and dull from her head. Her expression, what he had seen of it in profile, was vacant, hopeless as if she had experienced an entire lifetime of disappointment since he last saw her.

What he had seen of her now frightened him, hurt him. He had been naïve enough to think death had sheltered her, that it had allowed his memory to bestow upon her an eternal unalterable youth. That, at least, had been some compensation for her having been taken from him. But this was the punishment for his foolishness, for his selfish need to keep her only for himself: she existed in a world that had nothing to do with his fantasies.

And she was alive.

She was alive.

That astonishingly simple fact stirred the ashes of what had long since died in him, gave him what he thought had been lost to him forever: a sense of hope, a purpose.

And the wonder of that reduced to secondary importance, for the time being at least, the host of burning questions that waited for answers. What was she doing with Mooney? Why were they parked in front of his building? Where were they leading him?

The Merc turned away from the EL and crossed 149th, going south on St. Ann's past the park. It was clear now where they were heading.

It seemed, he thought, at this point in his life all roads led to the Kill.

And maybe they always had—since the first time the Renegades had gone there, when but for Charlie's strength, he would have drowned in the river. As a kid, he'd always thought of his life as a linear thing, a line that you followed from one point to another, a line you could use to measure how far you'd come. But he saw now that he'd been imprisoned for a long time in some kind of holding pattern, an endless circling, at the center of which was the Kill.

Tom Mooney had turned onto the marginal road and Danny stopped before reaching the corner. It was almost completely dark but he waited a full minute before edging forward. When he turned the corner he pulled immediately to the curb and waited.

Save for the Merc, the street ahead was empty. No Camaro in its usual spot. No sign of Short Fat Fannie or his Hispanic sidekick. Halfway down the avenue, Mooney's car with its motor running had been pulled in against the curb.

Nothing changed for what seemed like the longest time, though it could not have been more than a few minutes. Insects hummed in the empty lots and from somewhere, carried on the breeze, came the smell of decay, of rancid garbage. Overhead a gull screeched, a long forsaken cry that hung in the air like a curse.

It seemed to Danny his life would be stalled like this forever. Locked. Unresolved. With nothing for comfort or even distraction save the dull hum of flies, the fetid odor of rot, a bird's lonely plea to a darkening sky.

Close to Julianne but not able to reach her.

Close to the man who wanted to kill him but not able to stop him.

Without warning there was movement on the street. The passenger door swung open and Julianne lurched from the car, almost falling, as if she'd been pushed. She clung to the door to balance herself but the car jerked forward, the door swinging on its hinges, ripped from her hand, as the Merc drove off. She stumbled backward toward the sidewalk before righting herself.

Alongside the weedy edge of the lot, she stood there alone on the empty street, watching the car drive away. Like an abandoned child, Danny thought. Bereft. No purse, no belongings of any kind. A thin stick-like figure—much thinner than he remembered her—in a black T-shirt and jeans, looking uncertain.

She began walking unsteadily along the cracked, uneven pavement, her back to Danny. Fear tightened a knot in his chest as if she was about to vanish from his life once again. With purpose now, she picked up her pace and turned into one of the vacant lots on the old Renegade trail, moving through the overgrown grass in the direction of the Kill.

CHAPTER 38

The promontory stretched like steps into the dark water.

Nearby she sat on the bank where they had undressed before their final swim, the point at which the Kill emptied into the East River. It was full dark. The only light came from behind her, the long climbing arc of the bridge lamps and, from across the water, the yellow lights of the Con Ed plant. Her face was cast in shadow but her eyes, brightening when she saw him, bore through the darkness.

In the time before they spoke, the silence was filled with the collective breath of the river—lapping water, the distant thrum of boat engines, a ship horn sounding its warning—and the hum of insects barely heard beneath the more aggressive hum of bridge traffic.

Her voice came to him, it seemed, from another lifetime. "You don't look surprised to see me."

"There were rumors."

"Ah, rumors. There always are."

At their best, he thought, rumors teach us what we don't know. They prepare us for what is to come. They prepare us for things like *this*—what was in front of him right then: this girl, a woman now, this person he loved. "I didn't think it was possible."

"The river?"

He nodded.

"It's possible. If you want it enough."

"You must have wanted it awfully bad."

"I did." Leaning forward, she sat with her arms folded on her knees, rocking herself ever so slightly.

He was struck again by how much weight she'd lost. *Gaunt* was the word that came to mind. She'd always been thin but now she looked gaunt. Even in the poor light he could see her hollowed-out cheeks, the washed-out color of her face.

"Why?" was all he could say.

She laughed at that. "The eternal question. The root of all questions. *Why* was I born? *Why* am I here? *Why* don't I understand?"

She laughed again and he thought even her laugh was thin. Dry, brittle, without joy.

"It's the question that keeps us going, makes us get up in the morning," she was saying. "It's what some of us have instead of hope."

"You didn't answer me."

"Didn't I? I thought I had."

She was playing with him now. The brittle light in her eyes gave her away. There was even, he thought, a hint of her old flirtatiousness. But he wasn't in the mood for games.

"Why'd you disappear?"

"You want the obvious answer?"

Any answer, he thought. I want any answer there is. "I want to know why."

"You know why." She looked at him as if he should understand. "You always knew more than you thought you did, Baker. It was one of the things I liked about you."

Even that small admission, back-handed compliment that it was, eased his resentment, his feeling of having been betrayed. How pitiful, he thought, to need her approval still, after all this time. "Your father, you mean."

She sighed heavily. "My father, yeah."

"I thought—I—" He knew only what she'd told him, not what she'd left out. He knew it was bad, she'd told him that, but not *how* bad.

She hesitated before letting the memory return. "He'd decided definitely he was moving us upstate. He was going to put my mother in a home. That's what he called it, a home, but it was some kind of state asylum, some awful place. Me and him were going to live with his brother." Her eyes had narrowed, as if she could see all this happening again. "I couldn't stand the thought that now I'd have *two* brutal fathers. Especially 'cause my uncle, you see, in addition to having a nasty temper, had this thing for me."

"You never told me—"

"There was a lot I didn't tell you. The really bad stuff we don't tell anybody."

"But that doesn't explain—"

"Why I stayed away? Why I didn't contact anybody?"

Me, he was thinking. Why you didn't contact *me*.

She read his thoughts. "Because you were part of the problem. You, Charlie, even Timmy."

"The competition, you mean?"

"The competition, yeah. The tension every time we got together. Toward the end I thought you guys were going to kill each other. Over *me*. Pathetic little me." She laughed now at the memory. "What a group we were. The Moon, the Whales, the Big Boss Man, and you—the Baker, the guy who always had something cooking but didn't have the words to talk about it. And then there was me. What was I?"

"The object of desire."

"Not to Whales. He would have been too guilty. He could never have admitted to himself that he felt something for anybody but Lorraine." She bit her lip, considering this again, clearly not for the first time. "And maybe not to Timmy, either. I never could be sure. Sometimes I thought yeah, he really digs me. Other times I wondered if he could ever really love a woman. It seemed sometimes he was beyond feeling, that *he* was the true object of desire. Everybody wanted him, *needed* him in some way, but he needed nobody. It was like he wasn't human, really. The man on the moon. Who no one could reach."

"You were in love with him." It came out like an accusation.

"Yes," she said softly, "I was in love with him. It's an addiction for girls like me. Loving what's beyond reach."

He was surprised how much hearing her say those words could still hurt him. After all this time. About a dead man, no less. Words that came as no surprise. Words that he had always known were true. It was hearing her say them that opened the wound again, made it bleed. And yet hearing her say them was a relief in its way. There was nothing that could cut him more deeply. He'd reached, he believed, the rock bottom of hurt and anger and jealousy.

He stood with his shoulders back, his hands thrust into his jeans—his favorite stance as a teenager, his tough guy pose—and faced the breeze that came off the water, a stiff steady assault of air that blew back his hair, ruffled the sleeves of his shirt, as if it were life's adversities he was standing up to, defying.

The tough guy stands tall while inside him the baby curls up and cries. He lowered his head, stuffed the tip of his shoe into the mud and pushed it forward as if looking for something there.

"I couldn't find him at first," she was saying. Her voice was so low it seemed she was talking to herself.

He stepped closer, afraid he might miss something. "Timmy,

you mean? In the river?"

"I heard you shouting to him, telling him to go back."

He felt the need to defend himself, but what he said was: "He was grinning at me in some terribly odd way, like he knew something I didn't. Like—like—"

"He wasn't grinning when I saw him. He was way past that. He—" She stopped as if she'd changed her mind about something, then started again. "It was only him and me out there. I was a good thirty or forty feet ahead of him. What I was doing out so far I have no idea. Proving something to you guys maybe. To my father, too. That I was as good as you, I wasn't some weak thing who needed protection, I had a mind of my own, I was strong enough to fend for myself."

"Nobody thought you were weak—"

"Proving it to myself then. I don't know. Maybe that's why I'd gone so far ahead. But the real reason I'd gone into the river in the first place was to keep an eye on Timmy. I knew he couldn't handle it, that he was just trying to be one of the guys. At the playground, when Charlie suggested coming here, I had a bad feeling. That's why I came back. The bad feeling kept getting worse."

She stared out past the promontory as if she could still see it, the bad feeling, as much a part of the river's world as it had been of hers. "After Charlie and Whales turned back, after you'd turned back, I could see Timmy floundering there, so tired he could barely keep his head above water. The bad stuff I felt wasn't just something inside my head. It was right there on the water with me.

"But as I got closer to him I could see he wasn't trying to stay afloat at all, he was trying to keep himself down, *he was trying to submerge himself.* And when I grabbed him by the shoulders, when I lifted him he was completely limp, his eyes had this weird look, like they were saying, "Let me go, let me die," and with what strength he had left he tried to push me away."

She said nothing for a time, staring hard at the water.

"He said something else but it was hard to hear. His arms were slick, like they'd been greased, and he was too slippery to get a good hold on. He said something again, and this time I *could* hear it. His mouth was pressed against my ear. He said, "Let the river take me," and his eyes had that same weird faraway look like he was already gone. Then he slipped out of my grasp.

"The water was swirling so fast I could barely stay afloat

myself. I saw him ahead of me bobbing, bobbing, then he went under and I couldn't find him. I'd swallowed so much water, I was choking so bad, that for a minute I couldn't see or hear and, when I finally caught my breath and I could blink my eyes clear, he was gone. I was screaming loud as I could but he was gone, he was gone."

She held her face in her hands so he couldn't see her eyes but he knew by the sound of her voice there were no tears. They had come and gone long before, leaving in their wake the dry, hard, irrefutable truth.

He sat on the rock beside her. She inched over to give him room, said, "The not so obvious answer. Why I didn't come back." She still wasn't looking at him. When she spoke it was to the rocks of the promontory, the black water rushing over their raised surfaces as if to erase them. "What was there to come back to?"

He was thinking about the promontory, the long narrow pile of rocks forcing its way into the river, dumped there ages ago perhaps by some construction company truck looking for an easy way to dispose of unwanted debris, thinking about how he had thought of it *then*, as a teenager, as a magical bridge into the world of adventure: the river and all that lay beyond the borough he'd been born into. But all that had waited at that makeshift bridge's end, the stairway into the sea, was his *near*-death by drowning and Timmy Moon's *real* death by drowning. It led nowhere really where anyone would want to go. As for why Timmy wanted to die, he had no idea. No one who knew him would have predicted that. No one at all.

But the fact that Timmy wanted to die didn't absolve himself of anything. Of that he was sure.

It had been some time since Julianne had finished her story. Neither of them had spoken. Neither of them had even moved very much on the rock they shared. But he was as aware of her as if they were locked in an embrace, aware of her slightest tremors, the slightest shifts of her body, aware of even the space between them, the narrow channel of air infused with her heat, her muted energy.

She leaned forward, her eyes focused somewhere across the water, on the blue runway lights of the airport, or maybe on the flickering tail-lights of the arriving jets as they dropped from the murky sky, one every sixty seconds.

Finally she said, "What does this remind you of?"

He was thinking about the heavy silence, the nearness of her, the stirrings of old feelings that were both welcome and disruptive. None of it was simple enough for words to convey. "I don't know."

"Our first date. When you took me here."

"Our first and *only* date."

"At least we had *one*."

"And it was about Timmy, wasn't it? Our date? Making him jealous?"

"Only partly. Not completely."

Which left him with muddled feelings again, the emotional no man's land he had lived in all that summer of their youth. Give a little, take a little. She'd been good at that. Giving and taking in equal measure. One canceling out the other. Net result: zero.

She got up from the rock. "Let's go see what's left. The secret treasures."

They walked side by side past the railroad bridge, till they reached the ramp to the Tri-Borough, entering its tunnel-like underbelly crossed by thick shadows. He had little fear of who they might meet here, roving bands of teens or homeless druggies. Charlie's .38, for the time being at least, gave him peace of mind. As he walked, he could feel the holster strap rub his chest.

Besides, in the face of those who were out to kill him, any danger he faced here seemed insignificant by comparison. Julianne, too, seemed indifferent to any harm that might befall them. When he'd asked her a few minutes earlier why she wasn't afraid to come into the Kill alone, she'd said she always had protection. And what was that? he'd wanted to know. Sergeant Mace, she'd said and tapped her back pocket.

Walking beside her now, he found another reason for her apparent lack of fear. Her face, old before she was thirty, with its strain around the eyes, its hollow cheeks, said she'd been through too much to care very much about anything.

They passed the assorted hulks of junked cars upon which five years' worth of additional rust and decay had been laid. When they reached the red, white and blue American flag car, it was barely recognizable. The flags were gone and the car had been so spray-painted over with graffiti the stars and stripes were mostly undetectable. Nor could they find, in the grey light that filtered in between the bridge supports, even one of the red and gold rocks that had formed the makeshift ground wreath. And what remained of the driftwood tree was a single tinfoil star that he found half-buried in the mud.

"At least there's something left," she said.

He cleaned it off with his fingers and handed it to her, an offering of sorts, though what he expected in return he couldn't have said. She brought it to an open space between the stanchions and held it to the light that drifted down from the bridge ramp.

"Sometimes I think everything's dead inside me," she said. "Then something like this, a piece of plastic wrapped in foil, makes me think it's not."

Standing beside her, he said, "I was in love with you."

"I know you were. But you couldn't tell me." Her eyes in this light looked grey and flat and heavy with remorse. "You couldn't say it."

"Would it have mattered?"

"Love has to start somewhere. It can't be something you hoard inside like a dirty secret."

"But would it have mattered?"

"Then? Maybe not."

She stared off at the lights of Manhattan, considering something. "But afterward when I'd made it across the river, maybe yes. It might have helped me want to get out of bed in the morning."

He wanted to drive her home but she wouldn't let him. "Just drop me at the subway," she said.

"I'd like to drive you."

"Thanks, but I'd rather be alone now. I really would."

Before she got out of the car he said: "You know, I want to see you again."

She thought for what seemed like a long while. "Tomorrow's Timmy's birthday. I always say a prayer for him at St. Cecelia's on his birthday."

"When?"

"After work." She offered him a weak smile and pushed open the door.

"One more thing."

She stood on the sidewalk and waited.

"What were you doing with Tom Mooney?"

Her eyes turned inward. She drew a breath and released it

The Bronx Kill

slowly. "That's a long story."

"I'd like to hear it."

"No. You wouldn't."

"Try me."

She studied his face, looking for something. "Not now."

"When?"

"Sometime."

He watched her move away from him, a thin shadow of a figure climbing the stairs of the EL.

CHAPTER 39

He was crossing the park on his way to St. Cecelia's when he spotted Julianne. She was standing in front of the church, leaning forward, speaking through the driver-side window of Mooney's black Merc.

He watched the conversation continue, a minute or so more, before the car pulled away. Once it had turned the corner, Danny approached her.

"What did he want?"

She shrugged, her look one of resigned exasperation. "The usual. Tom being Tom."

"Meaning what?"

She waved her hand in dismissal and started up the steps to the church. "I want to light a candle for Timmy."

He knelt in a back pew while she moved down the center aisle to the altar. He tried to form a prayer but no words he could believe in came to him.

Beneath the high vaulted ceiling, kneeling before the bank of candles, she seemed even more ethereal and waif-like than she did on the street. She used a taper to light a candle precisely in the center of the middle row, the red glass dish around the candle suddenly aglow. And it was that gesture, her choosing the candle in the absolute center of the bank, that reminded him of something he'd long forgotten: Timmy's pre-occupation with lighting one of those candles whenever he was praying for something he wanted badly. It was always that same candle, the one in the center.

When she was finished with her prayer, she came down the aisle and they stepped outside into the greying light of dusk.

"I didn't think you were religious," he said.

"I'm not. But Timmy was. It was a side of him he didn't show anyone."

"I *do* remember his thing for candles, though. He thought if you lit one it doubled the power of your prayer."

She was staring across the park, beyond the shadow of the

The Bronx Kill 189

EL, at the neon sheen of the MoonGlow sign. "He would have been twenty-five today."

They were driving to the beach along his favorite of all Bronx roads, surrounded by patches of forest and meadows of green marsh grass.

At first she'd been resistant to taking a ride. "I've given all this up," she'd said on the church steps. "I'm a Queens girl now."

"A short ride, that's all." He surprised himself by what he said next. "This is the hardest part of the day for me. Twilight." He would never have begged her like this in the old days, but his heart was breaking and he couldn't help himself. "You'll help me get through it."

She looked at him as if she, too, were surprised at his admission. "Me, too. This time of day."

"Just a short ride," he said. "I promise."

When he pulled into the beach parking lot, images of their times here came at him with frightening persistence:

Julianne in her bathing suit. The soft curve of her shoulders, the deep honey-color of her skin, her half-smile, half-smirk telling him she knows what he's feeling and that he doesn't have to hide it, she doesn't mind being liked by more than one boy.

Watching her watching Timmy. Her eyes flashing with light when she looks at him. Her voice rich with laughter when she kids him.

Julianne at the shore-line, standing close to Timmy, speaking fast to him in a way that seems urgent and necessary.

Laughing, taking his hands, pulling him toward the water.

Lifting her hands to shovel water at him.

Chasing him as he stumbles into deeper water, Timmy's body thin and graceful, delicate and fluid and faun-like as he tries to avoid her cold water torture.

The two of them, finally, falling together in an embrace.

He stopped the car now at the edge of the lot, engine idling, thinking that hurt is the burden that holds you down while life rushes on past you.

He asked her if she remembered that song they used to sing. That golden oldie Uncle Sal refused to have taken off the jukebox.

" 'Course I do."

"What was it, like, fifty years old, right? But we loved it, anyway."

Her head was resting back against the seat, her eyes staring off at the grey sky above the beach. She half-sang, half-whispered the words: "*Do I love you, my oh my. If I lost you would I cry.*"

They had always sung that line twice in succession and so he joined in for what he thought would be the second time around. But she had stopped and he was singing alone, getting as far as *Do I love you*, leaving the words to float in the air, unfinished. *If I lost you would I cry.*

They sat in silence and he thought if this were a movie this is the part where they would take a melancholic stroll along the beach. But they were both already melancholic enough, so to lighten the mood he drove to a dockside café on City Island where they ordered clams on the half shell and watched two immaculately white long-necked swans glide gracefully past them on the dark, sullied waters of Eastchester Bay.

One of the waiters, a tall dark-skinned boy, had come outside on break. He was leaning against the railing and throwing crusts of bread into the water for the seagulls when he glanced over at Danny. Simultaneously, they recognized one another.

"Rashad?"

"Mr. B?"

The boy came over and they shook hands.

"You remember Julianne, don't you?"

"Sure, sure I do." His wide grin lit up his face. To Danny, he said: "Heard you were living in Florida."

"I'm back now. How are things going with you?"

"Great. Just great. Finished up my first year at St. John's. Made Varsity and all. Even joined a frat."

"And you were the one wanted to hide in the corner of the playground, too scared to play with other kids."

"You the man, Mr. B. Couldn't hardly do nothin' before I met you. Couldn't handle a B-ball, for sure."

Someone called to him from inside the café. "Sorry. Gotta go. Boss in a bad mood tonight." He extended his hand one more time. "Be seein' ya around. Now that you're back."

"I'll come out for one of your games."

"I sure would like that, Mr. B."

He walked away with an easy, loping stride. Nothing like the halting, tentative step of the boy Danny first knew.

"That was so great," Julianne was saying. "What you did for him back then. Taking him under your wing like that. He had to be the shyest boy in Chester Hill."

"That, he was."

"And you were so shy yourself. That's what made it so amazing. You were so lost within yourself and still you went out of your way to help him."

"I wasn't *that* lost, was I?"

She looked at him as if she couldn't believe he didn't know. "Remember how I used to have to go find you at the dances? You'd always be hiding behind one of the columns, writing in your notebook, sulking and sniveling."

"I wasn't sniveling."

"No? What do you call it?"

"Reflecting on life's inequities."

She laughed at that, and he felt hope return again to his world. "And remember how you'd never let me see what you were writing. Not once. Ever."

"I was afraid you'd laugh at it, at me."

Her face turned serious again, and thoughtful. "I wouldn't have laughed. I liked it that you were always thinking, that life for you wasn't just some blind thing you shoved your way through, like most guys."

"I was pretty blind, I'm afraid."

"Not with the kids in the playground. Not with Rashad."

"No, that was one of the few things I don't regret."

"What," she said, "what else do you regret?"

"You mean besides the obvious, besides Timmy?" He stared across the water as if the repository of lost things was a tangible item, something to be found among the detritus of the shoreline. "I regret I didn't get to know my mother better before she died, that I never got to tell her how much I appreciated her, all that she'd done for me. I regret I lost the closeness I had with my dad. I regret that I didn't get to spend more time with *you*." He turned to her. "And that's only the short list."

"Second chances," she said.

"What about them?"

"Our best hope, I guess."

On the way to the car he asked her again what Tom Mooney

had wanted in front of the church.

"He was threatening me. If I refused to testify against you guys, he said he would see to it that I suffered serious personal harm."

"That makes four of us," Danny said. And he told her about the attempts on their lives.

CHAPTER 40

On the drive back to Queens she told him about her addiction.

At first she'd refused his offer of a ride—she said she'd take the subway, the way she always did—but he insisted. He was driving her home, he didn't want to hear another word about it. She said she was too tired to fight and so, in a matter of minutes, they were on the ramp to the Tri-Borough, looking down at the railroad bridge and that overgrown, forsaken wasteland of their youth.

The traffic on the ramp was barely moving. Her voice came low and steady, filling the silence of the car, filling the space of the years between them.

It was more than a year after Timmy died when she started. She'd been holding her own till then, she said. Working at a supermarket, living at a woman's shelter in Astoria. Life was tough but she was hanging on, trying to deal with Timmy's death, the grief and rage it brought up in her, the bad feelings she had for the Renegades, the life she'd left behind.

She was strong, she said. For a while.

She was finally earning enough to afford a single room/no private bath in a fleabag hotel, which was a step up—though barely, she said—from the shelter. She was doing okay. Till the depression started. Nights mostly, when she'd be in her room alone, no friends, nothing to do but think. She was sure it would pass, the depression, that it was just a phase she had to get through, but everything kind of boiled up inside her, all the negative stuff, the hurt of Timmy leaving her and something she hadn't expected, this anger she felt for him because he'd given up, because he'd taken the coward's way out, and the anger just got blacker and blacker until it took over, until she couldn't see or feel anything else.

That's when it started, she said. Harmless stuff at first—weed and hash, a little coke, some meth—whatever she could get her hands on. She made enough money to buy distraction from her grief when her shift ended. That distraction soon took the form of pills, painkillers like Percocet and Vicodin and Oxycontin and eventually, over the course of another year or more, it took the form of what she called *the real thing*.

"That was when I met Tom Mooney," she said. "Or rather it was that homeless man I met first. The one we used to see at the Kill."

"Ellis."

"Yes, Ellis. You see, by then I'd started returning to the Kill, where you found me last night. The first day—or night—of every month I'd pay a visit. It made me feel closer to Timmy, though I didn't have to actually go there to feel close to him. He was with me all the time really—whether I was hating him or loving him—every minute of every day, even when I was high; but when I was high it didn't hurt as much. And when I was there at the Kill it was like we hadn't yet gone into the river, like I could fool myself into thinking nothing bad had happened yet, that the future hadn't already been painted black."

She stared ahead at the cars on the ramp, still inching along. "Ellis, you see, crazy old Ellis happened to be working for people who happened to be selling the very product I was most in need of."

She studied him then, as if deciding something. "You know that, though, don't you? You figured that out. You figured out his connection to Tom Mooney. That's why you killed him. At least that's what Tommy thinks. But I'm getting ahead of myself. I'm telling you things out of order. Which, I guess you could say, sums up my life since we last saw each other. Nothing's in the right order. That's why it's important I keep things straight, I've *got* to keep things straight—even now, telling you what happened."

"So, Ellis put you in touch with Mooney."

"Ellis remembered me from the times we hung around there, from that last night. And he knew, of course, it was Mooney's brother who'd drowned. Even someone like Ellis could put the pieces together."

"And Mooney wanted to know what you knew, what you could tell him about that last night."

"He came at the right time, yes, for both of us. I'd lost my job by then 'cause of my habit. I was about to get thrown out of my fleabag digs. Tommy descended on me like the angel of salvation. He paid for an apartment in a decent neighborhood, made sure I had food, clothes, dope, everything I needed. He was sweet to me, at first. Kind, too. And maybe most important of all, though I don't think I

The Bronx Kill

realized it at the time, he was my direct connection to his brother, as close to Timmy Moon as I was going to get."

They had made it finally onto the roadway of the bridge itself, traffic moving at the same slow crawl. Car horns blared around them in impatience. Danny relaxed his grip on the wheel. "A wolf in sheep's clothing," he said.

"Yes, I've been finding that out, slowly but surely. At first all I knew was that he hated you guys. It's all he talked about. The little bit I told him about that night confirmed what Ellis had seen, made him think he might be able to build a case against you, after all. I began to see his whole life was focused around that, his whole future. He'd just been transferred into narcotics from walking a beat. He wasn't a detective yet. But he was going to be. And he seemed to get angrier every day. Or maybe, as time went on, I just became more aware of it. Whenever he'd get insecure, which was happening more and more, he'd throw everything at me. Said, if I didn't cooperate, he was going to charge me with leaving the scene of a crime, withholding evidence, with whatever he could find to charge me with. He could guarantee me, he said, that I'd be doing time."

"So you talked to him, helped him build his case."

"Yes," she said weakly. "I talked to him. I told him what happened at the dance. I told him everything that happened that summer. I told him everything I thought he wanted to hear." She had broken down finally, not completely, not uncontrollably, but a low steady sobbing that sounded more like a cough she was trying to choke back.

"But by then," she said, "he didn't have to threaten me, he didn't have to force it out of me. I was giving him all this, this material for his case, willingly. It was a simple deal. He supplied me with what *I* needed; I gave him what *he* wanted. I told him I'd testify in court, if he wanted me to. I'd say whatever he wanted me to say."

For the first time, Danny thought he heard shame in her voice. It wasn't an apology she was giving, she wasn't going that far, she wasn't asking forgiveness for what she'd done, for betraying them. It was regret she was offering.

"The will is a fragile thing," she said softly, as if she might be speaking to herself. "It follows its own rules. It can disappear so easily."

Danny figured she was referring as much to herself as Timmy Moon. Ahead, the traffic still barely moving, he watched the bridge roadway climb upward, bright under the umbrella of lights above which the sky, dark and starless, held its grip on the city.

He said nothing for a while, trying to lose himself in the throb and rumble of idling engines, the slow grind of tires. The lights of Manhattan eventually fell behind them; there was no longer that dazzling panorama to distract him. There was nothing but the sounds of the road and the snail-paced movement of cars in the lanes ahead and the now silent woman to keep him from bearing alone the details of her story.

"I'm clean now," she said. "I've been clean over a year already."

"Good. That's good. That's real good." He looked at her across the seat, her face pale in the dashboard light. She turned to him with a faint smile. This is who I am, the smile said. This is the girl you were in love with.

He took a deep breath, held it in. This was her truth. He had to make it his now, too. Because this was the girl he cared for, the object of his desire, the one around whom—even in her absence—his life had been centered.

And he saw again why this was so, why he could never forget her. Because even in the darkest of times, her spirit had pulled her through. Not unscarred, but intact. A strength that never quit. That made her ready to face whatever the world offered next. Somehow he had sensed that—even in those days so long ago—when the deepest of feelings were kept secret inside them. It was a strength that he himself aspired to, that he had never been sure he was capable of. She had given him *something to hope for*. With her beside him, he felt that hope again now, despite or maybe because of the story he'd just heard.

There was an accident ahead. He pulled himself up and strained for a better look. Brake lights flared red for as far as he could see. But what did it matter? he reminded himself. He was in no hurry. There was no other place where he wanted to be. No other person he wanted beside him.

He settled back in the seat and looked at her. She sat close to the window, no seat belt. She didn't believe in them, she'd told him when she first got into the car. He hadn't argued the point. There seemed less tension now in her shoulders, her face seemed less burdened, the tightness in her eyes had eased.

The traffic had funneled into one lane. They crept forward slowly until they finally reached the problem: two cars in a fender bender taking up the two right lanes. The police hadn't arrived yet. Two men stood arguing behind the conjoined cars.

When they moved past the accident and the lanes opened up again she said, "Take the first exit. I live only three blocks from the highway."

Her words brought him back to a reality that had been pushed aside temporarily by the effect her story had upon him: the danger that would be awaiting him when he returned home that night, when he crossed back over the bridge. And the danger to her now, as well.

"So Mooney, getting you the heroin. Is he working for a drug gang?"

She shook her head. "I don't know. *He* says he's building a case against them. That it's part of his job. But I don't know."

"Has he said anything about wanting to kill us, about *trying* to kill us?"

"No, but he hates you guys enough to do it, that's for sure. Especially Charlie. Like I said, he talks about that all the time." She thought a while before adding: "He likes to play with people, torment them into giving him what he wants. That's probably why you're all not dead yet."

CHAPTER 41

She lived on the second floor of a house on a street of modest houses, close enough to the bridge to hear the constant drone of traffic when the wind blew right. A kitchen, a bathroom, and one small room with a futon on the floor, a TV on a stand in the opposite corner and in between a battered arm chair resting on a 6x9 gold-braided throw rug.

When she turned on the light, she looked at him and shrugged. "You shoulda seen the place I lived in when I first got out here. I'm working my way up."

The room, small and barren as it was, depressed him. "You'll be manager of that damn supermarket before you know it," he said, trying his best to keep things light.

"No more A&P. I work in a bar now. Two blocks over."

"You and Charlie'll have something to talk about then. You can trade war stories."

She grimaced at that. "I'm not real keen about seeing Charlie any time soon."

"Just making conversation," he said by way of apology. "I wasn't thinking."

"I can't believe how much effort that guy put into hitting on me. Day and night. Every which way imaginable. I wouldn't have believed there were so many ways of trying to get into a chick's pants." She laughed in spite of herself. "Remember his flagpole bit, at the beach? Daring you guys to scale it with him? You were the only one to take him up on it. And, what, you guys get about halfway up when the cops come. And you come sliding down so fast you both get third-degree burns on your arms and thighs. And we had to haul ass into the woods beyond the picnic area to escape."

"Guess I was trying to impress you, too."

"Noooo!" she said, straight-faced then laughed again. " 'Least you were a little more subtle. And you were so shy about it, I don't know, it was kind of adorable."

The memory embarrassed him. He didn't know whether to

defend himself or laugh at himself.

She watched him intently and he lowered his eyes.

"It's awkward as hell, isn't it?" She gave him a sheepish look. In the light he could see the barest of lines that had begun to spider from her eyes, from the edge of her lips. "The two of us here. Together like this."

It was his turn to deadpan. "You think so?" Then he laughed.

"You're still the guy I remember."

"What do you mean?"

"You still hold a lot inside you. There's still so much going on beneath the surface."

"Is that such a bad thing?"

"I think it overwhelms you sometimes. Leaves you high and dry."

"You always could see inside me like nobody else could. Why is that, you think?"

Instead of answering, she said, "I can offer you juice or water. Can't keep anything else on hand just yet, you know?"

"Water's fine."

She slipped into the kitchen and flicked the light switch. "Look around," she called. "Take the grand tour."

The first thing he noticed was that nothing remained from the old days, no photos, no memorabilia of any kind: only the bare essentials of a life: a place to sit, a place to sleep. He crossed to the window beyond which a small grassy back yard ended abruptly at a stockade fence. In the center of the yard a once-bright red and white swing set was succumbing to age and rust.

When he turned from the window he saw it on the floor, wedged between the futon and the wall, mostly concealed by the thin mattress. He bent to retrieve it, holding the blue chip in his fingers like a coin he was examining, as she came out of the kitchen carrying a glass of water. She saw what he'd found, read his expression and stopped short.

"Mooney comes over here?" Disappointment filled his eyes like tears. He had wanted to believe theirs was a purely business arrangement.

"I assumed you knew," she said hesitantly. "I assumed you understood—"

One more shock in a day of shocks, he thought. I didn't know. Or I didn't *want* to know. I didn't want to understand.

He tossed the chip on the mattress and turned back to the window: the small boxed-in backyard, the decaying swing set, the stockade fence that separated this house from the identical house next street over.

"When I'd been using a while, when I lost my job," she was saying behind him. "I was living on the streets till Tommy found me. He—"

"Tom the hero," he muttered under his breath.

"That's the way it was," she said softly. "That was my life."

Through the open window he thought he could hear the hum of cars coming off the bridge but maybe he was being deceived again, he thought, maybe it wasn't traffic at all he was hearing but simply the accumulated sounds of the Queens night disguised as motion.

"Once I got clean and got back on my feet, I broke it off with him. I changed my locks, told him not to come over anymore. I pay my own rent now.

"Then, a week or so ago, when he told me you'd come back, I began to change my mind about testifying like I'd promised. I told him I wasn't sure. That's why we were outside your building last night. He thought if I saw you face to face, you and Charlie and Johnny, I'd get angry all over again about what happened to Timmy. But being outside your apartment had the opposite effect. I knew I still had feelings for you."

At the window, Danny brooded over her story. She was telling him the truth; he didn't doubt that. She'd been through too much, she'd revealed too much about herself, to lie to him now. And what she was saying would help explain why Tom Mooney was trying to kill them. First he lost Ellis, now he was in danger of losing Julianne. In a matter of days, he'd seen his case collapse. Vigilante justice was the only path left to him.

"Tell me," he said, "does he know his brother committed suicide out there that night?"

"No." She hesitated and the way her voice choked he thought she might be fighting back tears. At the window, she stood beside him, still holding the glass of water. "I haven't been able to tell him. I don't want to hurt him. And besides, he won't believe me, anyway. I'm afraid of what he'll do to me for saying it."

"He has to be told."

"Yes." But the way she said it, weakly and without conviction,

The Bronx Kill

made it clear *she* wouldn't be the one doing the telling.

He felt anger rising inside him like a weapon—at her, the choices she made, at Tom Mooney for invading both their lives—but when he saw the fear in her eyes, the tremble of her fingers as she held the glass, he choked back what he wanted to say.

"That swing set," she said, "it always makes me sad. Abandoned like that. Nobody using it."

He was thinking about what she'd said: *that's the way it was, that was my life*. Not a life anyone would have wanted. But he knew he'd have to adjust to it, *accept* it. Or risk losing her a second time.

"My life's always been about choosing the lesser of two bad situations," she was saying. "But I want that to change now. I want to have better choices."

"Julianne—"

She cut him off before he could finish. "Julie," she said. "I call myself Julie now."

CHAPTER 42

The next afternoon Danny found Murphy's Dublin Rose, where she tended bar. A working class hangout. Blinds on the two large plate glass windows kept the light to a minimum. The place resembled a tunnel with a bar running down its entire length.

He made his way in, past three men in work clothes hunched in silence over their beers. At the end of the bar Julie leaned against the counter, reading. When she saw him she straightened up and closed the magazine. It wasn't that she was expecting him, but she wasn't surprised to see him, either.

"Got more of a selection to offer you here," she said as he lowered himself onto a stool. She was dressed as she was yesterday: black T-shirt, ripped blue jeans. Her hair in a ponytail.

"Beer's fine. Something on tap."

She moved down the bar in the shadowed light. When she raised a glass and drew the tap, she was caught in the slatted diffuse-yellow light from the windows. Then she was coming toward him in shadow again, holding his beer. Even the murky light couldn't hide how thin she was. Her arms like sticks attached to a sapling.

"They like it dark like this, my customers. Kind of got used to it myself." She placed a coaster in front of him and set the glass on it. Her own glass of cola, half full, sat on the counter behind her. "Peaceful, you know. Like the feeling you have when you're getting ready for an afternoon nap."

The place, by his assessment, was older and grimier-looking than the Glow. Plaster walls with no wooden trim. Few decorations of any kind. Simply your bare bones beer and shot watering hole: a place you crawled into when you didn't want to see what daylight had to offer.

"It's only a temporary thing." It was as if she anticipated his disapproval. "Till I figure out what's next. School maybe. I don't know."

"Isn't it hard? Having all this access?"

Her eyes answered for her. "I think of it as a test. How committed I am. So far, I always come out on top."

The Bronx Kill

He sipped the beer and stared down the length of the bar. The three patrons, all middle-aged, were loners. Silence hung like a penance, drifting like dust in the slants of light. This is the way my life might have turned out if I'd stayed in Florida, he thought. I might have ended up like this, killing time without purpose. Waiting for—*what?*

Julie, nursing a Coke, seemed lost somewhere inside herself.

There was so much he wanted to know about her life, how she'd managed to survive, how she kicked her habit, how she beat the odds and didn't end up dead; but he was afraid to ask, afraid to hear the gritty details.

He hadn't yet given up his fantasy of the girl he first knew. Not completely, he hadn't. There was this woman standing across from him who bore a resemblance to the girl he knew, who was—in his wishful thinking—merely the front for the Julianne of his youth. If he searched hard enough, if he dug deeply enough, he would find that original girl. Unravaged. Unshaken. Shining and beautiful, determined and laughing. And he would devote his life, every moment of his day and night, to shielding her from life's assault, from all that had brought her to where she was now.

But he stopped himself. He had come too far—they both had—for the fantasy to persist. He was no hero, and she was no damsel in distress. Without doubt, she was her own person now. The face that looked back at him across the bar, worn and weary perhaps but still determined, was proof of that.

So what he said was the consequence of the watered-down but still-lingering need to be her knight in shining armor. "These guys. They give you a hard time? You get hit on a lot?"

She laughed. "Getting hit on a lot's the least of it."

"What's the worst of it?" He braced himself for what she might tell him.

"Figuring out how to get the most and give the least." She laughed again, more edge to it this time. "Story of my life since I crossed that river. 'Cause they all want to take more than they give. To a man." She sipped the Coke. "Correction. There was one exception. The man who found me wandering along Astoria Boulevard in my bra and panties the night I crossed. He didn't ask for anything. Drove me to a city shelter where they fed me, put me up for the night. He didn't want anything in return. But the others—"

She laughed with the same edge again, her eyes heavy with

experience. "So, by the time I got here I'd had a lifetime's worth of practice, you see. I knew how to de-fuse these guys, 'specially at night when they get a little too rambunctious. I'd learned how to bring them down to where I wanted them to be. And believe me I've used everything to do that: logic, pleas, threats, tears, free booze. Even this." She reached below the bar and held up a foot and a half long lead pipe.

"You could kill a man with that."

"That's the point."

"*Would* you?"

"If it's him or me?" She turned the pipe in her hands. "It's not gonna be me, if I have any say."

"Guess we're alike in that regard. It's what the streets taught us."

"Our decisions are made long before we act." She took a last look at the pipe and returned it to the shelf. "I read that somewhere."

"Life—" He didn't finish. Two men had come in and she went off to serve them.

The silence was killing him. He pushed his stool back and walked to the front where he fed a dollar into the jukebox and pressed buttons without bothering to read the song titles. It was noise he wanted, of any kind.

When he glanced up, he could see the street through a gap in the blinds. Directly across from the bar a black Escalade was parked. Leaning against it, wearing sunglasses, his arms folded as if he was waiting for something, was the Jamaican.

Danny motioned for Julie. When she stood beside him, she said, "Yeah. He was outside my house this morning. It's the same guy you were telling me about, right?"

"Same guy."

"Figures," she said, without expression.

"Why didn't you tell me?"

"What for? If Tom wants to hurt me, he knows where to find me. Not much I can do about it, right?"

"You should have told me."

She looked at him and shrugged. "Okay, so now you know. How does that change things?"

"It's why I came out here today."

"Thought you came to see sweet little me." Her smile was part playful, part cynical.

He waited before replying. "I need your help."

The Bronx Kill

CHAPTER 43

Even now, long after their break-up, Tom Mooney still came into the Dublin Rose once or twice a week. She'd asked him not to, again and again, but he wouldn't go away. Told her it was a free country and he'd drink in any goddamned bar he chose to. So she'd learned to treat him like any other stranger who wandered in—polite, but impersonal and distant, too. Get his drinks, then move away down the bar. Keep to herself. Up till this point, it had worked. Other than his insistent stares and his grousing about what he called her bitchiness and her ingratitude that she had to endure each time she refilled his glass, he had kept his distance.

She was ready for him when he showed up the following day, mid-afternoon, before his shift. She poured his usual—a double Jameson's 12 in a rocks glass, no rocks—said, "Need to talk to you."

He grunted. " 'Bout time."

"In the back," she said.

It was slow, the after work crowd hadn't yet begun to filter in, so she could sit with him at one of the tables wedged between the bar and hallway to the rest rooms.

He sprawled in one of the wooden chairs, back to the wall, heavy arms pressed into the table's poly-urethaned surface. She felt a wave of disgust at his shapeless body, the weight he put on recently, the slight but insistent smell of his sweat and the not-so- slight smell of the cologne he used to mask it. How could she have let herself be intimate with this man? He was nothing like his brother or Danny Baker—the only men she'd ever had a real physical attraction to.

"Why don't you join me in a drink?" He smirked at her, making a slow-motion production of raising his glass, breathing in the whiskey, sipping it and smacking his lips. "For old times' sake."

"No, thanks."

He slid the glass toward her. "Come on. Just a sip. What's the harm? And if that's not strong enough, I got something stronger in my pocket. Something I *know* you'll like."

She stared at the glass and thought how easy it would be to

lift it to her lips. *Just a sip.* A moment's release from the ghosts she couldn't shake. From the men of her past. From the man before her now. *Just a sip.* She hesitated another moment before sliding it back to him.

"You know," he said, holding onto the smirk. "You were a lot more fun when you were a junkie."

"I guess I don't see it that way."

"Guess not." He tilted the glass in her direction. When she stared back at it expressionless, he brought it to his lips, swallowed deeply, then set it down with a bang. "You're all business now, right Babe?"

"That's right. That's why we're here."

"What kind of business we talking about?"

"*Your* business. The case you're building. Against the Renegades."

"What about it?"

"I've been thinking it over. Since the other night. Since we were parked outside Danny's apartment."

"And—?"

"You were right."

He grinned at that. "Usually am."

"I can't forgive them. Danny, Charlie, Johnny. I can't find anything in my heart to excuse what they did. No matter how much I try to give them the benefit of the doubt, there's no way around it. They're the reason Timmy's no longer here."

"What I been telling you all along." He sipped the whiskey, watching her closely, trying to root out any deception. "What made you change your mind—*again?*"

"I haven't been able to sleep. It's been eating me up."

"Your conscience—"

"Something you said. About not letting myself be influenced by the way things were *before* the drowning. No matter what I thought about them, no matter how good friends we were, what happened that night is the only thing that matters. It's what you said. At the least, at the very least, their behavior constituted negligence, *criminal negligence*"—she was careful to include that phrase from the penal laws, a phrase that he had drummed into her on the many nights he'd engaged in a tirade detailing the possible ways he could make a case against them—"which is simply unjustifiable by any reasonable standard of conduct. Even for teenagers."

He drew his shoulders up and couldn't hide a faint smile. One of his weaknesses, she knew. His inability to conceal his pride when something he did or said brought her around to his point of view. She had given him what he wanted on two counts.

"So you'll testify then? When the time comes?"

"Yes," she said. "But first I want to show you what happened. I want to take you through it, step by step."

"What do you mean?"

The wariness in his eyes had slipped into his voice, as well. Careful, she told herself.

"Tonight. At the Kill. I want to show you exactly what went down."

"I *know* what went down. You've already told me."

"Not all of it." She laid the bait carefully. "I've told you some of it, but not all. There are things I left out. And there are things I have to *show* you. *Where* the fight took place. *Where* they dragged him into the water. *How far out* he was when they left him there. Things like that."

He slouched in the seat, thinking it over, his eyes fixed not on her but on some inward place. She didn't think he could resist watching a re-enactment of the scene. She was pretty sure, no matter what his reservations were, he wouldn't be able to pass on that.

"It won't make sense unless I show you."

He nodded in agreement. "What about *this* place?"

"I have the night off."

"We could do it tomorrow. In the daylight."

"It happened at night. I want to show you at night."

He seemed satisfied with that, his eyes for the present at rest. "I'll pick you up later."

"No."

"What do you mean, 'no'?"

"I'll get there myself."

"That's crazy."

"We're not getting back together, Tommy. I want that to be clear. This is strictly business. I'll get there myself. And I'll come back home myself."

A flicker of wounded pride, of anger, passed across his face. "I did everything for you."

"And I'm giving you everything back. Everything you wanted."

He dropped his eyes then, staring into what was left of the whiskey, turning the glass slowly on the table. "Not everything."

"Hey, life's life," she said, refusing to be drawn into anything heavy. "You get and you don't get. And you never know which it's going to be. That's the fun of it, right?"

His eyes, weighted with a sorrow he hadn't shown her before, studied her closely. "Tell me. We had something then, didn't we? It wasn't all in my head, was it?"

She waited, considering his question, watching his heavy eyes watching her. "It wasn't all in your head."

He nodded then and pushed himself up from the table.

"I have to be sure of something," she said.

"What's that?"

"You have to come alone. This is only for you. I'm willing to make it public later on. But this is only for you."

She called Danny to say the meeting was set for 9:30, at the point where the Kill emptied into the East River. "But I don't think this is a good idea. The more I think about it the surer I am. I have this bad feeling."

"If there was another way—" He simply saw no alternative. They would either come to some arrangement or they would shoot at each other. But at least this uncertainty would end.

"I can tell him what I told you. That it was a suicide—"

"*I* can tell him just as easily. And it will be safer—for you. Besides, like you said, no matter which of us tells him, there's a good chance he's not going to believe it."

She scrambled for other ideas. "You can add to your photo collection. Get more pictures of him with those dealers. I can help you, pretend I'm hooked again. We can get him on camera giving me drugs—"

"I've thought of that. Too risky for you. Besides, photos or not, he can always claim he's just building a case, doing what he has to in preparation for a bust. Whether he's truly undercover or playing a dirty cop, or whether he *is* a dirty cop, he's smart enough to cover himself."

Silence filled the line while she considered this.

"Promise me something," he said. "Don't call the police tonight. No matter what you're thinking, or how worried you get. If they show up, I don't stand a chance. I'll have a tough enough time dealing with Mooney. I don't need an army lined up against me."

The Bronx Kill

CHAPTER 44

The first thing Charlie said when Danny told him of Julianne and the plan she'd set in motion was, "I can't believe it." He held the phone away from his ear as if it was the cause of his shortness of breath. "I can't believe she made it across."

"Believe it."

"She's been, what, hiding out all these years?"

"You could say that."

"Doing what?"

"Lots of things."

"How's she look?"

"Older."

"You mean, what, she's lost her looks?"

"I didn't say that."

Charlie considered the situation. "You're going to need back-up. You can't do this alone."

"I've got back-up. Me, myself and I."

"It's no joke, man."

"You hear me laughing?"

"You're gonna need help."

"Yeah? Who?"

"The Renegades. Who else?"

"Now who's joking?"

"Hey, just because I'm laid up at the moment doesn't mean I can't fire a gun. My infection's clearing up. My fingers and hands are fine. All I need's a little help walking."

"Forget it."

"And Johnny—"

"Johnny's upstate someplace. We have no idea where."

"We can find him."

"Yeah? How? He doesn't even have a cell phone."

"*Some*body's got to know. Johnny's mother. Or Lorraine's parents—"

"Johnny couldn't even hit the target, remember?

"That was years ago."

"Has he improved?"

"Hey, a wild shot's better than no shot at all."

"Forget it."

"I *can't* forget it. I'm dying here. I'm—Hold on a second, will ya?"

An orderly wheeling a cart had come into the room. Did he need anything? Did he want anything?

"Yeah, I need something. Yeah, I want something. I want to get out of this damn bed, this damn room."

"I got apple juice," the orderly offered.

He waited until the man left and the room, save for himself, was empty. The one thing he had to be thankful for this past day and a half was that he'd been spared a roommate. It wasn't bad enough you had to be laid up yourself, but to have to witness another prime example of human suffering a few feet away only added to the torture.

"Listen," he said into the phone. "I'm going crazy here. All I do is lie around and think. I feel useless, washed up. Like my life has no point—"

"The point is to get better."

"You know what I mean. I'm no good at this waiting game. I'm not doing something, might as well be dead, might as well put me in the ground."

"You try and come to the Kill tonight and most likely you *will* be dead."

"That's my point. You can't be out there alone. We're all in this together."

"That's what we believed."

Charlie stared at the phone as if it had insulted him. "What's the matter with you?"

"Nothing's the matter with me."

"Sounds like there is. You being so negative and all."

"I'm not being negative."

"We're the Renegades. One for all and all for one. We still believe that. No matter what's gone down."

Danny's sigh came through the line. "I know all that."

"So what's your problem?"

"This is different."

"Sticking together's gotten us this far, hasn't it?"

"Yeah? Where's that?"

"Negative, man. You're bringing me down."

"Better I do this alone. It's simpler and easier that way."

"You're not making sense."

"Things have been complicated in my head for too long. I *want* it simple. I want to take care of it *my* way."

"Wait," Charlie said. But the line had already gone dead.

Into the empty room, he said: "Don't want to lose you, old bud."

He lay there on the bed, staring at the hospital room's unblemished white ceiling. It was like a blank slate that had to be filled. And what did he have to fill it with but his thoughts.

Thought

after

thought

after

thought.

How worthless he felt. How pathetic. How he should be the one on point, not Danny.

After all, he had been head honcho from the beginning. He should be leading the charge now. That was only right. It was like being a General, training the troops, then dying before the battle was won. It wasn't fair. Not fair at all. He'd been robbed of the sweet taste of victory.

Bad fate, that's what it was.

He'd been reduced to a pansy, a wimp.

Bad fate. Bad fate.

If he hadn't been shot, if he hadn't turned his back in the alley, if he had been a half-second quicker, if he'd gotten to the stairs faster. If he'd twisted his body a half-inch to the left the bullet might have missed him, he might not be lying here now.

If, If, If

Thinking, he had come to believe, was nothing more than a form of self-torture. The ultimate prison. And the only escape was action of some kind.

So he forced himself up, tightened the belt on his robe and grabbed his crutches. He thumped his way to the door and into the hall, picking up speed as he went. The doctors had said to exercise, he would heal faster, and so at least once every hour, sometimes twice, he dragged himself five times up and down the long hall. Now he would double that. At twice the speed.

Eyes straight ahead, shoulders hunched, body leaning forward aggressively he traveled from the nurses' lounge at one end to the sun room at the other. He refused to acknowledge the discomfort in his muscles, the pain, the bed sores chafing against the cloth of his robe. He wielded the crutches in a plunging motion, veering around the obstacles of carts and gurneys, nurses and doctors and meandering visitors, taking grim pleasure in the unfaltering thumps of the rubber-tipped metal striking polished tiles.

Within minutes he had erased the senseless thoughts from his mind. He was working up a sweat, he could feel the glorious moisture building under his arms, collecting on his neck and chest, and he took this as a sign of victory, a vindication. See, I can function. I'm not an invalid. I may be down but I'm not out. Not by a long shot. No way, no sir, no thank you.

Ahead of him, at the end of the hall, the sun room was ablaze with the late afternoon light. He thumped his way toward it like a man who sees paradise on the horizon. He had no idea how fast he was going, only that he *was going*.

"Slow down," one of the nurses called to him. "You'll hurt yourself."

But life was on the line again, his buddy taking the heat this time. For all of them. And that just wasn't right.

He was not a pawn of fate. He wasn't. There was no way he would let himself be, as long as he had an ounce of strength within him. And he could feel it, his strength, a tangible thing building inside him, slowly, slowly, but surely. Legs, arms, chest—stronger than they were yesterday and the day before that, strong enough to do some damage.

The gold-suffused light at the hall's end grew closer, closer, brighter.

His body was covered in sweat now, his breath coming fast and with greater effort.

When he was within range at last, he stopped to raise his arm and, with his fingers shaped like a gun, he fired silently at the potted plants in the sun room ahead, picking them off one by one.

CHAPTER 45

Julianne's shift at the Dublin Rose ended at four that afternoon but she didn't leave until nearly five-thirty.

She dreaded her nights off, particularly this one, fearful as she was for Danny. If anything happened to him, she would blame herself.

Second thoughts.

They were driving her crazy and she didn't want to be alone with them. That's why she sat on a stool, sipping a Coke, chatting with Cory, the part-time bartender.

Small talk or no talk, he was easy to be around. He was the least judgmental person she knew. He didn't care where you'd been or what you'd done. His focus, always, was on the present moment, in finding the laughter in it and she loved his sardonic wit, the way he could laugh at people and things without demeaning them. He was one of the two people she'd ever met with whom she felt she could be herself. The other was Danny. But that, for so many reasons then and now, had become far too complicated. With Cory there was no complication. He wasn't interested in women in *that* way—a fact that he kept well-concealed from the Dublin Rose's outer-borough, working class clientele—so there were no lingering after-effects, no expectations, no recriminations. Hello, let's have a few laughs, then so long till whenever. In this, her new life, he was the closest thing she had to a friend.

By five o'clock the bar was filled and she thought she should leave. Cory had his hands full, not much time anymore for chit-chat. But still she stayed. She even helped out a little: serving drinks to the impatient, re-filling the bowls of pretzels and chips that kept their patrons going until they went home to their wives for a proper dinner. One thing the job had taught her was that she *liked* serving people, even if only drinks and snacks, especially since she'd broken it off with Tom and she had nothing more significant to give anyone.

"You don't leave soon," Cory said finally, "somebody might think you don't have a life."

"You already *know* I don't have a life."

"Never too late to start looking."

"I guess."

I guess, she said again to herself on the way home.

In her apartment, without bothering to turn on the lamp, she lay on the futon and let her fingers smooth out the creases in the coverlet. She was thinking: only one man had shared this bed with her, and even that had been a mistake. No, not a mistake, she corrected herself. She had been fooled, that's all. She had mistaken her needs for love.

It was a common human failing, she had come to believe. Need was the ultimate trickster, ever practicing its subtle magic, and she had been simply one of its many victims. In her darkest moments she believed that's all that love was: need to the hundredth power. Nothing more, nothing less. When your need changed or vanished, you broke up, moved on to satisfy your newest, strongest need.

But Tom had been a trickster, too, hadn't he? So tender at first, so comforting, here on this bed, with his words, his touches. Until, over time, even the bed became a podium from which he delivered his tirades, denouncing his brother's "assassins" in fitful rants, before and after their lovemaking, and sometimes—she thought—*during* their lovemaking, judging by the rough and near-violent way he handled her. He, too, had been a partner in destroying whatever need bound them.

From time to time—like right now, right this minute—she thought it might be time to find a new man, but that was her anxiety talking. She knew she wasn't ready. Though her nights off were slow and long and hard to endure, she didn't want to be close to anyone—lover or friend—at the moment. She was, as best she could understand it, adrift, waiting for something to make her feel *normal* again, whatever that was. Maybe, she thought, being normal meant having a reasonable hope things would get better. Not that they *would* get better, but at least the *hope* that they would.

What she had instead of hope, she told herself, was a fantasy or two. The first of these involved her father and mother: she would return to Peekskill, where her father was living in his brother's house. But she would do this only when she was healthy. When she'd gained back her weight, when her skin was once again aglow, her hair shiny, and when she'd gotten her life moving forward again. Because then she could say to him, see, I turned out fine, despite you, despite

The Bronx Kill

having you for a father.

Or maybe she would go back simply because she wanted him to approve of her, to *like* what she had become. One way or another, she *would* go back. And afterward she would visit her mom, too, in whatever hospital or asylum she'd ended up in, and she would be strong enough to endure whatever condition of deterioration the poor woman had fallen to, and she would be able to lift herself above her own fear and revulsion and tell her she loved her.

The other fantasy involved Timmy Moon: that she would, at some point, feel less anguished about his death, that she would make peace with not only *that* he died, but the *way* he died, as well, the despair that made him give up.

These fantasies, at least, made it possible for her to get up in the morning, made her believe it might be worth it to go through another day.

For a moment her mind seemed to shut down, be absorbed by the window's grey light. In that time there was no time; it seemed her mind didn't exist. Then she was back in time again, thinking of Danny, thinking he would be hurt this night and she was doing nothing to help him. His words came back at her like a slap in the face: *No matter what you're thinking tonight, or how worried you get, don't call the police.*

He'd made her promise.

But sitting on the futon now, in the dim light from the street, she felt the pressure mounting to break that promise.

But what if he was right? What if calling the police only made things worse, put him in even greater danger?

To distract herself, she turned on the TV and watched without comprehension as figures moved across the screen, spoke words she knew but could not unlock the meaning of. When she left the apartment she didn't even bother to turn it off, leaving it to mumble its gibberish to the empty room.

On the street she passed pizzerias and corner grocery stores with take-out food, but she didn't feel like eating. She passed theatres that showed movies about made-up people in made-up stories, nothing real, nothing but a diversion from what truly mattered.

Turning west, she walked toward the water—it seemed that in her free time she was always walking toward water—and when she reached the riverfront park it was already deep twilight. She walked to the park's end where, if she looked slightly north, she could see the section of the river she had swum across and beyond it the tip of shoreline that was the Kill. She had come here often in the years she had lived in Queens. It was her vigil from afar. When she didn't have time to travel to the Bronx. When she tried to pinpoint exactly *where* in the river she had last seen Timmy.

But now it wasn't Timmy she was thinking of, but Danny. *Don't call the police*, he had said.

So she didn't.

It was Charlie she called.

From his car a block away, watching her make the call, Tom Mooney felt the uneasy pieces of their last conversation fall into place. Her not wanting him to pick her up, her insistence they meet at night, that he come alone. His conviction grew stronger: she had been setting him up. She had never intended to meet him this night at the Kill.

Earlier he had waited across the street from the bar, waiting long after her shift ended, following her home, waiting for her to re-emerge, trailing behind her as she made her way to the park instead of the subway she would have to take if she were to meet him. And now the phone call.

Which of them was she talking to?

For surely, he thought, the call had to be part of the plan, the concluding act of her betrayal.

She had come out of the booth now. In no hurry, it seemed, she stood at the park's edge as if deciding what to do. She started back into the park but halfway to the water's edge she abruptly turned around and came back to the street, walking faster and with purpose. Momentarily, he entertained the hope that he'd been wrong, that she was in fact heading for the subway.

When she reached the EL, however, her step didn't slow. She walked beneath it and crossed the street, even as the Bronx-bound local that would take her across the river clattered into the station.

The Bronx Kill

CHAPTER 46

Johnny had awakened that morning feeling troubled.

Bad dreams, he figured, was the easy explanation but the truth was he'd been troubled since they arrived at the hotel early yesterday. Bad dreams were simply the latest manifestation. Although he couldn't remember the entire nightmare, images lingered: he was wandering through tunnels and basements and alleyways in search of Timmy. Until he met Danny who had been running hard and was out of breath. *Timmy's not here*, Danny said. *He's in the water, remember. That's where we'll find him, if they don't kill us first.*

If they don't kill us first. Those were the words he'd uttered in a semi-conscious state, upon waking.

Lorraine had turned to him in the bed and said, "What? What are you talking about?"

He hadn't told her about the danger he was in. He'd passed off the attempt on his life, and Charlie's life, as random acts. Unrelated. Unprovoked. And senseless.

"Bad dreams," he'd told her, dismissing it.

But as the day wore on and the troubled feeling persisted, grew even stronger, he knew he couldn't keep it from her much longer. It was Danny, the danger he was in. He'd been bothered by that since they drove up here, forty-five miles upstate, forty-five miles from where he knew in his heart he should be.

But Lorraine needed him, too. And he had struggled all day yesterday to keep his attention on her, the issues that had to be resolved, as he had struggled, even in his distraught state, to find the frame of mind to make love to her at night.

"I'm sorry it wasn't better," he'd said to her afterwards, I'm sorry *I* wasn't better."

With her usual optimism and good cheer, she had brushed away his lamentations. "We'll make it better," she promised. "Together, we'll make it better."

Then, in the soft light from the night sky that drifted through the latticed windows of their room, she had added: "They'll always be problems in a relationship. I don't mind that, working them out. It's *not having* a relationship to work on, that's what makes me crazy. All this time since you came back when nothing was happening, I felt so useless and alone. There was no *us* to hold onto."

"I know," he said by way of apology, "I know."

And also by way of apology he had devoted himself nearly a hundred percent to listening to her, her concerns, her grievances, her hopes for their future. And he had done all the things she wanted to do: long walks on the old carriage trails that wound through the hilly terrain of the property, kayaking on the lake, even swimming in the lake's clear dark water, despite its bone-numbing chill. And they had held hands in the gazebo on the rock wall above the lake. They had kissed there and made plans. And he knew that all of it, in one form or another, was a part of his extended apology.

But now, pacing the ornately furnished Victorian room where he waited for her to return from her walk—she needed some time alone, she had said—he could no longer keep at bay his worries about Danny.

He checked his watch and went again to the window that overlooked the lake. She was not in sight. Putting on his jacket, he went down the marble staircase and into the bright morning to find her.

He hurried on the path above the lake. The water below, surrounded as it was by limestone cliffs, was a deep shimmering green in the sunlight. This place she had chosen with its lake, its cliffs, its pine trees, its rambling white clapboard inn was a magnificent retreat from city life. Perhaps another time he would be able to appreciate its isolation, its remove from the grit and grime, the hard streets of the neighborhood.

At the lake's far end, she sat on a rock ledge overlooking a long wooded valley that reached nearly to the horizon. If he squinted, he thought he could see the city's skyline etched there. Or maybe it was only the way the light struck the clouds.

In her corduroy jacket and carefully pressed slacks—even in hiking clothes she managed to look adorably fashionable—she was sitting cross-legged and contemplative on the rock ledge. He stood tentatively above her, hands dug deep into his back pockets. The breeze pulled her hair back, which made her face more vulnerable, exposed like that, and smaller too it seemed, almost child-like in its fragility. He thought maybe he shouldn't say anything.

"I don't want to intrude," he said. "I know you needed some time to yourself—"

"It's all right. I've done my thinking," she said, indicating the space beside her. "This rock's big enough for both of us."

Again he thought maybe he should keep his mouth shut. When he looked to the horizon, though, he was certain this time that it *was* the New York skyline imprinted there: the jagged cluster of buildings lifting through the clouds like a taunt. "I have to go home," he said finally.

She looked bewildered. "Home? Why?"

"I have to."

"But why?"

"I have to see Danny. And Charlie."

Hurt and anger fell across her face like a veil. "We've been having such a nice time. We were going to have dinner tonight in the grand ballroom. We were going to go dancing—"

"We will. Soon," he promised. "We can come back here as soon as—" He sat beside her on the rock and told her about the attempt on his life. It wasn't a random thing, he explained, and he went on to describe the trouble he was in, that all of them were in.

When he finished, she looked at him with concern, incredulity. "Why didn't you tell me this before?"

"I didn't want you to worry. I thought I could handle it. I—"

"But don't you see?" She took his hand and held it in hers. She leaned close to him, a pleading look in her eyes. "This is exactly what I've been talking about. This is what a relationship is. Sharing our innermost thoughts and concerns. That's what we haven't had since you've come back. We've been strangers to each other."

"Yes," he said and he was beginning to understand at least some of the deeper things she needed from him.

"This kind of openness. It's what's been missing. It's what two people in love have to learn to share."

He wanted to learn it, he did. It would take time, he thought.

"The way you told me you used to talk to God. Telling him your deepest fears, your deepest needs. It should be the same with us. Don't you see? That's what intimacy is between a man and a woman."

Intimacy. It had always been a word that frightened him.

She was frowning now. "I had no idea you were still so tormented by Timmy's death. Why didn't you tell me?"

"Ashamed, I guess."

"Maybe I could have—it helps to get things off your chest. Sometimes just talking about it helps."

"I know. I should have—I'm sorry."

It was concern not reprimand that shone in her eyes. "I had no idea this crazy man was after you."

"He is," he said. "Right now he's after Danny. That's why we have to go back."

On the drive home they stopped at a Service Area so he could call Danny but his friend didn't pick up. Then he called Charlie.

"Where the hell you been?" Charlie wanted to know. "I'm going nuts here trying to get a hold of you."

"Sorry. Guess I'm going to have to get a cell phone eventually."

"*Eventually*, right," Charlie said with sardonic understatement. "Take your time. No rush."

"Sorry."

"No time for apologies. Something's come up."

"About Danny?"

"Yeah, it's about Danny. "You're gonna have to get the hell down here."

"We're on our way back now."

"Good. Good."

The day's worry had found its way into Johnny's voice. "He's okay, isn't he?"

"At the moment, yeah."

"Thank God. I've been praying for—"

"No time for prayers, either. Stop by my house first, before you come to the hospital. Jimmy's got the key."

"What for?"

"Clothes. I need them. And my .38. In the dresser. Third drawer, right side."

CHAPTER 47

Charlie came thumping down the hospital corridor, heading for the sun room.

It was past dinner hour but visiting hours were still in progress so there were people about, too many for his purposes—nurses, orderlies, visitors—moving in and out of rooms. If he could have swept them aside and cleared the hall by wielding his crutches, he would gladly have done so. He charged ahead, muttering under his breath, *Out of my way, goddammit. Out of my goddamn way.*

As he approached the north stairwell he slowed his step. The glass window had been empty the last time he passed, but now a familiar face bobbed in the small square pane, offering an encouraging smile.

Not the right time, though. The orderlies were too close behind him. A nurse was coming toward him.

He ignored the beaming face, pushed on, the nurse warning him not to over-exert himself.

"Who? *Me?*" he said, his tone incredulous.

She gave him an indulgent smile. "Mr. Romano, whatever are we going to do with you?"

Not one more goddamn thing, he said under his breath. *I promise you that.*

When he reached the sunroom, he found it even more crowded than usual with families, *extended* families, grandpas and grandmas all the way down the generations to little tykes crawling across the floor, a babel of foreign tongues—Spanish, Russian, Middle Eastern, Asian—filling the air space with a relentless cacophony.

No good. He would have to make another pass.

Reluctantly, he swung around and came back down the corridor. Slower this time. Assessing the enemy. There was an orderly working each side of the hall, ducking in and out of rooms to collect dinner trays, sliding them noisily onto a large metal cart, itself one more obstacle to his journey. When he passed the nurses' station he was glad to see all four of them gathered there, busily occupied behind the counter. So it was the orderlies now who posed the greatest danger.

Again he slowed his pace as he neared the north stairwell. The orderlies had moved farther down the corridor behind him. He stopped and waited until both of them stepped out of the hall. Ahead, the crowd in the sunroom seemed to be paying him no mind.

He signaled with a nod and the stairwell door opened from inside. In the next moment he was on the landing, standing on his good leg while Johnny helped him pull an oversized pair of pants over his cast and up over his hospital gown. Shirt and sneakers next and then, with the help of one good leg and a crutch, he was hobbling down the stairs, Johnny descending ahead of him to act as cushion in case the crutch Charlie was leading with slipped off a riser and he went plunging downward.

When Johnny opened the basement door, Charlie's Caddy was waiting, Julianne sliding over to the passenger side as Johnny took the wheel, Charlie barking orders from the backseat, "Take Westchester Ave to 149th. Fastest to go down Webster this time of night."

Johnny knew the way, he didn't need directions, but that didn't stop Charlie from staying in command. "Step on it! Beat this light! Give this jerk the horn! Turn right here! Cop car ahead, watch out! Okay, okay, clear shot now, gun it! *Gun it!*"

He kept at it non-stop—the way Johnny remembered him spitting out pepper in the infield whenever their pitcher was falling behind in the count—until they were driving through the deserted streets close to the Kill.

Several moments passed when he said nothing. Then his voice came again from the backseat, less frantic this time, slower and more measured: "Hand to hand combat."

"What about it?" Julianne asked.

"If we get close to Mooney. Go for the balls. If all else fails, go for the balls."

The Bronx Kill

CHAPTER 48

At nightfall, from the western edge of the rail yards, Danny followed the tracks onto the railroad bridge. A cement ledge alongside the tracks allowed him room to walk as the bridge climbed above the yards and arced eastward toward the Bruckner Expressway. He walked to the point where he could see the juncture of the Kill and the East River. It was early yet, not quite nine, and there was no sign of the detective.

From this vantage point he had a commanding view of the area below. He could follow the line of the Kill to the west until it disappeared in darkness beyond the rail yards. Under the ambient light from the Tri-Borough, he had a view across the entire breadth of the yards—not a clear view, but enough to see the movement of shadows. Between the yards and the East River he could see, almost directly below him, into the Skeleton Zone with its tall grass and reeds and its many paths, some traversing it end to end or side to side, others dead-ending at random, like passages in a maze.

It was too dark to see the broken-down Chevy with its stash of contraband but he could see the avenue beyond it, the abandoned warehouses sulking in the murky yellow glow of the street lamps. No Camaro parked in its usual place. No pedestrian or vehicular traffic at all. In fact, across the area he surveyed, there was no motion of any kind, not even near the make-shift foot-bridge over the Kill where the band of teenagers usually hung out.

It was an unsettling stillness, the first sign that made Danny suspect Mooney had seen through his ploy.

To comfort himself he let his hand rest on the shoulder holster beneath his jacket. He hoped he would not have to use the weapon that it held. But he knew he would, if it came to that. As he had said to Julie, it's what the streets teach us. And he thought again about what she had said in return: *Our decisions are made long before we act.*

Again the unbroken stillness sent a chill of uneasiness through him.

For what seemed like a long time the night held its breath. Then in the stillness a shadow moved. The figure of a man came along a path from the avenue. He could tell from the heavy drooping shoulders, the plodding gait, that it was Tom Mooney. He was smoking, the tip of his cigarette a red glow that lifted in an arc each time he raised his arm.

When he reached the Kill he stopped, drew again on the cigarette. The man wore a light raincoat over a sport jacket, as if he were stepping out for the evening. He seemed unhurried, completely relaxed, as he stared at the water beyond the promontory. His ease of manner added to Danny's anxiety.

So engrossed was Danny in watching the man, it took him some time to notice the shadow moving toward him from higher up on the bridge. The figure, coming from the East River side, suddenly broke into a run. Then Danny was running too, back the way he had come, toward the rail yards.

So, in the end, it had been himself not Mooney who'd been set up. He cursed himself for having been so naïve, for thinking the bridge would give him an advantage. He'd put himself in a bad situation.

He saw just how bad when he caught sight of a figure emerging from the rail yards and climbing the bridge toward him. This figure moved slowly, unlike the one behind him who was running hard.

Caught between them, Danny was running hard too. He didn't want to get trapped in a shoot-out up here. Not two against one with himself in the middle. Not with odds like that.

Which left him one option: jumping.

At its highest point he figured the bridge was almost ninety feet. But he was running downhill now. The closer he could get to the yards, the less of a drop. So he pumped his arms to gain more speed. His one advantage was that the figure coming up from the yards—he could see him more clearly now, a heavy-set man moving slowly toward him—seemed to be laboring under the strain of the climb.

The man behind Danny, though, hadn't lost any ground. Each time Danny glanced behind him the man was coming hard in pursuit, keeping pace with him. So far, neither of his pursuers had opened fire. But even as he was feeling grateful for that he saw the heavy-set man reach for something behind his back.

Danny strained to see over the cement railing. Fifty or sixty feet to the ground, he calculated. Thirty feet was the most he wanted to jump, the most he thought he could do with some hope of not breaking his legs. Twenty-five feet sounded even better. As kids, on a dare, they'd once jumped from a third-story fire escape. Their record high: twenty-eight feet.

Just a little more, he coaxed himself. *Just a few more yards on this damn bridge.*

Sweat was building under his jacket and a rasp came now with every breath he took. He pushed his body, his sneakers slapping loudly against the cement. Beyond the Kill, the lights of Manhattan swirled in a crazy kaleidoscope of pinpoints and for one brief instant his eyes cleared and he saw, beyond the black water of the Harlem River, the headlights of cars flowing southward on the FDR.

When he looked down the curve of track he saw the heavy-set man—less than forty yards away—resting himself, leaning against the railing for support.

Take every advantage you can. Another rule of the streets that he put into practice now, sprinting another twenty or thirty feet before the man—he could see well enough now to identify him by his waddle-like walk as Short Fat Fannie—pushed himself away from the wall, took several steps toward him and raised his arm.

Danny grabbed the cement rail and pulled himself over as the first shot rang out.

He hung for a moment from the railing before letting go.

The air flew out of his lungs.

He was sucked downward in a blind, breathless plunge.

CHAPTER 48

Winded, his body feeling as if a truck had hit him, he lay there without moving. Then he felt the soreness in his palms, felt the bleeding, where he'd scraped them on the rough ground. He shifted his legs and felt the relief of knowing he could move them without pain.

Above him voices were shouting.

He crawled under the shadow of the bridge to conceal himself as he scanned the area in front of him for any sign of the detective. No sound, no movement. He had landed several hundred feet from the railroad yards. Directly ahead of him was an area of weed-pocked open land, and off to his right beyond the Skeleton Zone section of tall grass and reeds was where he had last seen the detective.

The voices above him had moved closer to the yards. At any second he expected the two men to appear. Squinting from the shadows beneath the bridge, and with the help of the newly-risen waning moon's light, he saw them come into the yard and move along the cement supports in his direction, Short Fat Fannie moving faster now on level ground and behind him, a taller man: the Jamaican.

The sight of them together turned his blood cold, brought back the horrific shrill of men screaming, broken bodies groveling in the dirt.

If he stayed any longer where he was, he'd be discovered. So crouching low he made his way across the open ground toward the tall grass of the Skeleton Zone, the temporary safety of the maze. If he could lure them into chasing him, he might have an edge.

"There!" a voice shouted and a second voice followed it with garbled, excited words he couldn't decipher. Footsteps came running in his direction but by this time he was overshadowed by the weedy grass around him.

It was risky, he knew, he could get trapped in here but at least he had cover. And he figured he had more chance of surprising *them* than they did surprising him, because he had played here as a kid, had both hunted and hidden from the other Renegades here, hundreds of times.

Here the reeds grew high, sinewy stalks taller than a man. Like corn rows, these thin wavy sticks with their feathery, flag-like tips rustled in the slightest breeze, made a whispering sound. Like an army of skeletons massed as a protective shield around them—that's how they saw this place as kids. Now it was his sanctuary again.

What he didn't want to happen was to get caught in a path that dead-ended, because the only escape then would be to strike out through the reeds themselves, a noisy proposition, a dead giveaway of your location. He thought he remembered the paths well enough to avoid that.

Broken stalks littered the ground, the newly fallen ones giving off a cracking sound underfoot. So he had to move slowly, testing the ground with the tip of his sneakers before bringing his full weight to bear. For the time being, the voices had died away. Only the rustle of the stalks broke the stillness.

He stayed on the main path until it began to reverse direction in a loose U-shape pattern, then he took a narrower intersecting path that continued in more or less a straight line moving away from the bridge in the general direction of the street. Doubt nagged at him. He entertained the idea of simply making an escape, forgetting about his original intention: it didn't appear, to put it mildly, Mooney was in a talking mood.

The voices went at it inside his head.

Don't chicken out now. You'll regret it later.

At least if you run there will be a later.

You know better than that: you run from an enemy, he'll find you. You'll have to face him sooner or later. You know that.

He'd learned the truth of that long ago on the streets. Your enemies don't just disappear. Like the menacing figures in nightmares, they hound you till you beat them down with greater strength. Or until you outmaneuver them in some other way.

He slid the .38 from its holster and took a path that broke away from the path he was on, thinking he might double back along the outer edge of the Skeleton Zone, get to Mooney directly if he was still anywhere near the Kill.

But two things happened to derail his plan.

First the path he'd chosen turned out to be a dead end and, secondly, his pursuers were closer than he'd realized. Above the feathery tops of the stalks, on a path roughly parallel to his, some fifteen or twenty feet away, he caught a glimpse of the head of the tall man, the Jamaican. And even closer, he thought, because he could hear the man's heavy breathing, was the short fat man. From what Danny could tell he was not far beyond where the main path made its U-turn.

He was boxed in, stalks on three sides of him, and only one way out. If either of them came down this path, he had no option but to crash through the wall of stalks, a prospect that made him sweat profusely in the cool air.

He dropped to his knees and felt among the broken stalks. What he found were several stones and an empty Yoo-Hoo bottle, half buried in the muck. He stuffed the stones in his pocket and held the bottle at his side, then moved away from the dead end toward the main path, one tender minuscule step at a time.

When he was within sight of the main path he could hear the short fat man loudly and clumsily moving away toward the bridge. No way a man that wide could walk with finesse on such a narrow path.

At present, the Jamaican wasn't visible, but he couldn't have gone very far. What he had to do, Danny knew, was to distract them enough to allow him to get off the dead end path and find one that extended deeper into the Zone. And so he employed one of the tricks from their childhood games. He flicked a pair of stones beyond the point where he'd seen, a few moments earlier, the Jamaican's head.

He waited, aimed a second pair of stones onto the main path to the right of where he thought the fat man was. He wanted both of them to move in a westerly direction, away from him.

A breeze sent whispers through the stalks.

He stood frozen, waiting.

Out of the whispers another sound rose, distinct and more determined. Danny raised himself until he was eye-level with the tops of the stalks. The fat man was coming back toward the U-turn.

Waiting until the Jamaican's head appeared in the thinning spaces between the stalks, Danny flung the Yoo-Hoo bottle fifty feet or so beyond him.

"Over there, mon," the Jamaican shouted, moving away from Danny. The fat man joined him, both of them abandoning their respective paths and thrashing their way through the reeds.

Danny found the path he wanted and followed it deeper into

The Bronx Kill

the Zone. A tight narrow passage that traveled through the reeds in the direction of the street, it brought him finally to the ravine.

A ditch, really.

But they had glamorized it as kids, called it a ravine. It was steep-sided and narrow—a good twenty feet deep, and long—running nearly the entire width of the zone. You fell into it, you couldn't get out. Unless someone threw you a rope.

It had been Charlie's theory that long ago, millenniums ago, it had been a tributary of the Kill, gone dry now. Danny had argued with him, said he didn't believe that at all. He thought it was probably caused by some ancient earthquake. It was one more of their arguments without resolution.

It was one more of their contests.

As teenagers, they had taken running starts and tried to jump it. Occasionally one of them made it.

Now two boards had been lain across it to serve as a bridge. Danny pushed one of the boards into the ditch and dragged the other one away from the path.

Some distance away the Jamaican and the fat man were calling to one another.

Danny dragged the wooden plank through the stalks to create a racket.

"He over there," the short fat man shouted.

Some time passed. Danny crouched in the reeds, held his breath.

The silence bore down on him, a burden nearly intolerable to bear.

Then footsteps came along the path.

The first to appear was the short fat man. He came half-running, half-waddling down the path. At the last moment he must have seen the opening because he tried to hold himself back but his momentum, his weight, carried him forward, arms flailing in front of him as he fell. A deep-throated, unintelligible gargling sound came floating up out of the darkness.

The Jamaican, coming soon after, out of breath and clutching a pistol, was able to stop himself at the ditch edge. He peered into the dark cavity, said, "You stupid fuck, mon—"

If he had more to say, he never had a chance to finish. Danny, stepping behind him and using the plank as a battering ram, drove it into the man's back, sending him overboard. One of the tall man's hands groped at the far bank but couldn't find purchase in the crumbling dirt.

Danny could make out their shadows—one unmoving, the other crawling—in the pit below. Their voices came up to him, indistinguishable at first, then one voice, clearly the Jamaican's, scratchy and trembling, saying: "Help me, mon."

His words drifted in the air like an unanswered prayer.

A breeze brought the sour smell of the river, rattling the thin stalks like ruffled paper. Danny remained crouched in the cover of the reeds. He listened for some sound of movement but other than an occasional shout or low moan coming from one of the men below, the Skeleton Zone offered no evidence of human activity. Apparently, Mooney was in no hurry to come to the aid of his boys.

Danny moved away from the ledge. Behind him, the fat man was saying something in the ditch. It came out as a croaking sound, garbled at first. In a louder voice, though still weak, the man said, "He right heah. He right heah," calling out to Mooney or whoever else was patrolling the Kill this night in search of him. Danny didn't think the voice would carry, certainly not beyond the Skeleton Zone itself.

He followed the main path back toward the railroad bridge in hopes of finding the detective. The reeds gave way to the tall grass and, before the grass gave way to open ground, he spotted the man standing in the shadow of the bridge, his arm down at his side, gun in hand.

From the confines of the grass Danny called out: "I want to talk."

Mooney grunted. "So come on out and talk."

"Put your gun away first."

"Be a dumb thing to do, wouldn't it? You being a killer, twice over now. Not counting, of course, whatever you did to those boys out there."

As a precaution, a few minutes before, he had called the club. "Could use some more back-up here," he'd whispered into the phone. "Under the bridge." And then he'd added: "Pronto."

Now he moved closer to one of the bridge supports, the heavier shadows making him less of a target.

"I want to make peace," Danny said. "Whatever it takes."

A hard laugh came out of the shadows. "Peace means you got to give something up. What you gonna give to compensate for my brother's life?"

"I want to talk. Face to face."

"So come on out."

"I'm coming."

"Throw your gun out first."

"Can't do that, Tommy, long as you have yours. It'll be down at my side, though. Not gonna raise my arm unless you make me."

"You're an insane son-of-bitch, you know that? I thought it was Charlie, but it's you, man. It's you."

"We got to talk, Tommy. I'm coming out."

When he stepped clear of the wall of grass he was met with a burst of gunfire, three shots in quick succession that sent him diving back onto the safety of the path. He scrambled to his feet and ran back along the main path until he found an offshoot that cut westward and brought him out to the side of the Skeleton Zone that faced the rail yards. Behind him, he heard Mooney thrashing in the Zone. First his head appeared above the stalks then his entire body, plunging forward, his face cemented with purpose.

Danny bolted across the open space between the grass and the yards. He heard panting behind him and when he glanced back he saw the detective coming after him at a pace he wouldn't have thought possible for a man who looked so out of shape. The man raised his gun and fired. The shot went wide, kicking up dust some fifteen or twenty feet ahead of Danny.

When he reached the first of the boxcars he glanced back again at the man charging toward him, coat flapping in the wind. Danny, holding the .38 with both hands, fired and the man went down. He didn't want to kill the detective, simply keep him at bay, though the necessity of that—killing him, or else be killed by him—was coming to seem inevitable.

It turned out the shot wasn't what felled Mooney. Apparently he had tripped over a piece of the lot's debris, because he was on his feet quickly, running hard again and Danny was on the move again too, making his way deeper into the yard's shadows.

CHAPTER 50

Gun drawn, Tom Mooney edged along the side of a boxcar, uncertain whether Baker was hiding at the end of it or if he had slipped away deeper into the yard.

He listened for breathing, the scrape of a shoe, or what he liked to call the *whisper* of a moving shadow. Because he had come to believe the night, and what belonged to it, had a pulse of its own: a living force more insinuating, more threatening and more thrilling than anything to be found in daylight. And he had developed an almost extra-sensory awareness of it, attuned to the subtleties of its energies and rhythms, hearing in its silence warnings or threats, sensing in its darkness what eluded the eye.

Too many hours on the graveyard shift. Too many post-midnight prowlings and chases on the borough's mean streets.

Yet he was grateful for that history, seeing his years on the force in the clearest light now: as a prelude to this, this hunt, this chase, the opportunity to bring to justice those who caused his brother's death. This was the justification for all that he'd endured to get here.

As he approached the end of the box car he stopped, waiting to read the stillness before determining it was safe to turn the corner.

Empty track lay before him. He followed it to the string of abandoned cars ahead, the skin on his arms and the palms of his hands tingling, his heart pulsating with anticipation. Like being in love, he thought, only more intense. Like what he might have felt for Julianne if she hadn't turned on him twice now, and counting.

He understood that this was what he'd wanted all along, to hunt them one on one, to serve them a cold plate of vigilante justice. Yes, a conviction in court would have given him added satisfaction but nothing compared to this. Nor would having had someone else do it for him been as gratifying on a gut level as this.

If we were freed from civil and moral law, if we held free rein over our needs, this would be one of our most basic desires: to inflict pain on our enemies in our own way, by our own hands. So he was beginning to think things had worked out for the best, after all. And though he wished it was Charlie Romano out there instead of Danny Baker, he'd take what he could get. Romano's turn would come; he couldn't hide out in a hospital forever.

And Baker, well, Baker had turned out to be as much of a menace as his buddy, as much in his own quiet relentless way a representative of what Mooney hated about the Renegades: their smug arrogance, their defiance of the law, their harassment of his brother. If he'd had any doubt about Baker's part in all that, he convinced himself now that the man he was chasing was as responsible for Timmy's death as anyone. The world would be a better place without him.

He moved along the line of cars that smelled of rust and grime. Every few feet he stopped to read the silence. The man wasn't here. He sensed it. Not between the cars, not inside them. He would have heard him climbing; he was sure of that. He had the ears of an owl.

At Ellis' old car, a surge of anger added to the intensity of his heart's throbbing. They had beaten him there, too. They'd beaten him and gotten away with it, *again*. Just as he'd been beaten by Julie, too, bitch that she was. He felt weighed down by her betrayal, by the misery of everything that had gone down: hurt upon hurt deepening the wound of the ultimate hurt: losing Timmy, *not being there to save him, his baby brother*. He saw that as his life's greatest failure.

He flashed his light inside the car. Barren. No trace of Ellis' belongings. The place had been picked clean by thieves. Only the smell of the man remained, welded into the car's metal, rising from its floor. There was no one hiding in the corners. If Baker was still in the yard he must be lurking at the far end and he started toward it, his pain like extra weight he was carrying.

Moving from car to car, he made his way quickly. In the few instances where he had to cross brief patches of open ground, no shots came at him and a curious thought occurred to him: what if the guy really did want to talk? But he dismissed it immediately. Such an idea was laughable. What was there to talk about? He'd had plenty of chances to talk, and he didn't. Why would now be any different? No, Mooney thought, talk at this point was no good to him. He was way beyond that. Way beyond. It was the blood pulsing hard in his veins that controlled him now.

He hurried alongside a line of cars, winded, and he stopped

to catch his breath. Head down, hands on his knees, he blinked to clear the sweat from his eyes.

Something made him look up.

A flutter of motion, a twitching shadow at the back end of the yard.

He stepped across a series of interconnecting tracks and ran for the broken down fence. On the far side of it he saw Baker, the back of him at least, fleeing through a scraggly patch of woods in the direction of the Kill.

When he reached the Kill itself, he spotted Baker on the far side running for cover beneath the ramp to the Tri-Borough. No time to get off a shot. He looked up and down the long channel for some way across without getting wet. Then he was waist-deep in it, holding his weapon high, wading in pursuit through the vile-smelling black water.

CHAPTER 51

Mooney's reinforcements—a tall, broad-shouldered hulk accompanied by a smaller and thinner blade of a man, each of them carrying a Glock 9mm—were moving through a weedy section of the Kill, away from the railroad bridge. They had found the area deserted. No members of the crew. No Mooney.

"Which bridge he said?" the thin man asked. "The small one or the big one?"

"Under the bridge. That's all he tole me. Under the bridge."

"Must be the big one."

"Must be."

"Let's move ass."

"I *am* moving ass."

"Move it faster then."

They were a pathetic cavalry, Charlie had to admit, the three of them making their way into the Kill on the Old Renegade Trail. There hadn't been time to get the Albanians together, which would have been his best option, so this was what he'd been left with: Julianne on one side of him with her lead pipe and can of mace, Johnny on the other carrying a Louisville Slugger in one hand and the .38 in the other so that *he,* hobbling between them on his crutches, could maintain his balance on the uneven path.

When the path was wide enough, they walked three abreast. When it narrowed Johnny went first, holding the gun by the butt and away from his body as if it might at any moment explode, Charlie came next, and Julianne in the rear. The plan was, if they encountered anyone, Johnny would hand the gun off to Charlie.

From a short distance ahead, where the path diverged—one going to the left toward the Skeleton Zone, the other toward the railroad yard—they heard voices, raised in argument, coming toward them.

Johnny, in the lead, had stopped dead. As he turned to hand

off the .38, holding it tentatively as he was, he lost his grip and it fell off the side of the path. In the next moment, two men—each with a pistol in hand—appeared ahead of them, having come around a bend in the trail. One of them held a cell phone to his ear and he stood frozen in that position, shocked. The other man, unusually tall and broad-shouldered said, "What the—?"

In one of those bizarre coincidences for which one is never prepared, Charlie recognized the tall man. Lou Jamal Robinson. One of his offensive line men the year he'd quarter-backed the Cardinal Hayes varsity.

The recognition was simultaneous.

"Big Lou!"

"Romano. What the hell you doin' here?"

The second recognition followed quickly.

"Don't think we're on the same team anymore," Big Lou said, stepping forward and raising his gun.

Charlie swung his crutch at the man's chest, preventing a shot, slowing him down, allowing Julianne enough time to send a blast of mace his way and swing the lead pipe against his knees which brought him down. She whirled and sprayed in the direction of the man with the cell phone who had stepped back in anticipation. At the same time Johnny, on his hands and knees, found the .38 and lifted it. No time for a hand-off. He pointed it at the cell phone man and, closing his eyes, fired off two rounds, one of which struck the thin man's hand, the hand that now no longer held a gun.

When he opened his eyes he saw the man's back fading into the darkness of the path as he stumbled away. He aimed the .38 at Big Lou—he'd been a hell of a lineman, Johnny remembered, the best the Cardinals ever had—who on his knees now had dropped his gun to rub his eyes, his fingers working so furiously it looked as if he was trying to claw the chemical from his skin.

"We had some of this stuff we might've beat the Mounties in the Turkey Bowl that year," Charlie said to his former teammate who, bent over now, had been reduced to whimpering.

"Ain't funny, man. This shit's burning my motherfuckin' eyes out."

"Think of it this way, Big Lou. That stuff might have saved your life. My buddy here's a killer with a .38."

Johnny, grim-faced, his arm shaking almost out of control, tried to hold the .38 on Big Lou as the man writhed and stumbled

The Bronx Kill

from side to side on the path. He wasn't ready yet to appreciate Charlie's wit.

"Help our fellow Cardinal here find his way home," Charlie said. And Johnny edged forward sideways, holding his gun hand back as he reached with his left hand and pulled the big man onto the path, pushing him in the direction of the street.

"Should have tried out for the pros," Charlie called after the erstwhile gridiron hero. "Big mistake, bro."

CHAPTER 52

The city's toilet, the detective thought as he moved through the junkyard beneath the bridge, *hell's sewer*. The repository for all that was useless, wasted and worn. Bald tires, tape decks, cassettes, phonograph records, videocassette recorders, typewriters, primitive looking cell phones and boom boxes, TVs with twelve inch screens and rabbit ears. He had seen the refuse grow over the years, a rising tide of obsolescence, filling the space between the bridge supports, extending the length of this cavernous, tunnel-like urban wasteland. The spoor of man that would eventually overwhelm and destroy him. It was a noxious place, he felt sure. It gave off fumes that were deadly. The proof of that was the headache pounding the walls of his skull.

He had come nearly to its end. Here was the parade of wrecked automobiles, an oddly neat line of them, as if they had been parked in formation according to some unwritten traffic law. Beyond them was a wall of cement, the last of the land-based bridge supports.

He stood there cursing the vault-like gloom of the place and the wet chemical smell of his pants. His socks felt thick and soggy; they shared the cramped space of his shoes with a generous helping of the channel's muck.

The worst of it, though, was the pressure inside his skull. The headache was merciless—they came on like this sometimes, swift and sudden as a summer squall—but still he could think clearly enough to realize that one of two things was possible here: either he'd cornered his man at last, or he'd been led into a trap.

In defensive mode, he sought the protection of the nearest bridge support, pressing his back against the rough skin of the cement, holding his Glock at arm's length against the surface of the wall.

For the first time that night he felt at a disadvantage. The roar of the bridge traffic from above compromised his hearing, and the force of his headache dulled his sensitivity to the nuances of his surroundings. To his left, the waters of Hell Gate stretched toward the city's upper east side. To his right, shadows bobbed and weaved

The Bronx Kill

like spirits across the junkyard.

He thought, he couldn't be sure, but he *thought* he heard a noise there and he edged along the cement, arm extended, gun pointed into the shadows. In the time before his full body left the safety of his cover, in the time before he fully made the turn to face whatever was there, something struck his arm. Not wood, he thought. Something harder, something metal: a pipe or a pole. The force of it knocked the Glock from his hand, sent pain shooting from the bones of his wrist to his shoulder and he fell forward, Baker coming at him again with the pipe, aiming for his legs this time, striking the fleshy part of his calf.

The swing knocked Danny off balance and Mooney was on him, both hands gripping his shoulders and slamming him against the cement hard enough that the pipe fell from his fingers. Then it was simply the two of them, weapon-free, save for their hands and their mutual rage.

Mooney's hands clawed at the face, the object of his blinding hate. He wanted to rip the skin from that face, gouge out the eyes, tear the fucker's ears off. He used his power, his superior weight in the mauling and then he became aware of it: the shoulder holster, the gun, thinking *the guy's so dumb he's not even using it*.

But when Mooney grabbed for it he shifted his weight in such a way Danny was able to jam his knee into the man's crotch, sending him backward into the dirt. The Glock lay close by and the detective lifted it from the dirt, turning his body with one motion and raising it.

"Don't! Please!" Danny yelled.

He aimed the .38 at the broad mid-section of the fallen man.

The bullet hit Mooney—on his left side, somewhere below his chest—before he could fire the Glock.

"Jesus, no!" Danny came forward, held his foot on the detective's wrist till he dropped the gun and settled back in defeat against the cement. Danny kicked the 9mm Glock, sent it scuttling across the hard ground.

"I'm gonna die, I'm gonna die," Mooney was saying. He had his hand clamped to his side, below the heart. He stared in disbelief at the blood spilling over his fingers.

"Not before you hear what I have to say. Not before you know what happened that night."

"I *know* what happened that night."

"Not enough to separate fact from your imagination."

The detective raised his head, his mouth twisted in a mocking sneer. "And you're gonna enlighten me."

"That's right."

Mooney raised his head to spit but the saliva, failing to reach its intended destination in the dirt, fell on his shirt. "Why should I believe anything you say?"

"I've been over this in my head a thousand times."

Moving his hand gingerly over his wound, he winced in pain. "But you're not exactly an objective source, are you? What makes you think you can separate fact from *your* imagination?"

"I'm the only source you've got right now."

Mooney grunted—whether in acknowledgment or dissent, Danny couldn't say.

"*Fact*," Danny said, holding the gun at his side, staring at the man slumped before him. "Charlie was the one who fought with your brother earlier that night. At the dance, yes, but here at the Kill too. When Timmy said he didn't want to swim the river, Charlie went off on him. He was jealous of Timmy, jealous of his charm, his looks, his easy manner, jealous of the way everyone loved him, the way everything seemed to come to Timmy without any effort on his part. He knew Timmy could have any girl he wanted, he knew he could have Charlie's girl, if he wanted. And Charlie couldn't stand that, couldn't stand that he—Charlie—wasn't in control anymore, that he was powerless against whatever it was that girls, that the world, wanted from Timmy."

"So what's your point?"

"*Fact*: At the Kill, Charlie began coaxing him into the water, pretending he was joking around at first, then pulling him harder, *dragging* him. Then we were all pulling him and pushing him in—me, Charlie, Johnny. He didn't want to go. He kept saying, 'I can't swim as good as you, I can't swim that good.' We knew that, of course, but we didn't let up. *Charlie* didn't let up. He kept saying Timmy wasn't a man, that he'd never be a man, that he couldn't be one of us anymore if he didn't do this. Once he was in the water, though, Timmy started swimming on his own. No one was forcing him then. He was swimming like the rest of us, striking out for the far shore."

"You drowned him. One or all of you together."

"*Fact*," Danny corrected. "We *left* him out there. *I* left him out there." He waited to make sure the man understood that. There were sins of *co*mmission and there were sins of *o*mission, as the sisters at St. Cecilia had so often pointed out. His sin fell in the latter category. In a softer voice, he said: "I was the last one to leave him. I should have gone after him, but I didn't. *I* let him swim away."

He was pacing now, along the edge of the junk pile, feeling full-force the buried shame he'd been living with. "I've regretted that ever since. Not a day goes by, not a moment, when it's not in the back of my mind. I've gone over it and over it. From every angle. From every vantage point. What I did, what I didn't do. What I *could* have done. Why I didn't try harder. Why none of us tried harder." The questions had become as much a part of him as flesh and bone.

He rubbed his eyes to clear his head.

Keep it clear, keep it simple, he reminded himself.

Tell him what you know.

"Like I said, Charlie had his reasons. Johnny's were more subtle. And buried deeper. He had this—this *fascination*—for your brother. It was kind of an obsession, an *adoration* of some kind. Maybe it was love, I don't know. If it was, he couldn't admit that to himself; he still hasn't. Whatever it was, whatever you want to call it, he didn't know what to do with those feelings, he was supposed to be in love with Lorraine, he was supposed to get married and have kids—the life we all grew up thinking we would have; but this ran deeper, this threatened all his basic values, his religion, his sense of himself as a normal guy, as one of the guys. He couldn't think of himself in any other way. It would have killed the identity he'd spent a lifetime building."

He stopped pacing, stood in front of Mooney, his judge and would-be executioner, who watched him with a flat stare that offered nothing.

"And *me?*" He held his breath before continuing. "Me, I've never been more envious and more jealous of anyone in my life. I was so in love with Julie I didn't know who I was anymore. There was no *me* really. Only this confusion of feelings, this blob of hurt and need, because she couldn't see anybody but Timmy. She was *nice* to me, she knew me better than anyone else ever knew me and for that alone I'll always love her, but she was crazy about Timmy Moon, crazy and wild in love with him. And I couldn't bear that."

He drew back his shoulders, took a deep breath, and tried to steady the quaking feeling that came with his confession. "I thought your brother was the greatest guy in the world but he took away—

no, he didn't take her away because she was never mine, he *won over*—the only girl I ever loved. And maybe that's why I did what I did, why I turned away and left him there. Oh, I have all kinds of reasons why I didn't go after him: the water was too rough, the currents were too unpredictable, I was scared of drowning. That's all true. But equally true was that he was right there, a few feet from me, like he was waiting for me to reach out and take hold of him. I could have. I could have. I *should* have. But I didn't. And when he saw I wasn't going to do anything, something flashed in his eyes. Some *recognition*. And that's when he began to swim away. It was like, I don't know, he was counting on me, and I let him down."

"I let him down."

He let the words hang in the air. His shame exposed.

"So the reality is," he said, his head bowed, "I have to live with that, no matter whether the law says I'm guilty or not."

He took a deep breath to steady himself, to finish what he'd started. "Afterward when I got back to shore I broke down, told Charlie and Johnny what I'd done or, more accurately, what I didn't do. That's when we made a pact never to talk about that night. Ever again."

In the shadowy light, he couldn't fully read the detective's face. Hatred, for sure. And something more indeterminate. Something that went deeper.

Some time passed before Danny spoke again. "There is something else you should know. About your brother." He had thought long and hard about telling him this. He would have preferred to spare the man, but the pain was necessary so that they all could live. "He had his problems, too."

Some disconnect, Danny thought, between what he felt and what he could or would express. Some distance he couldn't cross. Which must have left him always feeling alone, no matter how many girls loved him. "Timmy wanted to die out there in the river. After he swam away from me, he fought Julie off. He pushed her away when she tried to help him. He kept forcing himself under, holding himself down. He begged her to let him die. His last words were, 'Let the river take me.' That's what he wanted. *Let the river take me.*"

And Danny thought, but didn't say: that must have been the meaning of his cryptic smile as he swam away. He had already decided he was going to die.

He waited before continuing. "That doesn't change anything.

It doesn't make me less responsible for the decision I made. It doesn't make any of us less responsible. We all share in the blame. If we hadn't bullied him, if we hadn't dragged him into the river, maybe he wouldn't have tried to swim it. And if he hadn't tried to swim it, maybe he wouldn't have decided to drown himself. Every act is simply a link in a chain, and there's a responsibility attached to each event in that chain. I see that now. No act, of itself, is a beginning or an end."

The truth, according to Danny Baker.

He stood there watching the broken man before him. It wasn't animosity that he felt toward him so much as a humbling form of pity. For himself, as well, for all the Renegades. For their weaknesses, for those failings that made them fall short of who they wanted to be.

We could have been so much better, he knew, we *can* be so much better.

I can be so much better.

The thought offered him the promise of comfort.

CHAPTER 53

Tom Mooney was disturbingly quiet. Still slumped against the cement pillar, he stared past Danny at the shadows flickering across the junkyard. Animals or spirits? In his growing delirium, he couldn't be certain. He was holding tight to his wound, the blood having spread like a rising tide from his waist to his shoulder, the pain in his head ready to burst the walls of his skull.

"I'm gonna die," he said again, half-whispered, half-choked, and this time with the statement came an unappeasable sense of regret. Not because he had failed to avenge his brother's death, but for the anger and resentment he'd felt toward the kid from as far back as he could remember: for the way he'd cursed him for throwing a baseball like a girl, for swinging the bat like one too, no matter how much he coached him; for the way he'd ridiculed him because the kid couldn't fight his own battles on the street, which meant he always had to be there to punch somebody out on the kid's behalf, until Charlie took his place; for the kid's refusal to do anything but curl up and cry when their father became abusive, for his refusal to stand up to the old man or to the aunt who later had taken him in.

Regret. Regret.

For not having the kid live with *him* rather than their aunt, for leaving him at the heartless mercy of that old witch, for leaving him to fend for himself. For all this and more, and especially for the things he'd said to him earlier that day he died: *that he was no man at all, that he was a faggot through and through, that he was ashamed to call him his brother.* "You disgust me," were the last words he'd said to him.

You disgust me.

Aloud now, he said, without anger or bitterness: "What are you waiting for? Finish what you started. Finish me off." He laughed at the way this would look to the world. "It's a perfect crime. Everyone'll think it was a drug deal gone bad." Even in death, he thought, he would be beaten. Again.

Danny raised his arm and pointed the .38 at Tom Mooney's head.

The Bronx Kill

He held it there until his arm began to quiver.

He lowered it at last and said, "Call off the dogs."

Before he left he used the detective's cell phone to call 9-1-1. On his way past the Kill he stopped and flung the phone and Charlie's .38 far out into the current.

Danny, on his way out of the Kill, heard shots and cursed himself for having gotten rid of the gun so quickly. The familiar adage, *it ain't over till it's over*, repeated itself in his mind like a taunting child's refrain.

The shots had come from somewhere near the railroad yard, he thought. He figured it was more of Mooney's cronies or, at best, random gunfire unrelated to the detective's vendetta.

He kept to a crouch and edged along the path. When he reached the Old Renegade Trail he had a long straight view ahead. Some fifty feet farther on he spotted them: Charlie, the invalid warrior king to the rescue, lurching forward on his crutches, flanked by his two unlikely foot soldiers. The sight stunned Danny, and moved him.

He didn't know whether to laugh or cry.

CHAPTER 54

All summer Julie had been on his mind. It was as if he'd awakened from a bad dream, felt momentarily reassured, before being plunged back into another dream, equally bad, only different. This dream was a lonely dream.

Danny had called her at least a half dozen times. She was always polite, but he had the feeling she was only tolerating the calls, that it would be easier for her if she didn't have to talk to him. With one excuse or another, she declined his offers to get together.

One night in early July he'd driven out to Murphy's Dublin Rose. That way, he figured, he could *really* talk to her. He'd have her eyes, her face, her body language—not only her voice—to judge what she was feeling. But it was a busy night at the bar and she was constantly in motion. When at last the crowd thinned and they could talk for a few minutes without interruption, she listened to him patiently as if it was a duty.

Nervous, excited, he spoke in a rush, telling her about Johnny and Lorraine, how they were finally getting married after all these years, and how he'd joked with his dad about the wedding, telling him the only reason he'd been invited was they were expecting him to show off his moves on the dance floor.

"What did he say to that?" she asked.

"Promised me he'd give it his best shot."

Then Danny was talking about himself, how he'd finally gotten going again on his book, he was writing one or two pages a day, and how he'd spoken to Florida State and they said he could finish the remaining credits toward his degree at Fordham. The last part of his good news was that, come fall, he'd be teaching an after-school class in writing at St. Cecelia's. Seventh and eighth graders. If it went well he'd have a chance of teaching full-time at the high school next year.

Finally he'd worked up the courage to ask if she was going out with anyone.

No, she wasn't.

Had she heard from Tom Mooney?

Yes, she had.

"He still comes in once in a while," she said. "He does it to punish me. His way, I guess, of making sure I won't forget him. Or maybe," she added on second thought, "he does it to punish *himself.*"

Word in the neighborhood was that, after he'd been released from the hospital, he'd left the force and moved out to the Rockaways—about as far away from the Bronx as you could get in this city. If he'd been suspected of being a bad cop, it never made the papers. The NYPD had gotten a lot of negative publicity that year, for a number of reasons, and it was Danny's guess they didn't want to add to it.

Before he left the Dublin Rose that night he asked her if she was coming to the wedding. She said no, she didn't think so. She was still getting used to being clean, to all that had happened since they'd found each other again. For the time being, she said, that was more than she could handle.

"I'm still in love with you."

"No," she said. "You're in love with a memory."

He thought: *even if that was true he had enough love stored up from that summer of their youth to last a lifetime.*

"You're not just a memory," he said. "You're not."

She looked at him a long time before she said: "Maybe someday I'll believe you."

Those summer nights at the Glow, after the bar was closed and they'd sit around in the semi-darkness listening to the jukebox, Charlie would sometimes insist they all go out to Queens to see her, coax her into being one of them again; but Danny discouraged such a mission. She wasn't ready for that. She just wasn't.

In the Renegade tradition, they didn't talk much about what happened that last night at the Kill—other than Danny saying he felt he'd re-paid all his debts and that he and Tom Mooney had come to an understanding.

Instead they mostly joked about the raggedy band of musketeers who'd come to rescue him and how fantastically weird it was seeing Big Lou, the greatest football hero ever to graduate from Hayes, reduced to a gun-toting go-fer for a low-life drug crew. How mother-loving weird.

One night, Charlie stunned them by saying he'd been doing a lot of thinking about things. While he'd been in the hospital and after he got out. "I've got to square it all away," he said. "The Ellis thing."

His next day off he began volunteering at a homeless shelter off the Bruckner Expressway. It turned into a regular thing, every Thursday, working at their soup kitchen where he helped serve dinner to several hundred hungry and homeless men.

Not long after that—again it was late night at the Glow—Charlie for the first time on his own initiative brought up the night of the drowning. "It never should have happened," he said.

It was the closest he ever came to acknowledging openly his part in Timmy's death.

And Danny, too, had some unfinished business. He would have to tell Julie about what he'd failed to do in the river. He didn't want his shame a secret he kept from her.

Mid-August, on a warm, languid night when his loneliness was waging a particularly brutal war against him, Danny made another trip to the Dublin Rose. It turned out to be Julie's night off so he would have to wait for another time to tell her.

As he turned to leave, he noticed Tom Mooney slouched at the far end of the bar. He was alone, the seat on either side of him vacant, and he looked like he'd been drinking heavily. When he raised his eyes to meet Danny's, he did so only briefly, before turning inward again, shutting down the world around him.

CHAPTER 55

The early September sunlight flooded the windows of St. Cecilia's. The church, filled to capacity, had the festive feel of an Easter Sunday. A steady murmur of anticipation and impatience lifted from the lips of the congregation.

Lorraine was late.

"A good sign," a woman standing in the back of the church said to those who, like herself, had arrived too late to get a seat. "It means she's in charge now. Things are going to be done her way."

A titter of laughter issued from the women around her.

Danny, overhearing her from his usher's position at the doors to the vestibule, thought that was a fair assessment of the way things had turned out. Lorraine *says*, Johnny *does*. That's the way it had been between the couple since their time away in the Catskills.

Johnny had summed it up this way: "Basically I said yes to everything she asked for."

When Danny asked him what it was, finally, that made him overcome his doubts, his hesitation, Johnny thought a while before saying, "It was seeing how happy it made her when I promised that I wouldn't ever again let something I did keep us apart. She was glowing, I swear. Like she had the sun inside her, shining through. And I thought: this is what grace is, doing whatever I can to make her happy." He blushed as if he'd revealed too much.

Then he said something that surprised Danny. "You know, that whole seminary thing, I think it was my way of begging God to forgive me. I think I was just running away from that night on the river. Like your going to Florida."

After a moment Johnny added with a distant, dream-like grin, as if recalling something faraway and nearly out of sight, "Love sings in many voices at the same time. I'm choosing to hear just one of them."

Danny had a pretty good idea what he was talking about. Love was part-compulsion, part-choice. Although, with regard to his own feelings for Julie, he'd never thought choice had much say in it.

On the altar now, Johnny looked thin and willowy, his usual tentative self but he seemed contented too as he stood beside Charlie, his best man. From time to time he would glance up at Charlie in search of an attitude he might adopt, some hint as to what was appropriate behavior at a time like this. He stood with his shoulders back like Charlie's, his face tilted at a similar angle, jaw raised in stoic acceptance of whatever was to come.

They must have decided that until word came of Lorraine's arrival there was no sense waiting out there in plain sight doing nothing, because they turned then—Charlie with a slight limp the doctors said might be permanent—and retreated into the sacristy.

It was then that Charlie's new girlfriend, Annette, appeared in the vestibule and Danny escorted her to a seat at the front of the church. She was less flashy than Charlie's usual type—softer, Danny thought, more centered. He was pretty sure Uncle Sal would approve.

When he stood again at the door to the vestibule, he took time to appreciate the scene before him: the crowded church with its vaulted ceilings, gold detailing and ornate statuary. Most of the neighborhood had turned out, and many of those who'd fled to Jersey or Westchester or the Island had returned for the occasion. It was a sight to lift the spirits, an echo of the community that had once nurtured him.

And walking the streets these days, despite all that had happened, he could feel with a clarity he hadn't experienced before how much he loved even the most ordinary of things this place had to offer, like riding the El, gazing down at rooftops and the suddenly miniaturized world of pedestrians and cars moving street to street.

And the streets themselves, the tingle he felt simply *walking* them, the vibrancy of sights and sounds and smells and small miracles, like the way a playground turned even the dreariest and most unlikely space into a joyful arena of games, a fortress against the ever-changing, threatening world.

In Florida he had never gotten used to the expanse of sky, the continual bright sun. Here the sky could be observed only in bits and pieces, between brick towers, through gaps in the steel webbing of the EL. So you never took it for granted; it was something you prized. Like the open space the rivers offered, so that even the grimy weeds and gnarled grasses of the Kill were things of beauty to be cherished. More than his ethnicity, more than his Catholic upbringing or his schooling, it was this neighborhood that made him what he was, that marked him as its own.

Now in the church before him, in the vast high spaces of the nave he felt the presence of Timmy—a calmer presence than before, it seemed, less anguished. Like a true Renegade, the forsaken boy was keeping his pain inside. And Danny, who thought prayer had been lost to him forever, felt one forming on his lips. *Wherever you are, Timmy Moon, forgive me. Forgive us all.*

A commotion outside distracted him. He crossed the vestibule and stood on the steps of the church. Lorraine had arrived. Her mother on one side, her father on the other, she came hurrying up the steps with her eyes down and her hands tugging at her dress to keep it from touching the ground. When she reached the top she looked up and saw him, her eyes wide with expectation.

"He's waiting for you."

"Yes," she said breathlessly, her face flushed. "*Yes.*"

She rushed past him in a swirl of satin and lace and he was standing alone, searching the wide street for some sign of Julie, hoping that after all she might appear.

And then she did.

At the corner. Stepping from a cab. Her face still pale, worn beyond her years, but with a girlish look of hope and promise he hadn't seen since their first summer.

Turning, she saw him.

And offered a smile.

Philip Cioffari is the author of the novels: DARK ROAD, DEAD END; JESUSVILLE; CATHOLIC BOYS; and the short story collection, A HISTORY OF THINGS LOST OR BROKEN, which won the Tartt Fiction Prize, and the D. H. Lawrence award for fiction. His short stories have been published widely in commercial and literary magazines and anthologies, including *North American Review, Playboy, Michigan Quarterly Review, Northwest Review, Florida Fiction*, and *Southern Humanities Review*. He has written and directed for Off and Off-Off Broadway. His Indie feature film, which he wrote and directed, LOVE IN THE AGE OF DION, has won numerous awards, including Best Feature Film at the Long Island Int'l Film Expo, and Best Director at the NY Independent Film & Video Festival. He is a Professor of English, and director of the Performing and Literary Arts Honors Program, at William Paterson University.
www.philipcioffari.com